PR
FOR
THE CHILDREN OF THIS MADNESS

"A heartfelt yet clear-sighted novel about the gains and losses of immigration, both personal and political, *The Children of This Madness* masterfully explores the fascinatingly different worlds in which a father and a daughter exist, and what happens when these worlds collide."
—**Chitra Banerjee Divakaruni, author of** *Independence* **and** *The Forest of Enchantments*

"The elegant twined narrative of *The Children of This Madness* offers the reader an intimate view of a complicated familial, and geopolitical, drama. I've always found fiction the best, most compassionate and honest resource for learning about the real world. Wahhaj's novel is a wonderfully useful addition to my own education. I really enjoyed reading this; the author made a very complicated situation lucid and moving."
—**Antonya Nelson, author of** *Funny Once* **and** *Bound*

"In *The Children of This Madness*, Gemini Wahhaj weaves a moving, powerful story that spans generations and continents. Told through the lives of a Bengali father and daughter reckoning with their dreams and what they've lost, this work is an essential new addition to the Bengali diasporic literary landscape, one that deepens our understanding of how delicate internal struggles come head to head with seismic historic events. As inheritors of centuries-long imperialist, colonial power struggles, the interconnected and vividly drawn relationships at the heart of this novel reveal to us the ways in which desires for freedom and material security are inevitably, and tragically, entangled in the machinations of war and power. We remember by reading Wahhaj's work that love and memory is what remains when all else disappears."
—**Tanaïs, author of** *In Sensorium* **and** *Bright Lines*

"Centered around the US invasion and destruction of Iraq, *The Children of This Madness* shows us how the Global South enters the empire or, rather, how the empire assimilates the Global South. In clear-eyed staccato style, Gemini Wahhaj insists on a humane narrative here and elsewhere. Houston, Texas represents. But Iraq and Bangladesh are essential, reminding us that there's a world out there larger and more connected than the time-space capsule in which imperial wars exist. A fantastic novel. Unbeholden to the market powers that normalize destruction in the name of culture."
—**Fady Joudah, author of** *Tethered to Stars* **and** *Mizna: The Palestine Issue*

"This extraordinary novel has the texture of lived life, with all its ruptures and complications. Nothing in Wahhaj's propulsive story has been packaged for a foreign audience, nothing feels manipulated or forced. The Bangladesh she describes (but never romanticizes) is at once sumptuously beautiful and, in colonialism's wake, heartbreakingly corrupt. Rather than moving in one direction and looking back with regret, Wahhaj's nuanced characters are buffeted here and there by the convulsions of geopolitics and war, trying to figure out what it means to be at home in the world."
—**Nell Freudenberger, author of** *Lost and Wanted* **and** *The Newlyweds*

THE CHILDREN OF THIS MADNESS

by

Gemini Wahhaj

7.13 Books

Printed in the United States of America

First Edition
1 2 3 4 5 6 7 8 9

Cover art by Alban Fischer
Edited by Kurt Baumeister

Library of Congress Cataloging-in-Publication Data

ISBN (paperback): 979-8-9877471-4-8
ISBN (eBook): 979-8-9877471-5-5
LCCN: 2023940607

For Arif

"We are the children of this madness. Let us be whatever we wish."

—Saadi Youssef, from "A Friendship," translated by Khaled Mattawa

1. THE PARTY

Houston, March 19, 2003

Beena's friend Salma was throwing a housewarming party on a quiet cul-de-sac of a gated community in Katy. Besides Beena, six families and one bachelor had been invited. Earlier in the day, Salma had swung by Beena's apartment in the city and driven her back to Katy for the party with the singular purpose of introducing her to their friend Khaled, who had just moved to Houston with a lucrative job. She had dressed Beena in an embroidered, blue handloom-silk sari and hung a heavy pendant necklace around her neck. She had lined her large eyes with thick kohl and mascara, contoured her long, narrow face, and painted her wide mouth to a smooth, scarlet luster. Salma herself was dressed in a sequined, heavy silk sari a shade of onion pink. Her small, piquant face was heavily made up to a thick, smooth finish, and her bob-cut hair had been sprayed and glued in place.

Following the custom at these parties, the men sat separately in the formal living room at the front of the house, while half a dozen women, adorned in embroidered silk saris and matching blouses, stood glittering under the bright lights of the kitchen. When Beena said hello, a few of the women looked back at her with hard eyes, probably because she had rebuffed their invitations in the past. She stood to one side observing them, struck by the sameness of their makeup and by their squealed greetings and busy activity–slicing tomatoes and cucumber for a salad, setting out metal serving spoons, and preparing the percolator for tea after dinner. In all her graduate student years in Houston, Beena had stayed away from this crowd. She had too much work to attend parties, and no car to drive to the suburbs where the Bangladeshi engineers lived, forty minutes to an hour outside the city. Also, she didn't have money to buy the expensive gifts people hauled in the front door at these parties.

Salma's husband Ronny entered the kitchen shouting. "Salma! Where are the appetizers? The men are starving!" There was a feigned note of tyranny in his voice, but he was smiling and the eyes that met Beena's shone with a wicked humor.

Beena liked him. He was a relaxed person with a frank, round face. He was dressed in brand-name clothes, a blue-and-white-checked dress shirt with the Ralph Lauren Polo logo and wool grey trousers, and he reeked of cologne.

Salma turned from the oven, her hands deep in silicone gloves. She had been bent low, watching the large aluminum-foil pans in which she was warming the dishes she had cooked throughout the week. Her hair was plastered to her forehead in the heat.

"Khaled!" she shrieked, coming forward, grinning at the man who stood behind her husband, her pin-black eyes dilated with pleasure.

"Why are you acting so surprised? Didn't I tell you Khaled was coming?" Ronny said peevishly. "He only moved to Houston three weeks ago. Right, Khaled?"

"I'm so happy to see you, friend!" Salma cried.

"Thank you for inviting me. I was pining away in my hotel room," a thick voice answered.

Looking up, Beena saw a tall man with a chiseled face and a head of thick, tightly curled hair.

Salma pulled Beena toward her. "Khaled, this is my school friend Beena, our teacher's daughter. You remember Nasir Uddin Sir."

"Kemon achhen? How are you?" Khaled asked, smiling.

Beena nodded stiffly.

He looked like he was about to speak further when another man dragged him away.

Left alone, the women redoubled their activity.

"We have to get the appetizer ready. The men left without food. How embarrassing! Salma Apu, is the chotpoti warm yet?" Shona received the tray of chotpoti from Salma and placed it on top of a dish warmer. A young housewife and skilled home-maker, she was considered a great asset at these parties. Picking up a kitchen lighter, she started to light the candles under the dish warmers arrayed on the counter. "How did you cook so much food, Salma Apu?"

"I did a little bit every day after returning from the office." Salma pushed the beef back in the oven, saying that the foil was still cold to the touch. "What can I say? I have been under so much stress at work. I'm keeping a low profile at the office since all this business with WMDs. They keep asking me my opinion about Iraq, as if South Asia and Middle East are the same place!"

"I know, Apu! Bulbul has been saying the same thing. What a nuisance! Now they think all Muslims are bad." Shona wrinkled her thin, powdered nose to express her dismay.

Beena listened to them with a sudden intensity. Her jaw tightened and her eyes narrowed. As the threat of a US invasion in Iraq had intensified over the past month, she had been perusing the online newspapers anxiously. "I grew up in Iraq," she said, moving closer.

"These cabinets are so nice, Salma Apu!" Shona exclaimed. "Is the countertop made of granite?"

"Yes. We had the cabinets and countertops upgraded from what the builder gave us," Salma said.

"I keep asking Bulbul to remodel our kitchen, but he won't listen to me." Shona pouted. "How much did it cost you, Apu? Which company did you hire to do the work?"

"Oh, we have a great guy," Salma said.

"Apu, please give me his number!"

"I will." Salma turned to Beena. "I'll have to give you his number too, Beena. You will need it soon enough." She burst into laughter at her own joke.

"Is there something we don't know?" another woman asked.

As if to avert the other woman's curiosity, Salma said, "Our work is done here. The men can come and get the appetizer. Who wants a tour of the house?" She threw her shoulders back and placed her hands on her hips, looking archly at the group.

"Give us a tour, Apu!" the women cried.

Beena followed the women engaged in their favorite activity, taking the measure of a house. Salma explained that the builder had built only ten such Mediterranean-style homes in their subdivision, modeled after wealthy neighborhoods in California and Florida, with stucco columns and arches, terracotta-tile roofs, curved parapets, and white stucco walls laced with wisteria vines. Inside, there were all the features desirable in the new Houston homes. A grand entryway with a marble floor and high ceiling led to a curved staircase with a decorative balustrade. Salma showed off the new furniture she had bought to complement the expanded space: new leather sofas in the family room, floor-to-ceiling shelves filled with entertainment devices, and shiny satin curtains hanging from the tall windows of every room.

The men had been reclining on two white couches, hands clasped over paunches, when the women entered.

"Guys, the appetizer is ready," Salma announced.

The men stirred and rose to their feet. In their mid-thirties, they had acquired the same polished, round faces and they wore the same brand-name clothes from upscale department stores. From long association, Beena had gathered that the engineers only associated with other engineers. They were fond of saying that they were the crème de la crème of their country. Out of the lakhs of students who passed the higher secondary exam in Bangladesh every year, only five thousand qualified to take the admission test at the engineering university, and out of those applicants, only six hundred were admitted as students. After graduating, they had gained admission in various master's degree programs in the US. And immediately after completing their graduate degrees, they had been snatched up by companies eager to hire them at mouth-watering salaries.

Salma pointed out the Bangladeshi décor in the formal living room. She had bought some of the furniture and art pieces in Dhaka and had them freighted by sea. A teak-wood cabinet with a crystal-cut glass door and glass shelves displayed a golden brass horse, a silver rickshaw, and a silver cup and spoon. A vinyl turntable record player sat on top of a corner table. A framed nakshi katha covered the length of one wall, while an original oil on canvas by Shahabuddin, signed and dated by the artist, took up another. Only the sleek, flat-screen TV mounted on the wall above the gas fireplace clashed with these imported items of Bengali heritage.

Shona turned to Salma. "How did you bring all this, Apu?"

"Ronny's company paid for it all."

"Really, Apu? How wonderful!"

"Yes, the benefits at his company are unbelievable. They spoil you." Salma pointed to a view of the front yard through an expanse of glass panels. "We bought the house because of this view. We fell in love with these French windows. Large pieces of glass like this are very expensive. But because of these windows, during the day, this room is washed in sunlight."

The men returned with chotpoti in Styrofoam bowls and resettled on the sofas. Seeing the women still in the room, they kept their heads low and spoke in low voices.

"Did you have to cut down any trees to clear the yard?" Mehjabeen's husband Nazmul Bhai asked Ronny.

"We didn't have to do anything. The developer cut two trees and cleared the bushes before we moved in," Ronny said.

"Be careful. There could be snakes," said Nazmul Bhai. "This area used to be rice fields."

Ronny nodded. "I know."

"You can buy pellets at Home Depot to keep the snakes away," Nazmul Bhai went on. "Just sprinkle them on the grass."

"What about foxes, Nazmul Bhai? Raccoons? Jackals? What other wild animals are here?" Shona's husband Bulbul teased the man.

"Are you mad?" Nazmul Bhai expostulated. "How would jackals come here? Is this Bangladesh?"

All this time, Beena's eyes had been adjusting to the dark room. She kept her gaze fixed on the glass to avoid seeing the person whose presence she was most conscious of in the room. She had forgotten what he looked like. Only a genial impression remained of a conventionally handsome visage, a blank canvas standing in for the romantic heroes of Bengali movies.

"Khaled! How do you like your new job?" Shona's husband Bulbul asked. He leaned forward to listen to the answer with a rapt expression on his round face.

"Good," Khaled said. He spoke in a powerful voice with a rich timbre.

Salma turned to the other women. "Cholo. Let's go see the bedrooms upstairs! After that, we will come down and serve the food." There were four bedrooms upstairs, one of them turned into a recreation room where the children were sitting.

When Beena stepped forward to join the others, Salma shook her head. Drawing close to Beena, she brushed Beena's mouth with a feathery finger, as if to fix her lipstick, and whispered in her ear, "Stay." Aloud, she said, "Beena, Ronny was asking about Sir only a few days ago. Why don't you stay and tell him about your father?"

The women fluttered up the stairs, their high heels thudding on the wood steps.

Ronny gestured to Beena. "Sit."

Beena pulled a white leather armchair with a studded back and sat down near him, carefully arranging Salma's sari about her.

"How is Sir?" Ronny asked.

"Bhalo. He is well."

"Will he come to visit?"

"He refuses to visit," Beena complained. "He says he is afraid to travel. He is only comfortable in his own home, where everything is familiar to him. My mother likes to travel, but my father doesn't want to."

As she spoke about her father, some of the men turned to listen.

"Same with my parents," Ronny said. "They have become absolutely reluctant to leave home in their old age. They have become so timid!"

"Yes!" cried Beena. "It is hard to imagine that these same people once traveled far from their villages to the city and then to America, Canada, and England to study, and to the Middle East for work! My parents come up with all sorts of excuses not to visit, saying, how will they get their medicine here, and what if they have to see a doctor." Her mouth twisted in frustration as she complained about her parents' refusal to visit her. Since she had left home five years ago, they had not come once to see how she lived in America.

"Don't you have a brother? What is he doing now?" Ronny asked.

"My brother Lenin left for Bangladesh after completing his PhD. Ei to. It has been almost a year."

"Really? What is he doing in Bangladesh?"

"Teaching. At North South."

"What was his degree in?"

"Math."

"Uh-ha! Bolo ki?" Ronny cried, shaking his head and slapping his thigh. "Why didn't you tell me? He could have got such lucrative positions at companies here! I could have got him a job!"

"Is Sir still driving that beat up Volkswagen?" someone asked.

"Yes." Beena nodded.

"Sir was an eccentric." Ronny laughed, shaking his head. "He used to teach a concept by telling a story. The bell would ring, but he would hold us back telling his story, and we would sit there listening. Nobody wanted to leave." He creased his eyes and parted his lips, as if recalling a fond memory. Then, in the manner of someone remembering a thing he had to do, he stirred and sprang to action. "Beena, this is our friend Khaled. My batch-mate." He gestured at the sofa across from him, behind Beena.

"We met. Salma introduced us," Beena said, blushing as she turned around to face Khaled.

"Hello again." Khaled flashed her a grin. She was impressed with his even white teeth. "How is Sir?"

"He's well," she answered, speaking quickly and nervously.

His face was of a rich brown complexion, smooth and clean shaved, with a square jaw. Unlike his friends, who had acquired thick waists and broad chests, he was still lean and light. His hair was parted to the side like the others, but unlike them, he still had a full head of thick, black hair.

"I heard you are getting your PhD in May?" he said. "Congrat-ulations. What are your plans after that?"

"I applied for a few jobs, but I didn't get any offers. I will return to Bangladesh." Beena shrugged her shoulders.

"Don't go! You would be crazy to give up this life in the US! Get a job here. Stay!" He spoke innocently, in a high, guileless voice, gazing at her with a frank expression.

"I have to!" she stammered. "My F-1 visa will run out after my studies end."

"Any company would snatch you up like anything! Anyone would hire a doctorate! They would be lucky to have someone of your caliber." He spoke warmly and kindly, with an earnestness that suggested that he would go out this minute to find a way to keep her in America.

"Going back is not an option. Believe me," he went on passionately. "You invested so much in your education! You are so smart. Why would you go back? What would you do if you went back? That country is a mess. There are strikes every day. When we were students at the engineering university, we faced session jots that delayed our graduation by two years. You must have faced it too, at Dhaka University, during your honors and masters? Take my word for it. Going back is not an option."

"I think Bangladesh is very livable," Beena argued back in a lively voice. "Our parents' generation fought for liberation in 1971 so that we could have a country to call our own."

"That may be the case, but look how happy you are here," Khaled said. He had shifted his position on the sofa so that he was very close now, giving her his full attention, with his back to the men. When she spoke, he listened intensely. There was a sincerity and earnestness in his manner that she found disarming.

"Look at all the things you get here. Freedom to do anything you want. Recognition for your merit. You can't get any of those things in Bangladesh." Perhaps sensing that she was wearying of this line of argument, he asked suddenly, "Did you like your subject?"

"Yes."

"What was it?"

"English Literature."

"And...what is that about?" he asked, furrowing his eyebrows. His face was tense with admiration.

She laughed. "We study literature. Novels. Poetry. But also important essays that mark the ideas of a period. We discuss what novels are about, what they want to talk about. I like it very much."

"There you go," he said, smiling. He leaned back in his chair in a relaxed manner, with his feet planted apart on the white carpet, placing his hands on top of his knees. His fingers were long and tapered like an artist's, with the gathering of brown skin around the joints, ending in clear, moon-shaped nails. "My hats off to you. Reading and writing in English is a useful skill to get ahead in any career. As for me, even if you beat me with a stick, not one word would come out!" He laughed.

"You are right. I loved my time at an American university studying the subject I love," she admitted warmly.

They had been sitting in a cocoon, away from the others.

Now Shona's husband Bulbul called to Khaled. "What is it like working at H–? How did you get such a good job?"

Beena's eyes flew open. She parted her lips to ask Khaled to repeat the name of the company, to confirm that she had heard right.

"Aarre, Bhai, what can I say? They wouldn't let me be!" Khaled cried, slapping his thigh. His handsome face split into a big smile. "This headhunter kept calling me for months, asking me to meet with him just one time, to hear him out. Finally, we met at a Starbucks. He made me this incredible offer that I couldn't refuse. That's their way. They make an offer that is impossible to refuse, great salary and benefits."

"And they paid for your relocation?" Ronny asked in a thick and greedy voice.

"Yes. They said they would pay to ship everything I own."

Looking around the room, Beena saw the naked look of admiration mixed with jealousy in all the men's faces.

One of them prodded Ronny in his chest. "How much does a bachelor own anyway?"

"True." Khaled laughed. "I said as much to them. I said, unfortunately I am a bachelor and I have nothing to ship."

The room exploded in laughter. Ronny looked at Beena, arched his eyebrows, and smiled. Only Beena remained silent, stunned by the name of Khaled's company. That name, uttered so callously, carried her back to the developing news over the past few months about a possible war with Iraq, and further back, to her childhood in Mosul.

The men were still congratulating Khaled on his new job. He was smiling pleasantly, answering a barrage of questions.

"Next step is international assignment, am I right?" Bulbul said.

"Hopefully," Khaled said with a boyish grin.

The men's conversation turned to their companies. The promotion someone had received. How long it had taken each of them to get a Green Card. Two men were discussing buying stocks.

"I have a bit of money to invest. Should I buy shares in M–?"

"No, man, don't invest there." His companion shook his head. "Didn't you see how their shares fell recently? Oil is where you should invest now. Especially if there is a war."

As if on cue, Ronny reached for the remote control on the coffee table and switched on the large-screen TV in front of him. A newscaster spoke loudly about the impending expiration of the deadline for Saddam Hussein to flee the country. The camera swept over aerial footage of Iraq as someone discussed war tactics. Beena twisted her head to face the screen.

Khaled turned back to Beena. "Sorry. You were saying?"

She shook her head. "Nothing."

"Oh, come on! You were saying something. Say it!"

She smiled tightly. Her eyes were wet with tears. "You work at H–? How do you feel working for a company like that?"

"What do you mean?" Khaled stared at her blankly.

"Do you know that the US is about to invade Iraq? How can you be so pleased about working at a company that is involved with the war? A lot of people are going to die if there is a war."

"My company is involved with the war?"

"They stand to profit from the war." She leaned forward. "Do you know that half a million Iraqi children starved because of sanctions?"

"Half a million? Surely, not that many?" he began.

"Oh, I'm sure the actual figure is higher!" she scoffed. "Do you know that Iraq is only allowed to export its oil in exchange for food? And do you know how many Iraqis have developed cancer from depleted uranium?"

Bulbul called to Khaled again. "Can you buy shares at your company, Khaled? Take my advice. Buy company shares."

"I'll look into it," Khaled replied, as the women appeared at the top of the stairs.

"Beena Apa, you are still here? I didn't realize you had stayed behind!" Shona looked down at Beena with accusatory eyes.

The other women came down behind Shona, staring at Beena sitting among the men.

"Come, Beena Apa," Shona called imperiously. "We have to serve the food."

Beena rose awkwardly and followed Shona and the other women to the kitchen.

The women became busy placing serving spoons in aluminum pans, piling chilled soda bottles in a corner, and cutting lemons and cilantro to spread on top of the salad. The heat radiating from the oven beaded their lips with perspiration.

Beena approached Salma, who was stacking paper plates and napkins at one end of the island, working with a nervous energy. "I'm just going to the bathroom to freshen up."

Salma narrowed her eyes. "What happened between you two? Khaled's face was dark with fury. He did not even look at you or speak to you when you got up to leave."

Beena shrugged. "I don't know what happened."

Salma shook her head and looked away. When Beena remained standing beside her, she became very busy with the paper plates in her hands.

The bathroom was bright white, with white tiles and white paint, the whole effect accentuated by soft white mats. A large mirror above the white sink reflected the white tiles on the back wall. Beena washed her face in the cold water from the tap and stared at her reflection in the mirror. Her narrowed eyes and the foul expression of her mouth reminded her of her father. He used to sit alone at the parties her parents attended when she was a child. He would sit by himself in a corner of a room full of people with a thunderous expression on his face, not interacting with anyone. As a child, she had felt wretched watching him sitting alone like that. She used to wonder why he didn't laugh and talk with the others. Why couldn't he be part of the group? Once, Beena and Lenin had been discussing their father, how he had always parked himself on the periphery of things, ready to jump up and challenge the way things were. The topic of his PhD thesis had been *Stresses and Deformations at the Junctions of Axisymmetric Shells*, so they had joked, "He is interested in applying the stresses that would break the shells of every institution!"

He had loved his students, though, the men sitting in Salma's living room.

"Oh!" she cried, placing her icy hands on her cheeks, as the full weight of what she had done descended on her. She had spoiled everything by uttering words that didn't belong in that living room, by bringing in ugly politics like mud on her shoes.

In the mirror, Salma's ornate blue sari sat askew on Beena's shoulder. The lipstick that Salma had applied so carefully had become undone. She shifted Salma's necklace around her throat, lifting the weight of the heavy pendant from her chest, and felt lighter. These engineers, her father's students who said they admired him, shared nothing of his values.

2. MY MOTHER'S DESIRE

Dari Binni, 1944-47

I GREW UP IN the village of Dari Binni in Jessore, named after the Binni River that runs beside it. Our home was situated in the south-ernmost cluster of the village, consisting of several mud-walled huts with thatched roofs arranged around a rectangular mud court-yard. There was a main house with a long veranda in front, another smaller hut to the side, and a kitchen across a mud courtyard. Ours was a joint family, consisting of the families of three brothers, my father and his older brothers Boro Chacha and Mejo Chacha, my grandmother Dadi, and my youngest uncle Chhoto Chacha, who was yet unmarried. For a long time, I was the only child in the household. All day, I wandered alone, eating fruits straight from the orchard behind our house and bathing in the river with the other village children. The river was also where I went fishing with nets, poles, and boxes, returning with juicy puti maachh, which my mother salted and fried for me over the open fire of our clay stove till they became crunchy.

When I was four, my father's sister came to visit during the summer holidays, accompanied by my cousin Muazzem, who was only two years older than me. While everyone else in the house took their midday nap, we two played on the mud veranda outside my mother's room, drenched with sweat. I danced on the veranda, jumping and circling Muazzem, singing.

The next minute, I slipped and fell, cutting my leg on the jagged edge of the veranda. Blood spurted from my knee and seeped into the ground. I began to scream, waking up all the women in the house. My mother came running with her sari wrapped around her, long tangles of hair flying behind her. Seeing me lying on the ground, clutching my leg and crying, she cried out. "Naughty boy! You do nothing but make trouble all day! From tomorrow, I shall send you to school!"

"Ayesha, the poor child is bleeding!" My aunt Mejo Chachi pleaded with her, but my mother remained unmoved.

As Mejo Chachi washed my leg, bandaged it, and gathered me in her arms, she stood with her hands on her hips, trembling with rage.

In the evening, my father and uncles returned from their work in the agricultural fields, holding kerosene lamps in their hands. The family gathered on the veranda to eat. My mother and her sisters-in-law served their husbands fried bitter gourd, mustard greens, and lentils on top of hard, red grains of rice and fanned their husbands while they ate. Sitting by the dim flicker of the kerosene lamp, my father and my uncles talked about their day. They were land-owners. My grandfather, who had been a zamindar's manager, had left behind many acres of agricultural land for his sons. I sat beside my father and ate from his plate, listening to their talk of land and farming while my mother fed me balls of rice with her hand.

My mother listened quietly to the men's conversation, but her eyes carried a faraway look. She was perhaps twenty, slender and long, with large eyes and thick, black hair that fell to her hips. Among the villagers, she was considered a beauty. She may have been missing her mother's house, which lay a few villages away from Dari Binni, but she was close to her sisters-in-law, Boro Chachi and Mejo Chachi, with whom she cooked the family's meals and went bathing in the river. She was also a favorite of my grandmother Dadi, who put aside the best dishes for her. But when my uncles talked about the land conflicts they had to resolve, the activities of neighboring landlords, and their plans to buy some acres of rice paddy, I looked up at my mother's face and thought her most alone in the world. She smiled at me and fed me another ball of rice. What was she thinking? I did not know then that sitting in the circle of her husband's family, fanning my father as he ate, my mother dreamed of how far she would send me away.

She did not want me to become a landlord like my father, having gotten it into her head that a person's worth lay in their education. She herself had never studied beyond primary school. My father and his brothers also had studied up to class five only. My grandfather had had an unfortunate experience with education involving his eldest son. Since then, he had determined that no son of his should go to school. But my mother had the highest respect for education. She was a village woman, so it is possible that she thought that by becoming a doctor or an engineer I could bring home money, but my father belonged to a well-to-do family and my mother lived comfortably in her in-laws' house. It is also possible that she wanted me to become someone famous so that she could brag about me to the other villagers, but the most likely explanation is that she wanted me to get an education so that I could escape her prison.

"Shono," she said, addressing my father in a low voice, pulling her sari around her shoulders, "I am thinking of sending Ketu to school."

My father, who was a quiet, mild-natured man, looked up in astonishment. "But how? There is no school here."

A few days later, I accompanied my youngest uncle Chhoto Chacha to a school a kilometer from our home, housed in a single-room mud hut with a thatched roof. There was no provision for someone as young as me to study in this school, but I was allowed to sit beside my uncle while he attended class.

To reach this school, I rode on my uncle's shoulders, securing my legs around his neck. Chhoto Chacha was a lanky fourteen-year-old and could barely support my weight. On the way, we passed the Binni River where fishermen threw their nets on the water and agricultural fields where farmers planted rice in the sun-warmed, green paddy, their checked, bright-colored lungi gathered around their loins, out of the way of the mud. Their lean, muscled arms and legs and copper-colored torsos rippled in the sun as they worked.

"Where do you take the boy?" they called to Chhoto Chacha.

"School!" Chhoto Chacha shouted back.

"What for?" they replied, with wonder.

We seldom reached school on time. One day, my uncle and I arrived especially late. The other boys were already crammed together on the benches, crouched over their carbon slates, working on sums.

Seeing us, the master came forward. "You have come late again, you rascal?" He slapped Chhoto Chacha across the cheek and told him to set me down.

Thus dismounted, I stared up at him. His head was bald and shiny. A thick moustache covered his mouth entirely. Leaving us standing in the middle of the room, he waddled to his desk, prised out a thin wooden cane, and walked back slowly as I watched, transfixed on his exposed belly jiggling underneath his shirt.

"Put out your hand," the master commanded.

Chhoto Chacha extended his palm. The master began to beat Chhoto Chacha with his cane. The stick went flying all over Chhota Chacha's body, landing blows on the backs of his legs, on his shoulders, and on his head. Chhoto Chacha jumped to escape the master's lashes, crying out and trying to shield his body with his arms. This made the teacher beat him even harder.

A silence descended on the room. No one dared shift his position or breathe loudly. Outside, the sun beat down on the mud, and a mild breeze flapped the leaves on the trees. The trapped heat inside the hut produced a pool of sweat on the teacher's face, which was distorted in a grimace. Drops of perspiration slid off his quivering nose and slipped into his mouth.

I ran out of the school, past the rice fields, the hill, and Binni river, teeming with fishing boats and laughing bathers. I did not stop till I reached the fruit orchard behind our house. Plopping down under a tree, I gazed up at the bright blue, cloudless sky and took big gulps of air. School was a place of cruelty and injustice, I decided. I was determined never to return there.

To explain what happened next, I must present a clearer picture of my mother. She was a young girl, full of mischiefs and passions. Once, while she and her sisters-in-law were walking back from the river where they had gone to bathe, they were passing through the bamboo grove behind our house when she pulled down a branch of a bamboo tree. The sharp, thin blade cut her arm open from the elbow to the wrist. Her arms and her sari were covered with blood. Her friends carried her home and placed her on top of our bed, where I had been sleeping. Waking up and seeing her lying in a pool of blood, I began to scream. Her friends had to drag me off her.

My mother had pleaded with the schoolmaster to allow me to sit in his school. Now my failure to return there filled her with humiliation. She worked distractedly in the kitchen, making careless mistakes. Her sari caught fire from the clay stove. Her sisters-in-law scolded her, pointing out that nobody in the village had studied beyond primary school. My grandmother Dadi, a diminutive woman with a long, thin face, cried that I was too young for my mother's schemes. But my mother would not listen to anyone. She had begun to hatch her next plan. She was a quiet person, but when she made up her mind, nobody could stop her.

One night, I opened my eyes to find my mother's face bent over me in the dark. She was shaking me by the shoulder. I peered at her sleepily and tried to shake her off.

"Ketu! I am sending you to my mother's house," she said.

I nodded and went back to sleep.

Early the next morning, my father dressed me in the bitter cold, pulling a shirt and half pants over my shivering body. The leaves and the grass were drenched with dew. A pigeon rumbled in the smoky air as our cows stirred from sleep, lowing throatily. My grandmother and my aunts worked in the kitchen with their shawls wrapped tightly around their bodies. My mother swept the veranda and the mud courtyard, setting off a dust storm. My eldest uncle Boro Chacha sat on the veranda in a cane chair, rubbing his beard and chewing a neem branch, looking at my mother with fiery eyes. Mejo Chacha and Chhoto Chacha splashed their faces with cold water out of a drum. Through their stiff gestures and stern looks, all the members of the household made it clear to my mother that she was acting against their wishes.

Crouching in the frigid air, I gulped down the fermented rice, washed my fingers from a tin cup of cold water, and stood up. My father wrapped a shawl around my body and hoisted me onto his shoulders. Holding the edge of her sari over her head with one hand, shading her eyes with her other hand, my mother stood smiling, watching me as I set off for my maternal grandmother's house, my Nani Bari Hairnakunda, in another village nineteen kilometers away. I would not return until I was eight years old, already an outsider.

3. THE PHONE CALL

Houston, March 2003

After returning from Salma's party, Beena had called her mother in a rush of emotions—homesick and needy—but now that feeling was ebbing away fast. She was lying on top of her single mattress, relaxed after changing into a loose cotton T-shirt and pajamas. Her window faced the street, looking down into the brightly lit windows of the sprawling houses below. No matter how massive the houses, or how resplendent the lives inside, at least she had this majestic height.

"Hello, Amma! Can you hear me?" she repeated the same words from a moment ago, fighting static.

"Beena! Did you meet the boy?" Beena's mother's voice sounded high-pitched and muted at the same time, as if coming from far off.

"How do *you* know about a boy?" Beena demanded, sitting up.

"Salma told me. She said he is a very good boy. A brilliant student," her mother said.

"I want to return home." She said the words softly, pressing her ear to the cordless handset.

"What? You mean to come live in Bangladesh?" Her mother's voice rose in alarm. "Beena, don't make the mistake of coming back! Hai, hai! I'm begging you. Don't come!"

"Amma, I told you my visa is going to run out in May, or a few months after that. I want to return to my country. Didn't Abba return after his PhD?" Looking around the apartment, she thought, if she had to leave, what of it? There was not much to pack. All the clothes she owned hung in the closet, a slim array of cheap pants and skirts. Most of her belongings could be thrown away. There were some books she wanted to keep, but she could ship those.

"Beena, you shouldn't do this. It's a big mistake!" Her mother repeated, as if Beena had not heard her the first time. She belonged to a generation of educated, middle-class Bangladeshis who wanted their children to surpass their parents in achievement. "Can't you get a job over there? Get a teaching position at a university. That's the best option for you, in my mind."

"It won't happen just because you keep repeating yourself," Beena shot back in a cutting voice. Springing up with the cordless phone in her hand, she stormed to the kitchen sink to get a glass of water. When she moved away from the base of the handset, her mother's voice became faint. "I *tried* to get a job," she retorted in her head, standing in her bare feet on the cold tile, gulping down the city water. Her mouth was dry, and she felt a headache coming on.

"Don't be a dreamer like your father. When your father completed his PhD in Canada, his supervisor offered him a job. He could have become a Canadian citizen, but he gave up all those prospects and returned to his country. He said, my country, my country. That was a big mistake. And I paid for it all my life. Don't you think if I had a PhD from Canada, my career would have been made?" Her mother was going over her old complaints, words that Beena had heard a hundred times before. "Beena, are you listening?"

"Yes," Beena replied heavily, scanning the inky sky outside her window. Late at night, the street became quiet and peaceful.

"Now you are telling me to stay in America? You didn't even want to let me come abroad to study in the first place!"

"The other day, I fell from the rickshaw and hurt my back," Beena's mother said. "The roads are full of potholes."

"What happened to your car?"

"Didn't I tell you? The car broke down. It has been in the shop for months."

Beena had not known this. It had only been five years since she had left home, and yet she felt separated from her parents by a great distance. They knew nothing about her life, just as she knew nothing about their broken-down car. But Lenin knew. Lucky Lenin was back home, living with their parents. Beena was filled with a longing to join her family.

"Amma, I want to come back!" She lay back down on the mattress and locked her arms under her head. "Say something good."

"Say something good? Okay, say something good." The voice on the line faltered, as if Beena's mother was thinking hard, searching for something positive to say. "It's unsafe here," she said at last. "Don't come back."

"Where is Abba?" Beena asked, changing the subject.

"Your father is at the academic council meeting. They have been having meetings all week trying to resolve a situation. Two rival contractors are fighting over a bid to construct a new building on campus. Now the rival student groups have become involved in the disagreement. Each group wants a different contractor to get the job. I'm worried about your father, Beena. His health is not good. His diabetes is getting bad. Sometimes he is hypo. One time, when he was at his department, his sugar became very low, and he fell down the stairs. He is very weak. You understand, Beena? His life is up to chance."

Her mother had a gift for ringing alarm bells, as if the business of her life was to tell Beena every bit of terrible news, to agitate Beena to some great action. Perhaps it was some sort of psychological strategy, motivation through threat.

"Your father is very worried that you are not married. Some-times, he wakes up at night, worrying about what will happen to you. It's making him ill!" she finished triumphantly.

"May I talk to Lenin quickly?" Thinking of her brother, Beena relaxed a little. Her optimistic, handsome, pleasant brother Lenin was always at ease in the world. Perhaps she would discuss the guy, Khaled, with him, tell him what had happened at Salma's party.

"He is out with friends." Her mother cleared her throat. "Beena, I wanted to mention something to you. Don't be angry with me. You get angry if I try to say anything, but I think you will be happy if you get married. There are so many nice boys. You could marry and settle in America. That would be a great solution to your problem. That guy Salma mentioned sounds very nice."

"I just told you I'm coming back!!" Beena shouted.

"I'm sorry, Beena. Don't be angry. Are you angry with me?"

"There is someone at the door. I have to go."

4. A WORLD OF FEAR

Harinakunda, 1944

IN MY GRANDMOTHER'S VILLAGE, I learned the meaning of fear.
My grandmother Nani's house stood at a distance from the other
houses, beside a jungle that was home to jackals, foxes, snakes,
and the Royal Bengal tiger. At night, hearing the jackals' cry, we
understood that the tiger was not far behind. The villagers rarely
ventured outside at night. Besides the wild animals, they were
afraid of djinns and ghosts wandering the jungle, ponds, and agricultural fields.

The object of my own fear was our schoolmaster Noyon
Master. He was a short man, bulky in body, with a long nose that
was broken in the middle and a thick beard dyed bright red with
henna. Tufts of orange hair covered his forehead and the tops of his
ears like wool. The schoolmaster's goal seemed to be to drive terror
into the hearts of his students. Whenever he saw me anywhere about
the village, he made fun of me, calling out to me from a distance in
a high, mocking tone. "Ei, Oyon, Oyon!" This was because I could
not pronounce his name correctly.

Unfortunately for me, the master was a frequent visitor at my
grandmother's house. On many evenings, he ate dinner with us,

sitting on a jute mat on the veranda, complaining to my uncles about me as he partook of our bowls of fish curry, leafy greens, and hard rice harvested from our fields, while I ate with my head bent over my plate and swallowed his insults with my food.

One day, Noyon Master introduced his students to a difficult math problem.

"It's an impossible problem! You will not be able to solve it!" he cried with glittering eyes. "When you try to do this sum, you will be in the same situation as the puti fish in the month of Poush." He pulled back his lips and bared his stained, orange teeth, as if to demonstrate the plight of the puti maachh.

I copied the problem on my slate with a dry mouth, as I was aware of the tragedy of the puti maachh to which Noyon Master referred. Walking beside the river in the winter season, I had witnessed the puti maachh shooting out of the freezing water, only to asphyxiate and die on land.

That night, I sat on the floor at the foot of Nani's bed as she slept, trying to solve the problem by the shifting light of a kerosene lamp and wondering, "Would I really die like those fish before I have worked out the solution?"

All of a sudden, a strong wind blew through the window and snuffed out the flame of the kerosene lamp. Rainwater drummed on the roof and fell to the earth like bullets. The wind began to push hard against the walls and the roof, threatening to level the house. I jumped into bed beside Nani and hid my face in her back. The whole night, the wind carried on like this. The trees groaned, bending and snapping in the wind.

In the morning, the three boys with whom I walked to school arrived at Nani's house calling for me. I gulped down my breakfast of fermented rice, wiped my mouth on Nani's sari, and jumped up to join them. We started off for school, dressed in collared shirts and half pants, carrying our schoolbooks and slates in our hands. The school lay two kilometers from my grandmother's house, across a river. To get to the other side, we had to cross a narrow bridge constructed out of single spans of bamboo tied end to end. Curling our toes around the bamboo, peering down at the rushing water below, we felt certain that one of us would fall. This sensation of danger lent excitement to our walk. Farther ahead, we hung from the branches of an odorous jackfruit tree with large, bulbous fruit sticking out from the trunk in clusters, threw stones at a boroi tree to knock off the fruits till the owner came out shouting at us, and chased after one another on the mud path, pulling our shirts loose out of half pants.

A few weeks ago, one of our companions, a small boy with large, twinkling eyes named Shomu, had fallen from a tree and broken his arm. The village doctor had bandaged the broken arm with a splint, but an infection had developed at the site of the wound, and, within a few days, Shomu had died. Following this incident, the adults said to us, "A djinn threw Shomu from the tree. See what happens when you are naughty? Be good, or the same thing will happen to you!" Now, passing under the tree that had killed Shomu, we closed our eyes and ran, simultaneously fearing the djinn that had pushed Shomu and Shomu's ghost.

On the way, we came across the wide destruction caused by the previous night's storm. Flattened trees and snapped branches lay fallen across our path. The wind had blown the thatched roofs off some of the houses. When we arrived at school, Noyon Master informed us that there would be no lessons that day, as the roof of the school had been damaged in the storm. He told the students to go to every house in the village to collect donations for repairing the roof. I felt relieved, thinking that I had been spared from being grilled about the impossible math problem that would asphyxiate me like the puti maachh. All day, we walked under the hot sun, going from door to door, collecting money for our school.

When I reached my grandmother's courtyard, the sun was setting and the sky was ablaze with colors. My body was squeezed dry of every ounce of water. Gasping to take a breath, I was reminded again how Noyon Master had said that trying to solve his sum I would asphyxiate and die like the puti maachh. As I crossed the courtyard of my grandmother's house, one moment, there was the vegetable garden, the water well, the canopy of fruit trees behind the house, the cowshed, the chickens, and the goats walking across the courtyard, and then every object went dark. I staggered to the ground and lost consciousness.

With time, I began to believe fervently in ghosts. Five of my mother's siblings had been married in the same village. They lived near my grandmother's house with their own families. At night, my uncles and aunts sat on the veranda of my grandmother's house telling stories about the ghosts that lived in the pond. There was one ghost called Mechho Bhut that took the shape of a tall, thin woman covered in a white sari who came to fishermen in the night and extended a skeletal hand to beg for fish. If the fishermen refused, the Mechho Bhut would pull them down from their boats and drown them. After listening to these stories, I lay in bed, too terrified to sleep. Every sound appeared to be unnatural. The soft thud of leaves falling on the tin roof, the cry of an animal or bird, and even the whooshing of the wind through leaves would jolt me. All the familiar trees that I had climbed during the day were transformed into the abode of other-worldly spirits. The world seemed overrun with ghosts.

During the fishing season, the fishermen threw their nets on the water and pulled in unbelievable numbers of fish; not only small fish, but also large fish like silver carp, grass carp, tilapia, Bengal eel, and minnow. For an entire month, we feasted on freshly caught fish cooked in hot, oily curry, served over hot rice. My maternal cousins and I caught small fish with bamboo fishing poles and other contraptions in the small pond behind Nani's house. One of my favorite ways to fish was using a box. I constructed a wire mesh box, with two small holes on the bottom of one side. Then I waded into the river and laid the box down. The holes acted as funnels, drawing in the fish with the current. In this way, I caught ten, twenty fish at a time.

At this time, my mother's youngest sister Chhoto Khala came to visit Nani from her in-laws' house. She had been married recently, at fourteen years of age. During her visit, we came to know that a djinn lived with my aunt. Several times a day, she fell into a trance, uttering strange words in a thick, heavy voice. During her visit, Chhoto Khala shared a room with my Nani and me. One night, I rose to go to the outhouse in the middle of the bamboo grove behind the main dwelling. I went through the process half asleep, but when I reentered the room, my eyes fell on the space below my aunt's bed, where a massive fire burned with red-orange flames and a tremendous noise. *Dau! Dau!* My aunt lay on top of her bed in a state of semi-consciousness. Her body was shivering, and her eyes were flung open in a vacant gaze. She was muttering something through trembling lips. Shutting my eyes, I leapt into bed beside Nani and hid my face in Nani's neck. Sometime later, I gathered up the courage to look again, but there was nothing there.

After that night's incident, I never went to the bathroom in the middle of the night while Chhota Khala was staying with us, not for fear of tigers, jackals, foxes, or snakes, but for the completely fictional fear of ghosts conveyed to me through my relatives' stories. My fear of ghosts instilled in me a kind of respect for the villagers' rule never to go out at night. Had I remained in my grandmother's house much longer, it is possible that I, too, would have become a sensible, god-fearing villager, but when I was eight years old, my father came to take me home. I had graduated to class five by now, so I could attend a new primary school that had opened seven kilometers from Dari Binni.

A few days before my father's arrival, an upsetting incident took place in my grandmother's village. A tiger had been spotted in the jungle behind the cluster of the villagers' mud huts, and there was great excitement afoot. "Mama has come!" the cry rang through the village. The villagers never referred to the tiger by its name, bagh. Instead, we used the pseudonym Mama, meaning uncle, because we believed that merely uttering the word bagh would call the tiger into our presence. To scare away the tiger, a forest guard had appeared with his old rifle, and some villagers had brought sticks, nets, and shovels. Many people gathered to watch the fun. In the middle of this excitement, the crowd parted suddenly to make way for an Englishman carrying a shotgun.

Seeing the Englishman, the villagers began to jeer at the tiger. "This time, it has no chance!"

We watched with great respect as the Englishman positioned his body, cocked his barrel expertly, and took aim at the tiger. There was a loud bang, and everyone rushed forward to see the dead tiger. At that moment, the tiger pounced and snatched a man from the crowd, carrying him up a banyan tree. In front of our eyes, with one swipe of its claw, the tiger tore the entire skin off the man's back. The villagers began to agitate bravely with their sticks, until the tiger flew off into the jungle, dropping the mangled body to the ground. A few men lifted the injured man into a cow cart and rushed him to the hospital in Jhenidah, but the poor man perished on the way.

A few days after this incident, my father and I started on our journey to Dari Binni. As we walked together in the heat of the Joishtho afternoon, in the last month of summer, I hugged his long legs, overcome with gladness. My father gave me a piece of surprising news. My mother had given birth to another child. My father told me that my sister's name was Jahanara, which meant queen of the world.

"She is so beautiful that she could light up the whole world!" he said.

On the way, people stopped us again and again. Old men with bent backs, young farmers with sun-beaten faces, and bare-chested young peddlers came up to greet us, asking my father, "Your son? What is the boy's name? How old is he? Where was he living till now? Why so?"

I did not enjoy these conversations. While my father talked with the men, his tall frame clothed in a white cotton Punjabi and loose pajamas, his pointed black leather shoes planted in the mud, bending his neck to listen to the men, I skipped ahead and scaled up a lychee tree, hiding my face in its leaves and filling my nostrils with their sweet smell. More than ghosts, djinns, and wild animals, I feared that something in my world had changed permanently. I would go home only to find that I had no home to return to.

5. A PROPOSAL

Houston, March 2003

AT THE TOP OF the steep flight of stairs leading to the garage apartment stood the slightly stooped figure of a tall man, lit by a yard light below. His high forehead, skeletal face, slanted, almond-shaped eyes, and cocked ears gave him the appearance of a lean wolf.

"Roberto!" Beena cried. "What a surprise!"

"I've been calling you. Where were you?" Roberto asked, stepping inside the dark apartment.

Beena looked away slightly, pulling at a lock of hair and curling it around two fingers. Roberto was one of her closest friends. He was a graduate student in engineering at her university. They had known each other for years, almost since she had set foot on campus, but she wasn't comfortable telling him about being set up for marriage.

"What's up?" Roberto said, picking up the only chair in the apartment and pulling it away from the small, pine-wood desk. He was dressed in a blue T-shirt and jeans, smelling of soap and shampoo. Leaning back against the chair, he pushed his legs out and locked his hands behind his head. "So?" he said in a cheerful voice, smiling at her. His eyes had changed color from yellow to a warm brown in the light of the apartment.

Beena walked to her bed, the only other place to sit, and plopped down on top of the mattress. The mattress pushed back, giving her a bounce. A hand-stitched nakshi katha bedcover stitched out of her mother's old saris covered the mattress. She had carried the heavy blanket in her suitcase from Bangladesh, against her wishes, at her mother's insistence. Beside the mattress stood a pile of hardcover books stacked high on the wood floor. These were library books Beena had borrowed months ago and was still using for her research.

"Roberto, I've decided that I'm going home. My visa runs out after graduation."

"Beena! You didn't even try to get a teaching job," Roberto began in a complaining voice.

"I *did* try. I applied for many jobs. No one would hire me. I didn't even get any interviews, except for that one place in Houston, and they didn't even tell me that they had offered the job to someone else. Come on, admit it, it's hard for an international person to get a job."

He looked as if he was going to object again, but then he stopped himself, biting his lip. "That's true."

Roberto had an offer from Motorola in Chicago and another offer from a big organization in Huntsville, Alabama. He was waiting to hear back from other places before he said yes to one. Although Roberto was Italian, his parents had lived in the US briefly when he was born, so he was a US citizen. Not that he didn't deserve those offers. He had worked hard, was brilliant in his field, in fact. He had published two articles already in respected journals.

"Listen," Roberto said. He paused for a moment, looking at her through hooded eyes, then jerked his chin. "Perhaps you don't have to go back."

"What do you mean? Roberto, my mother called, nagging me about how I have to get married. Again! I swear, I'll become a conniving husband hunter in no time. All I can think of is marriage!

She gave me a headache!" Beena laughed, throwing her head back, then looked at Roberto for sympathy.

When he didn't respond, she went on energetically, eager to impress upon him her ridiculous situation. "I told you before, right? For years, my mother has been sending me the biodata of strange men and forcing me to meet with absolute strangers who drive up from Dallas and Austin, even Louisiana!" She went on in an animated voice about the humiliations she had suffered, but the part about being set up with Khaled stuck in her throat. It made her blush to tell Roberto about that set up. She had liked him, too, a lot.

She still didn't understand what had happened. She had challenged Khaled, yes, but she had been taken aback by his anger when she had simply criticized the company where he worked. She had assumed that he would agree with her when he found out the truth about his company and the role of oil companies and oil interests in destroying Iraq! She really wanted to speak to someone about him. She looked at Roberto with big eyes, the words on her lips, wondering how to begin.

"Beena, I've been thinking. There is another way for you to stay." Roberto unlocked his hands and sat up, spreading his hands on his knees.

"What is it?" she asked, full of curiosity.

Roberto picked up a ballpoint pen from the table and twirled it in his hand, pressing on the cap with a thumb and letting the pen spin in the air. "We could get married," he said.

6. THE STORM

Dari Binni, 1947-51

THE UNCLE WHOM I called Boro Chacha was not my eldest uncle. My grandfather had another son, the child of his first wife, who left home long ago. We referred to him as the Lost Uncle. My lost uncle was the son of my grandfather's first wife. After the death of his first wife, my grandfather had married my grandmother. As a Zamindar's manager, my grandfather had to oversee all the land holdings of the Zamindar. In this process, he created many enemies. In order to fight his enemies, he developed relationships with other strong families. One way to develop these ties was through marriage.

My lost uncle had been a student at Presidency College in Calcutta. When he came home to visit during the Durga Puja holiday, my grandfather married him to the daughter of a powerful family against his wishes. My lost uncle was so angry that he left home on the night of his wedding. He was never seen again. He did not return to college, and nobody in Calcutta knew anything about him. The incident had a bad effect on the family. While my grandfather was alive, he never sent another son to a distant place for studies. After many months of waiting, the family declared my lost uncle dead. His immediate younger brother was married to his deserted wife in a hasty ceremony, and the family property and propriety were both restored. This uncle who had saved the day became Boro Chacha, even taking the title of my lost uncle, and he became very religious.

Boro Chacha had turned to religion at a time when he feared that he would die childless. After years of a barren marriage, he was desperate for his wife to bear him a child. One day, he set off on his bicycle to Jhenidah town to see a pir. On the way, his cycle broke down, and Boro Chacha had to make the rest of the journey on foot. At last, he reached the pir's house in Jhenidah, a palatial building with many rooms, balconies, gardens, and ponds, and waited in the public hall to see the holy man. Several hours later, a wizened man with a beard that reached his waist emerged in the hall. My uncle stood up to pay his respects and explain his wife's situation.

The pir interrupted my uncle, holding up a hand. "I heard you faced a misfortune on the way."

My uncle was astonished. How did the pir know about his plight?

"Go home," the pir said. "Your wish will be granted soon."

Within the year, Boro Chacha became the father of a child, exactly as the pir had promised. In another year, he fathered a second child. After witnessing this twin miracle, Boro Chacha became an ardent follower of the pir, spending all his time traveling around the country to attend religious gatherings. Seeing the way Boro Chacha led his life, staying away from home for months and neglecting his family, I developed a vehement aversion toward religion.

On one of his visits home, Boro Chacha was eating his evening meal on the veranda. Seeing me, he wagged his forefinger and said to my mother, "Ayesha! What good will it do to send Ketu to school? He is supposed to take care of our lands one day! If you want him to learn something, teach him to read the Koran."

My mother was going around quietly pouring water from a jug into tumblers. Boro Chacha jerked his head sideways, eyeing her, but she did not reply.

"Hmm? Ketu?" Boro Chacha turned to me with sharp eyes.

I also did not make any response. I was unbothered by his comments because I knew that he would never dare to impose his will on me, for two reasons. He sensed my dislike of religion, and he knew that my mother would never allow it. Boro Chacha did not know, however, that despite my admission to Fulhori High School, I rarely attended classes. The main difficulty for me was that the school was seven kilometers away from our home. My mother gave me a man's bicycle to ride, but it was too big for me. If I sat on the seat, I could not reach the pedals, so I stood with a foot on each pedal and rode that way. I cycled to school with two older boys from Dari Binni. On the way, we had to cross a bridge over a river, dismounting our bicycles and carrying them on our shoulders. The older boys had to help me, as my bicycle was too heavy for me to carry. I held them up, and they became irritated with me. All these factors made the effort of going to school too much for me.

There were other reasons that kept me away. The path to school was full of temptations. We passed ditches, rivers, and ponds teeming with life. Fruit trees beckoned to us in every season—mango, guava, lychee, papaya, sugar cane, and date palm. Sometimes, we stopped at a village to watch a puja, a baul playing his one-string instrument, or snake charmers, monkey tamers, and medicine men claiming to extract insects from tooth cavities. I gathered most of my knowledge about life under the open sky rather than within the four walls of the school. School was a suffocating place for me. To be confined in a room, surrounded by people constantly playing tricks and hurling abuse at one another, was abhorrent to me. I got through class five and six somehow, turning up for exams only. The masters granted me grace marks to pass.

It was easy to stay out of my mother's sight, as the house was full. Besides Jahanara, I had two other sisters now, Kodom and Rajani, who kept my mother busy. One day, when I was ten years old, I was sitting on the branch of a mango tree, keeping an eye on my projects. I was trying to raise bird chicks by feeding them grasshoppers, but I could never induce them to eat my offerings, and they were dying. My other project was an irrigation system constructed out of a network of water channels. I had the perfect excuse to be up in the tree. My father and uncles owned many fruit trees, but they were too busy overseeing their agricultural lands to take care of these, so my grandmother had given me the responsibility of managing the family's orchard. The air was ripe with the warm scent of sun-ripened fruits. The treetop swayed gently in each direction, making the best possible swing. My eyelids drooped as a delicious drowsiness came over me, and I prepared to take a nap.

"Ketu!"

Startled, I looked down to see my mother standing under the tree, with her face upturned, her eyes dark with anger.

"Why aren't you at school?"

"Amma! There will be a storm today. Look!" I pointed nervously to a fine sky with willowy clouds and flying birds.

"Come down this minute!" she cried in a voice throbbing with fury. "If you wish to see my living face, you shall go to school right now!"

My face crumpled. I climbed down quickly from the tree, mounted my bike, and cycled away from her, leaving my books behind.

That afternoon, the three of us were cycling back from school, when the sky changed color abruptly and the rain began to fall in curtains. A wind started up, flattening the tall fruit trees on our path. Branches snapped above our heads, showering to the ground. At several places, trees lay fallen on the ground. Cyclones were common in the coastal area, with winds gusting at eighty or ninety kilometers per hour. Such a storm surge over the Bay of Bengal could flood the surrounding areas. The rainwater had caused the rivers to flood the fields and paths, making it impossible to walk farther. Finding a wayside primary school, we took shelter inside the building. Throwing down our wet books on the benches, we crouched together on the floor, shivering in our wet clothes.

Even here, we did not feel safe. The wind whipped the mud walls and bamboo splints of the hut, making them dance like paper, and the rain drummed on the thatched roof with a monstrous sound. We were terrified that the strong wind might carry the roof off. Every time the thunder burst, we squeezed our eyes tight. The other two boys began to pray loudly. Sometime during the night, we heard sharp raps at the door. After much discussion, we crept to the door together and opened it cautiously. My father stood outside in the black night, white teeth glowing in a dark face. Rainwater poured off his back and his wet shirt was stuck to his body.

The rain was still falling hard when my father and I reached home after walking the other boys to their houses. My mother ran out to the courtyard and grabbed me. Pressing her chin against the top of my head, she began to sob. My wet clothes were plastered to my body. I shook uncontrollably and my teeth chattered nonstop. My mother brought me inside the house, pulled off my wet shirt, and toweled me dry. That night, as I lay shivering in bed under the weight of two kathas, I heard my parents whispering in the dark.

"What if Ketu had been killed today?" my mother cried. "To think that I forced my own child out into a storm! It is madness for him to cycle seven kilometers to school!"

Hearing these words, I went to sleep with a smile on my lips, with the impression that I could stop going to school now. But a few days later, Chhoto Chacha took me to Jhenidah in a cow cart and admitted me to Jhenidah High School.

When I was leaving home, my four-year-old sister Jahanara ran up to me and made me promise that I would visit soon. "Okay." I smiled wanly. I thought her lucky that she could stay at home with my parents while I was banished. As the cart took off, she waved frantically, a purple periwinkle winking in her hair, till she disappeared in the distance. My mother stood beside her, her thin face glowing in the midday sun. Her lips were parted, and a smile flitted over her teeth. Much later, I understood that she had fought hard to give me an education, in opposition to every member of

her own family and her husband's family, including my tyranni-
cal uncle Boro Chacha. Just as the villagers in my grandmother's
village saw snakes, tigers, and jackals as signs that they should fear
the outside world, my mother read the sign of the storm that had
nearly killed me to mean that she should pursue her dream of
educating her son even more vehemently than before.

7. SHOCK AND AWE

Houston, March 20, 2003

OPENING HER EYES AND wiping her mouth, Beena thought at first that the sunlight pouring through the blind had woken her. Then she became aware of the pealing phone.

"Roberto?"

"Hi. Did I wake you?" There was a formal note in his voice.

The events of the night before flooded back to Beena, and she blushed. "What time is it?"

"Eight. Listen, I called because on the way to school I was listening to BBC..."

"You heard the news?" Beena cried. "Did the US bomb Iraq?"

"Yes, I think they bombed the presidential palace in Baghdad. Listen, I heard that there was a bomb blast in Dhaka, in Bangladesh, and I thought I would let you know. To see if your family is all right?"

"Thanks for letting me know, Roberto. I'll check."

"Sure."

There was a pause, as if they both didn't know what to say. Then Roberto hung up. Beena tried to remember how she had answered him the night before. She had pretended not to have heard, or not to understand his meaning. She had looked away and started talking about something else.

Setting down the phone, she bounded to the desk and sat down in front of her laptop. There were bomb blasts every day in Bangladesh, in addition to strikes and protests. To live in Bangladesh was to live with the possibility of falling in front of a bomb any day. Such reports were not as frightening to her as they might appear to a foreigner. Beena and her friends used to say, if you walked in one direction you could be caught in a crossfire and if you walked in the opposite direction a bomb might land near you. Still, squinting, she checked for news headlines and then started to read all the English-language daily newspapers in Bangladesh, catching up on a month of news. *Businessmen Terrorized in their Homes. School Girl Kidnapped and Killed. Two Brothers Hacked to Death in Property Dispute.*

There was usually a delay before the news outlets published on the Internet. Idling, she started to read other news on her search engine. There were reports about explosions rocking Baghdad, a bomb attack on a palace. An authoritative voice on TV announced with awe that downtown Baghdad was "lit up in explosions and balls of fire."

"The US used more than fifteen hundred bombs and missiles!" another site said. *The New York Times* reported that a few dozen cruise missiles had been launched to kill Mr. Hussein. "American jets attacked Iraqi artillery in the southern no-fly zone," cried a headline. President Bush had announced that American forces "had begun 'the opening stages' of a broad campaign to overthrow the Iraqi government." Closing the window, Beena searched for news from Bangladesh again. After reading the same reports on several Bangladeshi news websites, she walked back to bed. All morning, she was stuck, unable to do work or walk outside, reduced to checking the computer every few minutes. She did not make it to campus for her afternoon class, either.

Then there it was. Miscreants detonated several bombs at the engineering university in the late afternoon yesterday. Two groups were fighting over a building contract. Three students were dead. One bomb hit a residential building in the teachers' quarters. Dr. Nasir Uddin's wife and son were dead. Dr. Nasir Uddin had been at the academic council meeting at that time. There had been no other people in the flat, as the maid only came in during the day from the nearby slum.

Beena's eyes narrowed from the effort to focus. She rubbed her forehead with her hands, trying to understand. She could not absorb any of it. Her brain had stopped functioning. She called home. Nobody answered the phone. She called her aunts in Dhaka and her cousins in Jhenidah, Chuadanga, Khulna, and Jessore, but she couldn't reach anybody in Bangladesh. When she called her cousins in America, waking some of them, they were as stunned as she was, and they did not know any more than she did.

8. BIG BANG

Jhenidah, 1951-55

MY FATHER'S YOUNGEST SISTER Chhoto Phupu was a new bride in her in-laws' joint family home in Jhenidah, but she took me in readily at my mother's request. For the first few weeks in my aunt's home, I wandered with a heavy heart. Chhoto Phupu tried her best to cheer me up, feeding me boiling pieces of beef from the pot on the clay stove and chatting with me, but she could not raise my spirits. After some time, I began to explore the surroundings of her home. When I discovered the mature lychee, jum, and amra trees in her orchard, a canal that teemed with fish, and a dense shrubbery of woods in which I could get lost, I felt a lot happier.

I had been admitted to class seven at the Jhenidah High School. On my first day, I sat dumbly during the first lesson, which was English Grammar. The schoolmaster was testing the students on verb tenses, with his glasses hung low on the bridge of his nose.

"You! What is the past tense and past participle of fight?" The master pointed at me, glancing up from his book and scratching his neck above his wrinkled punjabi. He waited for a quick answer, tapping his feet in leather sandals.

I did not know that English verbs had tenses. I had attended school so rarely that I had no rules to depend on, so I copied the other students' answers for their verbs and replied, "Fighted. Had fighted."

"Good," the master mumbled and moved on to the next student.

I sat in the back row, so, luckily, the master had not heard me, but the boy who sat next to me sprang up from the bench and cried, "Sir, he is wrong!"

"Really?" said the master. He looked at me again over his glasses with a puzzled expression. "Can you tell me again what the past tense and past participle of fight are?"

Again, I stood up and said, "Fighted. Had fighted."

"Truly, he does not know the answer!" the master cried in an astonished voice. He called me to the front of the room and struck me on my palms with a sharp cane.

This same master also taught math. In the second period that day, our class was introduced to geometry. I discovered that my classmates knew all the theorems in geometry, but they could not apply these theorems correctly to solve the problems. I tried to crack the mystery. How could someone know a theorem by heart, yet not be able to apply it to solve a problem? The other students began to discover my ease with mathematics and approached me for help. The master also directed them my way for tutoring. As I helped my classmates, I discovered the reason for their difficulty. They had memorized the theorems without understanding them. That was why they could not solve the problems!

A few weeks later, we were in English Grammar period again when the school clerk appeared in class to say that the headmaster had sent for me. I followed the man with trembling legs, wondering what I had done wrong. The headmaster was teaching algebra in class ten. He was a round man who always dressed in starched, white dhoti and loose, white shirts. Seeing me, he called me to the front of the room. I stood beside the headmaster with my hands clasped behind my back, staring shyly at the senior students. They were a head taller than me, with hair on their upper lips and dark stubble on their chins. They stared back at me with stern eyes.

"Ketu, my students could not solve the Pythagoras theorem. Let's see if you can do it. In a right-angled triangle, the square described on the hypotenuse is equal to the sum of the squares described on the other two sides. Prove it."

I picked up a chalk and worked out the answer on the blackboard.

"See? He solved the problem!" the headmaster cried, his eyes shining.

The senior students sprang from their benches and rushed to the front of the classroom. Without paying me any attention, they crowded around the headmaster to see what I had done, speaking in excited voices with one another. Thus ignored, I relaxed. For the first time in my life, I realized that I possessed the skills to do well in school. I had a talent for solving math problems. Not only that, but also, these problems had begun to tease me and tantalize me. Slowly, I began to grow a love for subjects that were governed by logic.

Fetu, the boy who had told on me in English grammar on my first day at Jhenidah High School, became my close friend. Fetu's older brother Aplu Bhai had also graduated from Jhenidah High School and was now a first-year student at the Ahsanullah Engineering College in Dacca. He was considered a bright scholar in our town. When we were in class eight, the headmaster invited Aplu Bhai to our school to teach a class on the irrigation system of Pakistan.

Two days before Aplu Bhai was supposed to visit our school, however, an upsetting incident took place in Jhenidah. A tiger jumped onto a bus, dragging a passenger to the road and mauling him in broad daylight before running off into the forest. Several people saw the tiger up close and described its enormous, powerful body, almost three meters long, its orange coat and black stripes, the white fur above its eyes, and the black coloring of its ears. The news left us all stunned.

Aplu Bhai's visit cheered us up considerably after this tragic incident. Everything about Aplu Bhai made an impression on us. He was a slim man with a narrow face and a prim mustache. He was dressed smartly in a white shirt tucked in black pants, black laced shoes, and white ankle socks, and he wore a wristwatch with a black leather band. He had a serious, round-shaped face, with black glasses hooked over his large ears, and slicked back hair. While lecturing, he wrote in chalk on the blackboard, his fingers flying as fast as his thoughts.

In half an hour, Aplu Bhai finished his prepared lecture. There were still a few minutes left till the end of the period. He hesitated, holding the chalk, looking at us as he debated what to do next. Then, seeming to make up his mind, he rolled up his chalk-covered sleeves. For the next twenty minutes, he spoke to us about the history of the universe, covering the big bang, the expansion of space, the creation of gas and dust, and their compression into stars and planetary systems. When the bell rang, I emerged from the school building with shaky limbs to stand in the cold, smoky air outside.

Leaning against the yellow wall, I cried out, "There is no God! There is no need for God! Nature operates according to its own logic!"

Before that day, I had disliked religion because I disliked the behavior of my uncle Boro Chacha, but now I lost my faith completely. My introduction to science gave me a new confidence in my surroundings. The world appeared to be dependable and reliable. I decided then and there that from that day, I would not suffer any belief that could not be explained by science. I declared myself to be an unbeliever of God, ghosts, and djinns. Later, I found out that Aplu Bhai was a devout man himself, but that day he destroyed my faith forever.

9. SALMA TO THE RESCUE

Houston, 2003

"I CALLED YOU THE moment I heard," Salma said on the phone. "This is terrible news, my friend."

"Oh, Salma! Can this be true?" Beena cried.

"I'm coming. I'll manage everything. Just wait for me. I'll be there soon."

Beena had no memory of what passed in the hours before Salma arrived at her door. Her throat was parched, but she was unable to drink water. The news about the bomb blast still rang in her ears. She had tried to call her father several times, her fingers pressing the buttons repeatedly till she had used up an entire calling card, but no one had answered the phone.

When Beena opened the door, Salma fell on her.

"Oh, my friend!" Salma cried, enveloping Beena in her perfumed arms. "When I heard the news, I said I cannot believe it!" She had come in her office clothes, a silk shirt in geometric patterns draped over pleated slacks and pink stiletto heels, her hair glued in place with hair spray.

Tugging Beena to the mattress at the end of the room, she pulled her down beside her saying, "Auntie inspired me so much." She was always so proud of me for being a woman engineer..." She broke off mid-sentence. "Where will Auntie be buried?"

"I...I don't know. I don't know anything!" Beena said.

Salma sighed heavily. "I remember Lenin as a little boy. He would come running wearing these bright yellow half pants to show me a drawing he had done. I can't imagine that he's gone now!" She rose briskly to her feet, saying, "Stay. I'm coming."

For the next hour, Salma kept disappearing to make phone calls, standing on the landing outside Beena's apartment, at the top of the staircase. Beena could hear her on the phone, slowly wearing down her friends.

"You're coming?" Salma asked each time she rang someone, in a sweet, insistent voice, and always the answer came, so loud that Beena could hear it, *yes, yes, Salma,* or *yes, Salma Apu.* Salma's friends would do what she asked of them. Salma was the center of their social scene, and Ronny was in a position to help them career-wise, to give them jobs when they were laid off.

"Do you want me to get you anything? To eat?" Salma poked her head back into the apartment.

"No. Honestly, I can't eat," Beena replied.

Salma filled a glass with cold water at the tap and carried it to Beena. "Drink."

"I can't."

"Drink or you'll be sick. You can't be sick now. Uncle needs you."

As Beena swallowed the water, Salma went on, "Your landlord's crepe myrtle is very pretty, but she should cut down the two ugly pine trees. They cause allergies. The developer of our subdivision cleared all the trees in the lot. Then he planted top-quality St. Augustine grass."

At dusk, Salma's phone began to beep. One by one, her friends arrived, sending her text messages as they parked their cars. Salma stood on the landing, turning to Beena to announce the guests in a high-pitched voice. Beena came out to see a cavalcade of cars parked on the driveway and on the street, doors slamming and glittery figures emerging from expensive, late model cars as the long light of the sun fell across Beena's landlord Kate's yard.

The guests entered the apartment murmuring that they used to live in the medical center or some other neighborhood inside the loop, back when they were poor and rented apartments, before they bought houses and moved into their real lives. Soon, the tiny apartment filled up until there was no standing room. Other than Salma and Ronny, no one else had been inside Beena's apartment before. Many of the faces had been present at Salma's party, but there were more people today, all friends of Salma's and Ronny's. After they had expressed their awkward condolences to Beena, the men and women stood in separate groups, speaking in low voices. What would happen to their jobs, with the war? Oil prices would rise, they were certain. They were already rising, as a quick glance at the gas pump showed, someone said, so this meant their jobs were safe.

"Apu, I just brought some food I cooked for you. I will warm it up. Do you have a microwave oven?" Shona asked in a supple tone. She wore a cotton shirt over jeans. With her hair down, she looked much younger today.

"Thank you!" Beena pointed out the microwave oven, coming forward to help. She was surprised to find how sluggish her movements were, how difficult it was to move at all.

"No, Apu, sit. You should not work."

Some of the women asked Shona what she had cooked.

"Apu, nothing much. Just some beef curry, daal, polao, and a green vegetable, long beans with potato."

Shona became busy heating up the rice and curries in their separate plastic containers, sliding these into the microwave oven one at a time. The odors of mustard and cumin filled the air. "Apu, the kitchen is very cute, so small and efficient," Shona complimented Beena as she poured portions of each curry onto a large plate, piling fluffy rice in the center. "Apu, please eat. You must be hungry."

Now that the food was in front of her, Beena looked at the plate in confusion, wondering how to refuse. The last thing she wanted to do was eat. "Won't you all eat something?" she said.

A tall woman named Jahan Apa, who had graduated a couple of years ahead of Salma and Ronny from the engineering university, had brought along a Koran covered in a thin, white cloth. She pulled out the bound copy of the Koran and began to recite verses.

"Beena, do you have a prayer mat?" Jahan Apa asked.

No! She did not.

"Or a clean sheet? Anything to pray on?"

"Ah, let her eat," Salma said.

Jahan Apa pulled a sheet herself from Beena's closet and laid it on the floor. First the men, then the women, completed their Isha prayers while Beena ate rice and curries.

"Beena, do you have a pen?" Mehjabeen asked. "To write down how many dua each person makes? We are making the dua to make sure your mother and brother go to heaven."

"No need," Jahan Apa said briskly, rising from her prayer and reaching for her handbag. "I brought tasbihs."

"How many, though?"

"Several. Enough for all of us. I always come prepared." Jahan Apa chuckled as she produced several strings of prayer beads in brown, green, and black colors.

Their trivial discussions and even their laughter were comforting to Beena, whose inner thoughts were the most unpleasant thing to her. Everyone had been speaking in muted voices, the women reciting dua in an undertone, when Beena's phone rang loudly.

"I'll get it." Salma reached the phone before Beena.

"Who is it?" Beena asked, expecting it to be her father. Or Roberto.

"Kate, your landlord."

"Beena, I'm really sorry. Are all these cars…are there guests at your house?" Kate's voice sounded anxious and apologetic. "I

We stood and watched the fish leap out of the water, their silver coats glinting in the moonlight as they catapulted through the air.

Then someone cried, "Come on, let's catch some fish!"

Tearing off the colorful gamchha we wore around our necks, we spread them on the water to catch the fish. A thick mist seeped into our hair and clothes. We fished all night, standing in the cold air. When day broke, we realized that we had caught so many fish that it would be impossible to carry our catch back to Dari Binni. We were discussing what to do with our catch in excited voices when, through the morning fog, we saw a group of three men approaching us, their faces shriveled in the cold, with shawls wrapped around their heads. As they came nearer, we realized that the men were from our village. Their faces were ashen, and their eyes were red and watery. They said that they had been walking all night looking for us. Our families had sent out a search party in every direction, mad with worry about what had happened to us.

"What were you doing?" the men shouted angrily.

"We caught a lot of fish!" We showed them our catch with wild, excited eyes.

They were not moved by the sight of the prancing fish in our receptacles. Quickly, we gathered our prizes and followed the men meekly, struggling with the heavy weight of our catch. When we reached our village, it was bright daylight. My parents scolded me and sent me to bed, where I succumbed to sleep gratefully.

The next day, I rose from bed weak with hunger and started for the kitchen, but while crossing the courtyard, I fell down and began to vomit. Somehow, I was carried to bed, and my youngest uncle Chhoto Chacha was called. He was a schoolmaster now and also practiced homeopathic medicine on the side.

"He has a high fever," Chhoto Chacha pronounced after he had examined me. "He is suffering from a disease that is sweeping through many villages and killing a lot of people." A disease that I now know to be typhoid fever.

I lay in bed with my eyes shut while my mother, my aunts Boro Chachi and Mejo Chachi, and my grandmother Dadi pressed damp cloths to my forehead. Once, I heard my grandmother and my mother talking at my bedside.

"It is the work of the djinns, I am certain, Ayesha," Dadi said.

My other relatives also remarked with satisfaction that I had become ill because of the blasphemous things I had said in the past about djinns. For two weeks, I suffered with high temperatures, aches and pains, and extreme tiredness. While I lay in bed, Jahanara played barefoot in the sunny mud courtyard outside my room, but as soon as I recovered from my illness, she fell sick.

Jahanara's fever took a worse turn than mine. She had a high fever for several days. One night, my parents sat beside my sister on the bed watching her emaciated body. They washed her head again and again to bring her temperature down, but they could not shake off the fever. Her body burned as she lay motionless in bed with her eyes closed. We watched her limbs grow weak and lifeless. Chhoto Chacha entered the room and produced a vial filled with white pills. Dropping a few of the tiny white discs onto his palm, he fed them to Jahanara, saying that the medicine would make her feel better soon.

As promised, Jahanara seemed to recover the next day, but by night, she developed a high fever again. Her eyes turned white, and her skin became colorless. Rose-colored dots appeared on her chest and abdomen. My parents told me to go to sleep, but I would not budge. I stood beside her bed and watched her intensely. Her body was stationary, and she was barely conscious. Her scalp remained scorching hot no matter how much cold water my mother poured on her head. Sometime before morning, she died.

Jahanara's favorite game was to lie with her face hanging over the edge of the veranda, clawing the mud with her fingers and drawing figures in the clay. Several days after she died, the shapes were still imprinted in the mud. I lay face down on the veranda, in the same posture as my sister, studying the marks she had made and crying inconsolably. People said Jahanara had been beautiful beyond human comparison. Her pupils were large and dark like a deep river. Her movements were those of a wild deer that has just come out from the forest, stopping for a moment in the sunlight. My mother lay in bed inside the house, unable to get up. My aunts consoled her, running their fingers over her back and stroking her hair, saying that Jahanara had died because she was too beautiful for this world. As I listened to their reasoning, my head ached painfully and my mind wandered to the possibility that the djinns had challenged me one more time, by snatching up my sister in front of my eyes and carrying her off into the night.

11. ROBERTO'S HOME

Houston, 2003

"READY?" ROBERTO ASKED IN a tender voice.

He had piled all of Beena's possessions—two hard suitcases, five boxes, and a black travel bag with shoulder straps—in his car parked on the street. He had already talked to Kate, explaining Beena's situation, and Kate had readily agreed to allow Beena to break her lease agreement without a penalty.

They drove ten miles south on local roads to Roberto's apartment complex on the bayou. The buildings were new, of shining metal and glass, with exposed trusses and beams. The guest bedroom had been prepared for Beena. Roberto moved her things in easily, stowing the suitcase and boxes neatly in the closet.

"There," he said when he was done, rocking back on his heels, glancing up at her standing nervously in the middle of the room. "Now you have nothing to worry about, just your defense and graduation."

Beena nodded. She didn't know how to thank him for this offer of shelter. Over the next few days, she accepted his ministrations gratefully. She remembered how they had first met, on campus, in front of the old, crumbling engineering building. Beena had bumped into Roberto because she wasn't wearing glasses, trying to look nice. Standing on the wet grass, they had laughed about how divided the campus was, at least for graduate students, the liberal arts students completely separate from the science students. The air was damp and full of the earthy smells of soil and mulch. It had rained the night before, making the paths wet and treacherous. The gardeners had planted yellow milkweed in hedges around the campus. Three orange monarchs perched equidistant atop a hedge, feeding on nectar. Roberto wore a thin T-shirt in the chilly fall weather. Beena was dressed warmly in the heavy jacket she had brought from Bangladesh, holding her hair back with both hands in the wind. They discovered that they had both just arrived on campus and that they were both foreign students, enrolled in PhD programs.

When he had said he was a PhD student in engineering, she had laughed and said, "Really? I grew up on a campus full of engineers."

"And how is it that you wandered off into English?" he had teased.

"My father wanted me to study English Literature. He studied engineering as a practical degree, to be solvent, but he said that I did not have the same practical urgency."

"Ah!"

A week after moving into Roberto's home, Beena finally spoke to her father. He was incoherent, uttering short, scattered words, his voice cutting in and out. At times, his voice rose in agitation.

"They have destroyed me!"

"Who? Who has destroyed you?" Beena demanded.

"They! They!" he cried. "Beena, where are you?" he asked suddenly.

"In Houston. How are you?"

"Uh?" He made a guttural sound, as if he could not understand.

"How are you?" she repeated.

"Me? I am good."

Listening to his confusion, Beena's chest shrank. "Where were you all this time?" she asked in an accusing tone.

After some minutes, she gleaned that he had been staying with his sister in Jessore, but now he was back at the flat in the teachers' quarters, where she had reached him.

"Abba!" she said, leaning into the phone. "Where are my mother and brother?"

"Gone," he said. "They are no more!" Then he began to weep, and for the first time during their phone call, he sounded sane to her.

12. THE MAGIC MAN

Dari Binni, 1954

AFTER APPEARING IN THE national matriculation exam, I was waiting for the results in Dari Binni. I had only pretended to study for the exam, but now I did not even have to pretend. I was having the finest time at home, wandering through sugar cane fields chewing on the sweet stalk and catching fish from the river, dreaming about the food I would eat during the Eid holidays.

By this time, my uncles had moved away to separate homes. My youngest uncle Chhoto Chacha had married and built his own house in the village, taking Dadi to live with him. Since my sister Jahanara had died, my mother had lost the quickness of her movements and the sparkle in her eye. Without the company of her sisters-in-law, she had become intensely lonely. Mejo Chachi was my mother's shoi. Shois share everything, including secrets they would never tell anyone else. My mother was normally quiet and soft spoken, but in the company of her shoi she laughed loudly, making her eyes big and telling terrible stories. The two cooked in each other's kitchens and dropped off items to be eaten by each other's families.

On Eid day, I returned from Eid prayers to find my mother holding her back. She had recently had a difficult childbirth and was still suffering from the complications. She was constantly complaining of aches and pains. She had been sitting on a stool in the kitchen cooking my favorite sweets with date molasses. Seeing me enter the courtyard, she sprang from her stool and ran out.

"O Ketu, will you fetch your uncle Chhoto Chacha?" she cried in an animated voice, stepping down to the courtyard. "I'm feeling very bad. My back is hurting a lot."

I was a frequent visitor at Chhoto Chacha's house because my Dadi, who was my best friend, lived with him. I promised my mother that I would give him her message when I went there for my Eid visit, but when I walked to Chhoto Chacha's house he was not there. Dadi fed me sweets, and we started talking about girls, sitting on top of her bed beside the window. I was getting interested in girls, but I couldn't discuss them with anyone except Dadi. My mother talked with her sisters-in-law about the girls in the village as prospective brides for me, all of them falling apart in laughter, but I was excluded from these conversations. I was burdened with the reputation of being an ideal student. In keeping with this image, I was barred from meeting or talking with any girls my age. Now, chewing betel leaves between her red lips, my grandmother brought me up to date on any girl I asked about.

When I returned home hours later, after visiting many houses on the occasion of Eid and eating many delicacies, my mother saw me entering the courtyard and stopped me again.

"Did you deliver my message to your uncle?" she asked in an expectant voice.

"No!" I had to admit. I had completely forgotten about my mother's request.

"You will never be of any use to me!" she cried. She looked very angry.

Feeling bad, I left the place quietly to let her cool off. Muazzem was visiting for Eid holidays, so I went to greet him.

In the middle of the night, loud voices woke me from my sleep. Jumping down from the bed, I followed the sounds to my mother's room. All my relatives were standing in the room, crowded around her bed. My father, my uncles and aunts, and Dadi were all awake. My uncle Chhoto Chacha, whom I had failed to find the day before, was there in flesh and blood, his dark beard gleaming in the lamp light. My mother lay on her bed under blankets, shivering uncontrollably. I learned that she had risen in the middle of the night to go to the outhouse in the bamboo forest behind our house, where she had been bitten by the gokhra shaap, the Indian cobra. Mejo Chachi instructed me to run to the next village to fetch the Ozha, the witch doctor who treated snake bites by burning herbs and potions and muttering chants.

"Take Muazzem with you," she said.

Muazzem and I started out for the Ozha's house, which lay a few villages away. Instead of following the footpath, we ran across the rice paddy, as a straight line is the shortest possible path between two points. We could not see even a foot ahead of us in the dark. Leaf blades grazed our legs as our sandals slapped the wet fields. I kept moving without being fully conscious of what I was doing. At fourteen, I was too old and too rational to believe in quack medicine, but my mother was dying, and there was no time to think.

Reaching the Ozha's house, Muazzem and I pounded on his door, shouting and crying. At last, a tall, bare-chested man came to the door, tying a checkered lungi around his waist. His face was long and weathered, with white stubble on his cheeks.

"A snake bit my mother! You must come!" I panted.

The Ozha listened to our story with an unperturbed face. When we had finished speaking, he said calmly, "I cannot go with you. There is nothing for me to do."

When we insisted, pleading with him, he said, "I'll do whatever I need to from my home."

Unable to persuade him otherwise, Muazzem and I ran back to Dari Binni. As we approached the village, we could hear people crying far away. I broke into a run, moving as fast as I could across the paddy fields. When we entered the mud courtyard of my home, I lost consciousness and collapsed on the ground.

By the time I regained consciousness, I saw that my mother's body had been covered by a sheet and laid out on a jute mat on the veranda. I ran to the veranda and raised the sheet with shaking hands. My mother's body was cold to the touch. There was a sad expression on her face, which had turned an unearthly color of green. She'd had a buttercup yellow complexion when alive. I didn't know that the human body could change color that way.

By this time, all the people in the neighboring houses were awake. My sisters Kodom and Rajani, my brother Asif, and my newborn sister, who had not yet been named, were crying. At dawn, people were sent to deliver the message of my mother's death to our relatives in other villages. My siblings posed the most immediate problem. My youngest sister was two months old and the eldest only five. Who would take care of them? Dadi alone could not handle the work. Mejo Chachi sent for Nani, my mother's mother. She arrived in the afternoon, traveling by horse cart, but she was not much help. She looked feeble and confused, and she did not appear strong in health. She simply sat and cried for her daughter, wiping her eyes with the edge of her sari. In the end, it was Mejo Chachi, my mother's shoi, who took over the management of our household with the help of our neighbors.

From the moment I found out that my mother had died, I moved in a semi-conscious state. The world stopped. Every leaf on every tree stopped moving. I did not understand how life could go on after her death. I could not feel the earth under my feet. Only one thought moved through my mind constantly. Before her death, my mother had said to me angrily that I would never be of any use to her. Now I thought that my mother had died only to prove to me that I could be of no use to her.

My family members called me to eat, but I did not have the energy to get up from my bed. I got up only when I had to carry my mother's body to her grave. Returning, I climbed into bed again and lay there, with a still world standing guard over me. The windows next to the bed were open, with the shutters flung out. I could hear the coming and going of people outside and my siblings crying constantly.

Late at night, Mejo Chachi entered my room and sat down on my bed with a long face.

"Ketu, I have come to talk to you about a problem," she said. "Now that your mother has left us, who will take care of your younger brothers and sisters? We have all been thinking about that."

I opened my eyes and listened to Mejo Chachi, thinking about the problem. What was the solution?

"I think that your father should marry again," she said. "A bride is also available. You have seen my younger sister. She is also a widow, with no children. Your Dadi, Nani, and all other members of the family have approved of the marriage, if only you consent to it. What do you say?" Mejo Chachi looked at me, waiting for me to respond.

The moon shone through the window, filling the room with light as if it was daytime. It appeared to me that my father's remarriage was the first step to recovering from the mishap. I sat up and nodded.

The wedding preparations started, and I became very busy, but the crisis was not over so easily. My infant sister died from malnourishment a month after my mother's death. With time, my mother's roles were filled by other people and all traces of her vanished from this world. Yet, long afterwards, my heart stopped beating suddenly and a panic rose within me whenever I remembered her last words to me, cried out in anguish. *You will never be of any use to me!* My mother had given me an education and transformed me into a rational, scientific person, yet, for her, I had run through the night looking for an Ozha to spell away the poison of a snakebite. Long after I had stopped believing in gods, djinns, and ghosts, I had put my faith in a magic man.

13. ESCAPE

Houston, 2003

BEENA RECLINED AGAINST THE studded back of a rawhide sofa. Ambient lighting from a shaded chandelier washed the room in a soft glow. She watched TV as a distraction. A classmate in her department had recommended it as a way to manage grief. Now she remembered that her father used to watch American comedies on television, laughing merrily, his face open and his eyes constricted as he concentrated on the show.

"Life is just for laughing. There is no time to waste on serious things," he used to say, although he was generally a gloomy person.

Roberto was preparing pasta in the kitchen to the strains of Puccini. The sound of the metal blades of the blender grinding ice drowned out the TV momentarily.

"Sorry! I'm making a strawberry banana smoothie before dinner!" Roberto shouted from the kitchen.

The next moment, he entered the living room with a tall glass containing a frosted, pink drink. Beads of moisture clung to the outside of the glass. "Enjoy."

Beena lifted her head, smiled, and took a sip. The liquid was cold, frothy, and sweet. "Thanks."

"You're *welcome*," Roberto said in a sing-song voice. He was still dressed in a white office shirt, the sleeves rolled up to his elbows. "Dinner coming up soon."

He disappeared into the kitchen, humming a tune. Beena turned back to the TV, but sometimes even the comedy could not prevent thoughts from flooding in. Now she remembered her recent conversation with her mother's sister. Using Roberto's phone and an international calling card, she had called her aunt in Bangladesh. Her aunt had said that her mother had been feeling lonely and down lately, before her death.

"But I talked to her. She seemed fine to me," Beena had protested.

"Who knows," the aunt had said.

Beena thought that perhaps her aunt was hinting that Beena's mother had been depressed on Beena's account, not only because she was so far away but also because she was still unmarried. A cousin had called from Boston and said that Lenin's body had been blasted into pieces by the shrapnel. He could only be identified through a few items of his clothing, the cousin had said. Here, Beena had cried out sharply and the cousin had stopped.

Roberto returned with two large plates piled with pasta cooked in homemade garlic sauce and topped with more garlic, freshly chopped and raw. Beena handed the remote control to him. Roberto liked to catch the evening news. Embedded journalists on the screen described how the American soldiers were helping the Iraqi people. British and American forces had taken the port of Umm Qasr and flown the American flag over the port. All major oilfields in the south were under coalition control. America had established a base in the west of the country. Now the US was trying to gain control over the northern oil fields. A video showed Iraqis rejoicing and kissing American soldiers in helmets and uniform. Donald Rumsfeld claimed that the war was being covered transparently through the free press. Roberto lingered for a moment, glanced at Beena, and handed the remote control back to her.

"I'll get the dessert out." He rose with the two plates.

"Oh! There's dessert?" Beena arched her eyebrows.

With Roberto gone, Beena changed channels till she found an old sitcom with canned laughter. When she was alone, she usually avoided any news about Iraq, journalists and experts giving their opinions on cities that had suddenly become household names in America—Baghdad, Mosul, Kirkuk, and Kerbala. It felt so strange, because she had always known these cities, as places she had wandered through growing up.

The last time Beena had spoken to her father on the phone, she had asked him feebly, "Should I come home?"

"No," he had said. "Not yet."

The bodies were still in the morgue, waiting for the postmortem. There was no telling when the burial would take place. Beena had asked her mother's sisters and her father's family for direction. Nobody had any advice for her. *Should* she fly home? What would happen to her father now? What was she supposed to do? She was left to grapple with these questions alone. Certainly, her father could not live alone, but neither could she imagine returning to a country that had killed her mother and brother, where she now constantly imagined people being murdered, kidnapped, bombed, burnt, and drowned to death. When she thought of returning, images of capsized launches, building fires, floods, earthquakes, cyclones, strikes, armed cadres, collapsed bridges and buildings, crossfires, and cocktail bombs filled her head.

Roberto reentered with two bowls of mango ice cream.

"Mm. Delicious calories," Beena said.

"That's right."

"Roberto." She turned to face him in the dim room. The light from the TV screen flickered in her black eyes. "Will you marry me?"

14. THE PROBLEM SOLVER

Dari Binni, 1953

MEJO CHACHI LIFTED THE ruti from the clay stove and dropped it on a plate with boiling beef. The ruti puffed up, its two skins separating, then sank back down. Mejo Chachi's round face glowed brightly in the light of the fire. Her nose stud glinted when she laughed or talked animatedly. Even after my father had remarried, Mejo Chachi remained a constant presence in our household, making sure that her shoi's children were cared for. As I ate, she wiped her thin face with the edge of her sari and sighed. Neither of us spoke.

The previous day, I had cycled to Jhenidah to find out about my matriculation results. That morning, I had cycled back to Dari Binni with the heavy weight of my results in the back pocket of my pants. I had secured a dismal second division. I was glad that my mother was not alive to witness my poor performance.

When I had finished eating, Mejo Chachi took the plate from me and asked, "What will you do now?"

My mother was no longer alive to nag me or chase me to my studies, or to tell me what to do. I fished another piece of meat from the boiling pot, scorching my fingers, and stared into the wood kindling. Now that she was gone, I could see at last what she had wanted for me.

"I want to get admitted to college," I said.

A few days later, I returned home after spending time with friends to find my uncles and my father sitting on the veranda, waiting for me. They looked alike, their long backs bent forward, dressed in white cotton pajamas and punjabi and leather shoes. They looked at me through unsmiling, squinted eyes.

"Why does Ketu need any more schooling? He is fourteen years old. He is of age now to work for the family." Boro Chacha addressed my father.

"What use is a college education anyway?" Mejo Chacha said, echoing Boro Chacha's words. "Ketu needs to start managing our lands."

My father received his elder brothers' words silently. He was a tall man with muscular shoulders and a work-hardened body, but he was soft spoken, with a gentle smile around his eyes. I can only imagine his conflict now. He was respectful toward his elders, but he never imposed his will on his juniors.

"Ketu, you should give up this nonsense of going to college and start to help with the agricultural lands," Boro Chacha said, turning to me. "You are not a child anymore. You need to help the family. It is time to grow up and provide a solution to your father's problems." He looked at me with pinpointed eyes.

I faced my elders silently without making any reply. As land-owners, my father's family was well off, but a college education was still a great expense for a village household. Mejo Chachi had been watching the scene from inside the house, where she had been stitching a katha. Now she emerged on the veranda. She was a tiny woman, but she stood with her back tall, wrapping her sari around her sternly.

"It is my decision that Ketu shall go to college. Does anyone have anything to say to me?" she said.

Mejo Chacha looked as if a thunderbolt had struck his head. He stared at his wife, then he swiveled his head and looked at his elder brother. Boro Chacha's face was pinched, but he did not utter a word.

In those days, people from Jessore used to travel to India for higher studies, crossing the border to Calcutta to get admitted to Presidency College. Recently, however, colleges in East Bengal had begun to earn some prominence, so I decided to try my luck at Rajshahi College. With money from my father to pay the college admission fee, I set off for Rajshahi with my friend Fetu, boarding the train in Jhenidah. The smoking engine sped past rice paddies, lone homes beside the forest, and barefoot schoolboys already lost among the fruit trees. Perhaps they would never reach their school. With each station, the train catapulted us to new territory, until, at last, we reached the northern district of Rajshahi.

Having secured a first division in his matriculation exam, Fetu was admitted to the college immediately. Since I had a second division, the college authorities told me that I needed to sit for the entrance exam. The exam would be administered a week later, so I had to wait. Fetu returned to Jhenidah without me. The college authorities allowed me to stay in an empty hostel room. I had not brought enough money with me for the extended stay, so I tried to think what to do about food. Finding a roadside shop that sold essential items like eggs, bananas, notebooks and pencils, I bought the cheapest item available to eat, a bag of fried peanuts. I survived on these snacks for a week, after which I was able to take the exam, which consisted of several math problems. I solved them easily and was admitted to the college.

Now to return home. At the railway station in Rajshahi, I found out that I did not have sufficient funds to purchase a train ticket to Jhenidah. I asked for a ticket to the farthest station in the direction of Jhenidah. This turned out to be a station two stops away from Jhenidah. Here, I climbed down from the carriage and started to walk the rest of the way, expanding my chest and opening my nostrils to breathe in the smoky morning air.

15. PRACTICAL ADVICE

Houston, 2003

BEENA SAT ON ROBERTO'S couch watching TV after working on her dissertation for an hour. An hour a day is good progress, Roberto had said. They drove to school together, with nineties music playing on the radio. Beena enjoyed the drive. In Roberto's car, with the wind flying through her hair, she could be in her head. At home, they worked together on their dissertations, sitting side-by-side at the dining table with their laptops open. The weather in Houston was getting hot, so they stuck to the confines of Roberto's air-conditioned apartment.

Roberto handed the phone to Beena. "It's someone by the name of Salma."

"How did you get this number?" Beena asked.

"Uncle gave it to me. I called him when I couldn't reach you. Where are you?"

Beena scrunched her nose. "I got out of my lease."

"Why are you staying with Roberto?"

"What do you mean?"

"Don't do anything sinful, my friend!" Salma cried. "Turn back while there is time. I'll keep your secret."

"What are you talking about?" Beena made a movement, about to end the call.

"Listen. Don't be mad. This is why I'm asking. I spoke to Khaled. He feels sorry for you. He forgives you for whatever happened between you two at the party. He wants to marry you!" Salma squealed.

Beena was silent.

"He will marry you today if need be. Then he can take care of you. Auntie would have wanted this too," she added.

"It's too late."

"What do you mean? What have you done?" Salma raised her voice.

"Roberto and I are getting married."

There was a pause. Then Salma changed her tone. "Congratulations, my friend. I have to meet him. Is he American?"

"Listen. I have to file for immigration. We're looking for a lawyer. Do you know any lawyers?"

"Do you mean an immigration lawyer? Because that's what you need, an immigration lawyer. Someone who does immigration specifically." Salma's voice became efficient now. She began to speak in English, full of the professional polish that made her such a successful engineer at work.

"I'll have to ask Ronny. Oh, Khaled will know! He just went through the process himself."

"Thanks."

"So, did you get married already?"

"We went to a courthouse downtown and filled out an application. It takes two days. Then you go to court and a judge marries you."

"We will have to get you married properly, in the Islamic way." Salma's voice crackled on the phone. "Otherwise, your marriage will not be legitimate in the eyes of the religion. Oh! I'm excited. We'll have a wedding for you," she said brightly.

"Okay."

"You agree?"

"I suppose. I'll have to ask Roberto…"

"Don't sleep with him. *Are* you?" Salma asked Beena on the phone.

"No."

"First, we do the Islamic ceremony."

"Then hurry."

"Very good, it's decided then!" Suddenly Salma's voice cut off. She made an exasperated sound, blowing air into the phone.

"What is it?"

"*Oof.* On TV, they are showing some silly people in Boston who are protesting the Iraq war. Ridiculous. These brave American soldiers are risking their lives to save Iraqis from that evil man. You know, there are Weapons of Mass Destruction there. And what are these lazy people doing? Don't they have jobs?"

"I think protests have been going on for a long time? In cities around the world, actually, in America, Britain, all over Europe, Brazil, Mexico, Syria, Jordan, India, Bangladesh…"

"Never mind. We'll get you married properly," Salma interrupted her. "We'll throw a grand party for you!"

16. LOST DREAMS

Rajshahi, 1953

AT RAJSHAHI COLLEGE, I spent most of my time in the common
room of the hostel, playing chess, table tennis, and cards with the
other students. I only returned to my room to sleep at night. The
courses did not appear to be too difficult. I positioned myself to do
the minimum work possible. My class attendance was also abysmal.
Classes were held in large galleries. After the roll call, my friends and
I slipped out the back door. I only attended class at all because a fifty
percent attendance was a requirement for passing.

The days stretched ahead in lazy expanse. The mossy paths of
the college campus with its wide-girthed trees provided the perfect
grounds in which to lose ourselves. After dinner, we lay on the
muddy grass, our shirts stained by the straw underneath our backs,
and stared up at the night sky. If it was a cloudless sky with a full
moon, then each crater and ridge was visible on the bright disc
with its soft, bleeding circumference. On moonless nights, the sky
burst into a thousand stars.

Once a month, the dining hall held a feast. The students were
served roast chicken, polao, and beef rezala. At the end of the meal,
the dining hall provided each student a triangular khili of sachi

paan (a sweet betel leaf) and one local cigarette. At first, I passed
my cigarette to others. One day, I thought, why am I passing up
this free gift? I inserted the stick in my mouth and lit a match. After
that time, I began to crave the delicate aroma of tobacco. To this
day, I have not found a taste parallel to the combination of the
sweet betel leaf and the local cigarette.

Rajshahi College stood near the Padma River. During the
floods, the river reared its violent head, making terrible growling
sounds from its belly. The city had to be protected with a high
wall. At other times, the waters of the Padma flowed gently beside
the riverbank. Whenever we got the chance, we flew to the riverbank with guitars, drums, flutes, and cigarettes, singing and talking,
arguing about politics. On the way back to the hostel, we stopped
at a roadside shop to drink sweet, cloying tea with sugar and cream,
smoking and chewing paan while discussing politics and philosophy.

The days came and went. I continued my previous course
of life, studying as little as possible. Only one subject attracted
me. I began to read the writings of Marx through his Bengali
translators and Marxist Bengali writers like Muzaffar Ahmad,
Kazi Nazrul Islam, and Reboti Barman. As a child, I used to
follow the landless sharecroppers who worked in my father's
fields. My mother served them a breakfast of fermented rice
and date juice. Despite her repeated orders to the men not to
share their portions with me, they always gave me some of their
food. I used to think their lives romantic, working in the sun,
chatting together, laughing, sometimes breaking into song. Now
I realized that poverty drove the field workers to work for a
pittance on somebody else's fields.

I passed my intermediate board exams with only a second
division, but I still managed to secure a scholarship to pursue a B.A.
degree at Rajshahi college. Rajshahi College suited me very well,
so I decided to continue there, studying mathematics, a subject
that seemed as idyllic to me as the canopied woods of the campus.
However, as soon as I started my studies, I realized there was no

future in my field. The senior students in mathematics graduated and struggled to find a job. The only employment for mathematics graduates was teaching. There were only so many schools, and only so many math teachers were needed.

During the annual Eid holidays, Aplu Bhai and I were both visiting Jhenidah. I met up with him at a local roadside restaurant that sold paan, cigarettes, and tea. Drinking hot milk tea from chipped cups, we discussed the politics of East Pakistan.

"What do you think will happen to this country?" Aplu Bhai asked me.

"Bengalis shall never be granted equal rights in Pakistan," I said passionately, lighting a cigarette and blowing smoke in the air. "Can you imagine, how can we even be part of the same country? We don't even share a border with West Pakistan. We are on one side of India and West Pakistan is on the other side."

"It is madness," he agreed.

"When have relations ever been good between the Bengalis and the government of Pakistan?" I said.

He sipped his tea and shook his head. "Never."

"I mean, the whole project is madness, starting from partition, in 1947. Separating India into two parts based on religion, creating a Muslim majority state and a Hindu majority state, and dividing Bengal in two in the process, forcing millions of people to migrate on the basis of religion!"

"What do you think has gone wrong with Pakistan?"

"Oh, the whole idea of Pakistan was mad, making a country out of two regions so far apart! Then, in 1948, when the government of Pakistan imposed Urdu as the official language on the Bengali-speaking people of East Bengal, that was madness!" I cried. "That foolish decision alone led to the language movement and massive protests in 1952. And then, in 1955, when the government of Pakistan renamed East Bengal as East Pakistan. Why do you think they did that? To further challenge our Bengali identity. And don't forget the unfair allocation of resources. When

Suhrawardy tried to revive the joint electorate system in 1956 and allocate funds and resources equally to East Pakistan, he faced opposition from West Pakistan. We Bengalis are just second-class citizens of Pakistan."

After letting me air my political views, Aplu Bhai asked me about my studies. He listened attentively as I explained why mathematics appealed to me, not interrupting me once.

"Aar ek cup cha?" Aplu Bhai pointed to my empty teacup.

I nodded.

Calling a boy of about ten or twelve with large, black eyes in a dark brown face, Aplu Bhai ordered two more cups of tea.

"And make them hot. *Bujhli?*"

"*Ji*, Sir." The boy ran off.

Aplu Bhai turned back to me. "Have you considered engineering?"

"No." I shook my head.

"Engineering promises an easy life, whereas a degree in mathematics will consign you to the fate of all vanishing trades, lifelong penury."

"Nothing will deter me from my love of mathematics. I don't care if I starve in the gutter!" I cried sharply. I gulped the lukewarm tea at the bottom of my cup and puffed anxiously on my cigarette.

Aplu Bhai did not argue with me. Twisting his torso, he cried to the same boy again and ordered spicy goat curry and ghee-filled paratha.

"You should do what you want with your life. Live your dream," he said to me when the boy had gone away with the order.

"Yes. That's what I was thinking," I said, folding my arms and speaking in a forceful voice, but my spirits deflated. I held my cigarette between shaky fingers.

Aplu Bhai was aware of my family's circumstances. My father's resources were limited, and his household was growing every year. Half a dozen younger brothers and sisters now depended on me to make something of myself. Every time I visited Dari Binni, a new child had been born. During my last visit, Kodom and Rajani complained to me that my stepmother had tried to drown our brother Asif. I had scolded them and sent them away, but I had a headache for the rest of the day. During the long train journey back to Rajshahi College, acid juices flowed in my stomach. As the train whistled through Kushtia, Bheramara, and Pakshi, I bought roasted peanuts and shobri kola, the small bananas of Jessore, and drank the juice of young coconut to calm my stomach, but the pain was always there.

The boy brought our food to the table, setting down the tin plates. We dug in without further words. The fiery goat curry burned my tongue. The greasy paratha acted as salve. Aplu Bhai paid the bill. When I stood up, my head spun. I gripped the edge of the table. For what appeared to be several seconds, I lost my vision, seeing only black.

"Everything good?" Aplu Bhai peered at me anxiously, chewing a betel leaf.

I nodded and straightened myself. Right then and there, without another word, I decided to give up my romance with mathematics and move out of Rajshahi College to study engineering in the busy, bustling city of Dacca.

17. BURIED

Houston, 2003

"ABBA, WHAT IS IT?"

The red light on the alarm clock in Roberto's guest bedroom displayed the time as 4 AM. So far, it had been Beena who had been calling her father every day. For the first time, he had called her, at the wrong time. Roberto had brought the phone to Beena's door, his eyes red and irritated.

"Beena!" Her father's voice sounded shaky and hoarse. "The medical authorities returned the bodies to us. We will bury your mother and Lenin today. In the evening, after Maghrib prayers."

"But what about me? Shouldn't I come? Can't you wait till I get a ticket?" Beena cried, pressing the phone against her ear.

"The bodies have to be buried right away. You don't need to come. Concentrate on your studies. Your mother would not have wanted you to interrupt your studies. What is it? Why are you crying, Ammu?" His voice rose, filled with worry.

Beena could not bear the thought of her mother and Lenin buried under the earth. She had a sudden urge to dig them out of their graves. Now she noticed that her father sounded very weak. He was straining to make sounds. Her heart filled with pity for him.

"Abba, I have some good news to tell you. I'm getting married. To a friend. I want to bring you here to America to live with me. I want you to apply for a visa."

"Congratulations, Beena. I am very happy for you. I want to meet him. What is his name?" he spoke in a chatty, bright voice now.

"His name is Roberto. Come visit me," Beena said.

"Dekhi," he replied vaguely. He would not commit to anything. When Beena grew insistent, her voice nagging, he said, "I'll try."

"You don't care about me," she said.

"Of course, I care. You are the most important thing in the world to me, Ammu."

"Then apply for a visa, please. Come stay with me!" she cried. She wanted to say that she was getting married for *him*, as the best solution to their problem, so that they could be together, and she could take care of him.

18. HEAVEN AND HELL

Dacca, 1958-62

THE PRINCIPAL OF THE engineering college Dr. Rafiq sat in his office marking student papers. His desk was covered with bundles of gray newsprint. Heavy curtains had been drawn across the windows, leaving the room dark and cool.

"Take a seat," Dr. Rafiq said absentmindedly, without looking up.

There were no chairs in front of the desk, so I remained standing. The principal's personal secretary had fetched me from the students' hostel, saying that he wanted to see me. I was to come immediately. Now I wondered why he had sent for me.

Dr. Rafiq was a stout man with a thick mustache and a round, balding head. Among the engineering students, he was known as a man of high principles. He finished checking a paper, wrote something with his fountain pen, then pushed the pile away and glanced up, as if noticing me for the first time.

"Nasir," he said, leaning back in his chair and smiling at me with an expression of pleasure. "After your graduation, you can join the college as a lecturer. It is all set. Take the job. It'll suit you."

In such a manner, I received the news of my teaching appointment at the Ahsanullah Engineering College.

"Do you accept?"

"Yes, sir." I grinned, exposing cigarette-stained teeth.

Dr. Rafiq extended his hand. "Congratulations."

I shook his hand, feeling that I was the happiest man in the world. Dr. Rafiq resumed checking student papers. I escaped to celebrate by smoking a cigarette standing behind the canteen. I had four other job offers, each of which promised a higher salary and more facilities than the job at the college, as engineers were in high demand in East Pakistan. But I had decided that I wanted to be a teacher a long time ago, for three reasons. One, I liked teaching. Two, campus life suited my character. And three, I felt that the world outside the campus was extremely corrupt. Anyone working in government or in business had to be involved with either giving bribes or receiving bribes. Besides, I had enjoyed my time as a student at the engineering college. There was very little memorization required in engineering courses, and there was ample time to engage in other activities. My friends and I sat on the grass talking and smoking into the night, or we walked to Eden College to see the beautiful female students.

After graduation, I joined as a lecturer at the engineering college. At the time, there was only one two-story academic building. The machine shops and other offices were housed in tin sheds. The campus was surrounded by greenery and shaded by big trees with thick trunks. There were large fields for playing sports. I enjoyed teaching. I had enough money to buy anything I wanted. I was able to save almost my entire salary as my teacher's accommodation in the thatched barracks on campus was free. My students were highly intelligent and excited. I could share my thoughts with the students and colleagues who surrounded me. I felt that I was in heaven. I thought that this Earth was heaven, but people converted it to hell while aspiring to go to some imagined heaven. Earth was created to meet all the requirements of a human being. If this is not heaven, then what kind of heaven do people aspire to?

One day, I came home to the teacher's quarters to find a letter from my father. My father wrote that both Aplu Bhai and his younger brother Fetu were now working in government jobs. Aplu Bhai had built a house with his government salary. If I worked in one of the government engineering jobs, I could make a lot of money too, my father suggested. He was worried about our family's financial situation. Who would provide for my siblings? He urged me to find a job with a higher salary that would allow me to support him financially. I folded the letter and stored it under my mattress. I suspected that no government official could afford to build a house without taking bribes, but this fact did not ease my feelings of guilt.

When I had gone home to Dari Binni during the holidays, my uncles also had spoken to me about getting a job with a higher salary with my expensive education. I did not argue or reason with my family, but I left home with a heavy heart. I realized that my relatives were not in the least interested in my academic life. They were waiting to find out how much money I could make.

Slowly, the pressure began to torment me. I was constantly reminded in letters from my well-wishers at home that it was foolish for an engineer to be a teacher, that I should take a job at a foreign company or a government office. I was being advised to convert my heaven into hell. At last, after a year of teaching, this constant hammering made me apply for an engineering job.

19. IRAQ

By April, Beena blocked all news of Iraq. It seemed to her that she and Roberto were stuck in a surreal space, watching events unfold. The world consisted of just the two of them, with any news from outside trickling in only slowly. Beena's mother's and brother's dead bodies had been carried in an open truck to Dari Binni to be buried in the family graveyard in the fruit orchard behind the house. Nowadays, there was a proper road all the way to the village. In the old days, they had to hire a cow cart for the last leg of the journey, from Jhenidah town to Dari Binni. Beena's mother had hated the journey to her father's village, complaining about the bumpy dirt road and the jolting ride in a hard cart.

"Nothing is in our control, except our dissertations," Roberto reminded Beena. "That is completely within our control."

Roberto had asked the company in Alabama that had offered him a job if they could create a job for Beena and apply for a green card for her. Perhaps this would be a faster way to a green card, as Salma had suggested.

Two days after applying for their marriage license, Beena and Roberto drove downtown to get married. Beena wore a green

A-line dress. Roberto was dressed up in a buttoned blue shirt and khaki pants. Parking Roberto's Toyota on Congress Street, they walked to the courthouse. The courtroom was paneled in a rich, grained wood. The judge, a young man with a blonde goatee, sat in a leather swivel chair, with a US flag on one side and a Texas flag on the other. The judge donned his robe and came down from his bench to stand with them at the podium. After the ceremony, he took a picture of Beena and Roberto with Roberto's cell phone.

Returning to the apartment, they slipped into Roberto's room, holding each other on the bed without words. Beena's mind wandered through the rooms of her childhood, to her mother's and brother's deaths, the bomb blast, shrapnel flying, then to Iraq. She wondered what the people in Iraq were experiencing, with the constant bombing, the power outage, and whatever else was unfolding in the total darkness.

20. THE RINGING OF THE BEARER'S BELL

Dacca, 1964

THE PAKISTAN GOVERNMENT HAD recently issued a rule requiring foreign tea companies operating in the country to recruit for assistant manager positions from the local population. I thought that I ought to apply to one of these companies to fulfill the desires of my guardians. The British Finlays Group operated in the tea estates in Srimongol and Chittagong. I answered an advertisement for the post of assistant manager at a tea garden in Sylhet. A few weeks later, I received an interview letter that summoned me to the company's head office in Chittagong, to the bungalow of the general manager of one of their tea gardens.

The bungalow stood on top of a hill looking down on cascading slopes covered with tea trees. The general manager was a red-haired Englishman with pale white arms and a pink neck, dressed casually in a Safari shirt and shorts and a hat to keep out the sun. We sat on a long, stretched veranda facing a garden of fruit and flower trees, while a bearer poured tea made from fresh tea leaves into two cups.

"All this can be yours when you are a general manager like me

one day. A great thing to have, no?" The Englishman opened his
arms to indicate the garden, the hills, and the dark green slopes of
tea plantation.

I nodded, sipping my tea, enjoying the subtle taste of the fresh,
loose leaves.

"It is very sad what is happening in your country, Uddin,"
the manager went on. "It is a sad state of affairs. There is so
much corruption."

I could only agree, so I nodded silently.

"On this plantation, in this beautiful garden, you can be assured
of achieving everything you desire." He waved his hat to fan
himself, planting his feet apart. "Everything is fair here. You work
hard, and you rise to the top. In a few years, you shall be sitting
in your own bungalow on top of a hill, driving a jeep around this
estate, and eating meals like a gentleman. Small pleasures, selfish
pleasures, no doubt, but not a small thing to have, no?"

While speaking to me, the general manager signed several files
and received two calls on a phone that was brought out to him on
a long cord. I watched him in amazement. This Englishman was
doing the work of fifty government officers in my country!

A few weeks later, back in Dacca, I received a tentative offer
from the company, provided the tea garden manager in Sylhet
approved of me and I passed a medical exam. Soon afterward, an
envelope arrived with an invitation from the manager in Sylhet
to visit the tea estate in Sylhet, where the position had been
advertised. I was to stay as a guest at the manager's house for a
week to familiarize myself with the tea estate and my job respon-
sibilities. The letter was accompanied by a return train ticket.

At the station in Srimongol, there was a jeep waiting to take me
to the manager's bungalow. The view from the road was breathtak-
ing. Hills rose majestically on either side of the road, covered with
the dark shadow of tea trees. When the jeep passed through the high
gate of the tea estate, the beauty inside made me suck in my cheeks. It
was difficult to imagine that such a place existed in East Pakistan. The

manager's bungalow was built in a colonial style. A long, cane sofa and a white swing were laid out on the spacious front veranda. Gilt-framed paintings of the English countryside and long-coated gentlemen riding in horse carriages hung from the walls of the drawing room.

The manager had been reclining on one of the sofas. He was a stout, tall Englishman with blonde hair and a bushy moustache. He motioned to me to take a seat. As soon as I sank down on the overly soft cushion of an armchair, a uniformed Bengali man came running and started to pull off my shoes.

I sprang to my feet in surprise. "I am your guest only for a few days," I said sharply to the man. "I shall be able to manage putting on my shoes and taking them off by myself."

With these words, I walked to my bag, brought out my slippers, and quickly changed out of my shoes myself. The servant watched my actions with dismay. His large eyes in his tense, hollowed face shifted from the manager to me.

The manager frowned. "Bearer. Go, bring this young revolutionary a glass of water," he said stiffly.

I realized that my host was not pleased with my action. If I was going to work as an assistant manager on the tea estate, I would have to get used to the customs of the place.

Over the course of the week, I visited many tea gardens and tea processing plants and met with the managers of the other tea gardens in Sylhet. The managers described the problems they were having with their production. I inquired with interest into when the plants had been built and what changes had taken place in the equipment over time. They told me about the history of the company. The tea gardens in Sylhet had been set up in 1854. The British owners had brought in poor laborers from Bihar, Orissa, and Patna, telling them about a heaven wrapped in greenery. I remembered that these laborers had revolted against their mistreatment and started a movement to return to their homes, called Mulluke Cholo. Many tea garden workers had died in the revolt.

At the heart of the tea estate was the club life and the upkeep of colonial customs in the managers' bungalows. The tea managers' club still held on to the traditions of British India. The manager told me about all the perks of the job. In addition to the high salary, I would be able to live the life of an Englishman. An additional attraction of the job was that assistant managers were provided a return air ticket to visit England for their annual vacation.

In spite of all these attractions, several times during the visit, I was jolted by the manager clapping his hands and beating his hammer against a hand-held bell, calling for his manservant.

"Bearer!" the manager cried while we were seated at the dinner table, and the Bengali manservant appeared bearing drinks on a tray and cups of corn soup before dinner was served.

The more I saw the man, with his quick movements and darting, frightened eyes, the more I became embarrassed and uncomfortable about my own presence in that bungalow.

"You won't get this life anywhere else," the manager said to me, brandishing his bread knife and curling slices off the home-made butter onto white bread.

The bearer stood erect in his uniform, carrying the dishes around the table on a round silver tray and serving us each item.

"The salary, what is it, at least ten times higher than what you get paid now?"

I nodded.

"As an assistant manager, you get a motorcycle. And in four years you get a car. The best part," the manager winked at me, "is the club life. You have no wife to create problems, so you can spend all your time there."

As I tried to handle my knife and fork like a gentleman, the manager went on between bites, chewing his food with his mouth closed. "What do you think, professor? Are you ready to sign the contract?"

I nodded again, smiling widely.

On the last day, I was waiting on the front veranda with my

bags for the manager's jeep to take me to the train station. The bearer approached me nervously. This time, I readily allowed him to carry my bags into the jeep. As I climbed into the vehicle, the manager thumped me on the back and congratulated me, as he was sure that this was a dream job for any Pakistani. I returned to Dacca with the manager's assurance that it was only a matter of time before I received the magic envelope.

Sure enough, a few weeks later, I received another letter from the company, this one asking me to report to a physician at Baitul Mukarram for medical tests, the next step in the process.

"It's a very attractive prospect. You are fortunate to get such a job as an East Pakistani," the examining doctor said to me appreciatively.

I decided to take a walk before returning to campus. Turning toward Dacca University, I passed the peddlers with bronze faces and stubbled chins selling food on the pavement. Their dark eyes shone in the cold winter air. The pitha sellers had set up fires to steam bhapa pitha. As they waited for customers, they smoked cigarettes and chatted leisurely with the chotpoti wallahs who were bundled up in their bright shawls, stirring the spicy chickpea mix in a big pot. There was a festivity in the smoky air that called to me achingly.

I tried to make sense of the recent events of my life and the future that awaited me. If I accepted the position, I could help my father financially to raise my brothers and sisters. The money I sent home from my teacher's salary was not sufficient. My salary as an assistant tea garden manager, on the other hand, would provide for my family more than they could ever need. Reaching Palashi Road, I crushed the cigarette under my foot and passed through the gate of the engineering university campus. The next letter would be an offer letter. I had decided to accept the job. I headed straight to the principal's office in the low, yellow-walled academic building, wanting to tell him of my decision to accept the job offer at the tea estate before I could change my mind. I found him in the same

posture at his desk as when he had given me the teaching job at the
college. A ceiling fan rotated slowly in the dark room. I told Dr.
Rafiq frankly about my decision. He kept quiet, neither congratulating me nor expressing his disappointment. I came out feeling
confused, without a single word from the principal.

That evening, I was playing cards at a smoke-filled table at the
teachers' club when a reedy man wearing a dirty white shirt and
checked blue lungi appeared at our table.

"I am Dr. Rafiq's domestic help," the man explained. "He has
asked you to come immediately."

"What for?" I asked, stubbing out my cigarette.

He did not know, but he said I should follow him. I hurried
after the man with curiosity, certain that the principal would not
disturb my pleasure if he did not have some urgent business. The
principal's residence on campus was a brick bungalow occupying
a large area with mango and guava trees and a flower garden. The
man showed me into a drawing room with faded sofas and cane
bookshelves crammed with books arranged in a disorderly manner.
A ceiling fan rotated slowly overhead. Dr. Rafiq appeared in the
room almost immediately. He sat down abruptly on a hard chair
and addressed me brusquely.

"I have just been informed that your nomination for the
Colombo Plan Scholarship has been accepted. You have been
approved for your chosen area of studies, a master's degree in
Applied Mechanics. Get ready to travel to Canada in two weeks.
If you refuse the scholarship, they will take somebody from West
Pakistan, and East Pakistan will lose a scholarship. This is the second
year in the history of the college that a graduate has been awarded
this scholarship, so consider the meaning of your actions."

I stared at the principal with my mouth open.

"Above all," continued Dr. Rafiq, "you like teaching, so
forget everything else. Go to your village home tomorrow to say
good-bye to your family. Come back as quickly as possible and
finish the formalities for traveling."

"Yes, sir." I stood up and shook Dr. Rafiq's hand.

It seemed to me that I had been waiting for the principal's terse instructions all this time. Now I was back in my heaven. I forgot about the tea garden immediately.

The offer letter from the tea company arrived a day before I flew to Canada, instructing me to report to the Chittagong office within a month. I held the crisp pages in my hand and smiled bitterly, thinking that I had been saved from falling into a deep hole. If I had become a tea garden manager and accustomed myself to the ways of the tea plantation, the bell to call the bearer would have sounded constantly in my ears, tormenting me.

21. MORE TROUBLE

Houston, April 2003

BEENA ENJOYED CHATTING WITH Roberto's loud brothers and his soft-spoken parents, who called her *bellisima* and *amore*. Calling her own father was a different experience. Even dialing the number, Beena's stomach churned with panic. She had to get her father out in time before something happened to him. She remembered that Lenin had told her a fault line ran through Bangladesh. Within fifty years, there would be major earthquakes. And if there was a rise in sea level, the country would be underwater. "After all, most of Bangladesh is a low-lying delta!" he had said. Now, she thought of his words constantly.

"Hello? Is this Beena?" a woman answered the phone in a rich voice, uttering Beena's name in a sweet, elongated sound. "I am your Rajani Phupu." She spoke in the lilting accent of people from Jessore.

"Oh! Salam, Rajani Phupu!" Beena tried to remember her aunt as she had last seen her, a woman from the village who had visited infrequently at their flat in Dhaka, traveling on a bus from Jessore, crossing the Padma River on a ferry, her bony frame bound in a loosely worn cotton sari, a long, taut, sunburnt face that shone like cinnamon bark.

"O, Beena, your father asked me to stay in your home so that he can visit you," Rajani Phupu said.

"Oh. Thank you for taking care of him. Apni kemon achhen?" Beena asked, sitting up self-consciously. Her Bengali had become childish and foreign.

Growing up, she had visited her father's village only a few times because Beena's mother had been afraid that Beena and Lenin might perish there in the dangerous, unknown surroundings. In fact, it was true that every time they had gone to Dari Binni, something bad happened. Once, Beena had taken a dinghy on the Binni river with a cousin and almost drowned when the boat filled with water. Another time, her cousins were trying to teach her to swim when Beena fell to the bottom of the riverbed. For several seconds, she lay on her back, gulping water, unable to get up, thinking she would die.

"O, *Ma*, I am well," Rajani Phupu said, washing Beena with tenderness. "Don't worry. Your father is trying hard to visit you. He is trying to get permission from the government."

"Really?" Beena beamed at Roberto. Her father had been listening to her after all! "When will he come?"

"As soon as he can," Rajani Phupu said. "Your Mukul Bhai is helping him sort everything he needs to take care of before he can leave. He has to pay his bills and his taxes while he is gone."

"Great. Thank you, Phupu!"

"O, Beena." Again, Rajani Phupu drew out Beena's name in a soft caress. "A lot of things in the flat got destroyed, but whatever was in your mother's steel almirah is safe."

"Oh, thank you, Phupu." Beena smiled. Her mother had been the queen of steel almirahs. She locked away everything in her almirahs and trunks.

"We moved the gold to her locker at the bank. Most of it was in the locker, but the small things she wore were in the house. Your father can bring them with him when he comes to see you. And Mukul Bhai and your father are trying to convert the property that was in her name to your name."

Roberto and Beena had been pulling an all-nighter. Beena covered her mouth and yawned, trying to stay awake. Roberto looked at her, scraped back his chair quietly and rose, heading to the kitchen. In another moment, she could hear him grinding coffee beans.

"But *Ma*, do you know that your father's health is not good? His diabetes is not in control. Your Mukul Bhai took him for his checkup. The doctors think that he had a few small strokes."

Beena's response to this news was childlike. "Please tell him to come!" she repeated. Her parents had left her out of the loop whenever one of them had a major health crisis. Each time her father had been hospitalized; she had found out only later. All these years, she had been thinking that her mother was always complaining, when in fact she had hidden everything.

Rajani Phupu was still speaking. "O, Beena. O, *Ma*. Your father is not well. He is coughing up blood, and he has constipation. There are so many things wrong with him. Maybe it is because of the diabetes and not eating enough. But he has fainted twice since I came here."

"Please, tell him to come, Rajani Phupu. Please help him to get his visa."

"Don't worry, Beena. He is doing everything he can. He is settling his bank accounts and arranging for his bills to be paid in his absence. But he is very ill. I am just telling you."

22. THE PSYCHOLOGIST

Ottawa, 1967-69

BEING ONE OF THE youngest of eight children, my wife Rahela received little attention. Her family even forgot to send her to school until she was nine years old, at which time one of her sisters noticed and admitted her to class five. As a child, she spent long hours lying on her stomach on the floor, reading, drawing, or writing. From this peculiar circumstance, she grew an obsession with learning. Her writing was not confined to her discipline. She wrote stories and poems, and she kept a constant, daily journal. These are some pages from her journal about our life in Canada:

The year was 1966. I had just earned my M.A. degree in psychology from Dacca University, and my family had begun to try their utmost to arrange my marriage. I had resisted getting married so far, although there had been no shortage of efforts on their part. After I had earned my B.A. degree, my second sister Mejo Apa took me away to live with her. She was married to an army officer. Every week, the officers and their wives dressed up in their fine clothes to socialize at the officers' club. My sister dressed me in a silk sari, tied my hair in a tight bun on top of my head, and took me with her to present me to the dashing young army officers who were looking for wives. But when the proposals came, I refused them all. In the end, it became apparent to everyone, including my ageing parents who were anxious to see me settled, that I would not marry until I completed my master's degree.

After passing my M.A., I was spending time in my parents' home in Old Dhaka when my brother-in-law Boro Dulabhai, the husband of my eldest sister Boro Apa, fetched me to visit him and my sister in Tangail. They lived in a large house with gardens and a pond, surrounded by greenery. Boro Dulabhai was a high-ranking engineer in roads and highways. He dressed smartly in suits, waistcoats, and boots, and he drove an engineer's jeep. The house was full of his office staff. There was always a car ready to take us wherever we wanted.

I spent a month at my sister's house enjoying a leisurely time, playing with Boro Apa's three small boys, going to movies with my sister and brother-in-law, and learning how to bake cakes. But when I wanted to look for a job at the nearby school, my sister would not let me. Soon I learned the reason for her reluctance. My family had found a match for me, and preparations were underway for my marriage. My third sister Shejo Apa had brought the proposal. The boy in question was twenty-seven years of age, a teacher at the engineering university who was now pursuing a PhD in Canada. Seeing an eligible bachelor, all the married Bengali women in Ottawa had been trying to secure him as a husband for their younger sisters, but my sister had grabbed him first.

One morning, we were having breakfast with omelet, fried potatoes, and ruti when a letter arrived from my sister Shejo Apa in Canada.

My brother-in-law Boro Dulabhai teased me with a line from a Bengali song. "Uth chhuri, tor biya legese! Hey, girl, it's your wedding!" Boro Dulabhai was jolly and light-hearted. Life was a joke to him. He seemed to have only two concerns, showering my sister with affection and teasing the wits out of everybody else.

Boro Apa tore open the envelope and handed me a photo with a naughty smile in her eyes. "Look."

I grabbed the photo and ran away to my sister's roof. A breeze from the pond blew over the flowerpots arranged around the edge. Leaning on the parapet, I studied the photo in privacy. A dark, handsome face grinned back at me. I found myself looking into small, intense-looking eyes under thick eyebrows and a broad forehead. In his mouth was a pipe. He had a prominent chin, a long nose, a dark mustache, and thick, curly hair. A vertical line divided his forehead. Despite my intense scrutiny, I could not gather anything about his personality.

Alas, before the marriage could be formalized, my family received a terrible shock. My brother-in-law Boro Dulabhai was driving from Tangail to Dacca when his jeep was hit by an oncoming truck. He died on the spot. Forty days later, my poor father died from a heart attack. Only a few days before his death, he had turned to my mother and said, "I had thought to marry off one daughter. Instead, I widowed another."

My sister Boro Apa and her three little boys, all under eight years of age, moved to Dacca into a half-finished house in Dhanmondi that Boro Dulabhai had been constructing before his death. My widowed mother and I moved in with my sister to care for the children. We all slept in the only finished room in the house. One night, I heard my mother and Boro Apa talking, lying beside each other inside the mosquito net.

"This marriage is inauspicious," my mother said. "It is a bad omen that following the proposal there were two deaths in the family."

"Then you must stop it," my sister said.

But when my mother tried to talk to my brothers-in-law, now the guardians of the family, they overrode her objections. "Amma, that is just superstition. How can you object to such a brilliant boy?"

In April, three men from the boy's family came to see me at my fourth sister Chhoto Apa's house in Banani. They had traveled all day by bus and ferry from their village in Jessore. They asked

me many questions. *What did I study? What books did I read?* Before
leaving, they slipped a red ruby ring onto my finger. Baas! After
that, my marriage was finalized on paper. A trunk call was placed
to Canada from my sister's house in Banani. My future husband
and I uttered our vows on the phone over a muffled long-dis-
tance line between Canada and East Pakistan while a kazi held out
the papers for our signatures. By May, I was on a plane crossing
the Atlantic Ocean to Canada, a country that had assumed the
proportions of a dreamland for me. What kind of prince awaited
me there?

My flight companion was a middle-aged man with a broad face
and steel-rimmed spectacles. He was a friend of Mejo Dulabhai,
the husband of my second eldest sister Mejo Apa. Mejo Apa had
booked my ticket on the same flight so that my brother-in-law's
friend could act as my chaperone.

"Who are you going to see in Canada?" the man inquired,
leaning into me with a smile on his lips. He raised an eyebrow and
appeared to wink at me.

"My sister lives there," I said quickly, looking down at my shoes.

For the rest of the flight, I kept my eyes focused on my shoes.
I worried if they would bear out the Canadian winter.

My third sister Shejo Apa and my brother-in-law Shejo Dulabhai
received me in Montreal, and the three of us traveled by bus to
Ottawa. My first view of Ottawa with its quaint buildings and
flowerpots hanging from windows filled me with excitement. The
air was still mild and comfortable. We reached Shejo Apa's home
in the evening.

As we were entering the building, my sister's landlady who
lived on the top floor ran out, crying, "Mrs. Ahmed, your sister is
very pretty!"

Once we were inside Shejo Apa's tiny flat, the aura of spices
overwhelmed me. My sister had been cooking all day, preparing

the items that would be served at the wedding, polao, beef rezala, and roast chicken.

The next day, my husband and I were married in my sister's home. The two of us stood stiffly in the middle of her living room as we were garlanded and photographed by a swarm of Bengalis who were strangers to me. Then we sat down on a dais and a throng of people pressed in, surrounding us. Someone held a gilded mirror under our faces.

"Look in the mirror!" a voice cried to me from the crowd. "What do you see?"

Shejo Apa lifted my chin. My head hurt under the clasp of a hundred hairpins. My bridal sari, of the softest, purest red Benarasee silk, clung to my body. Raising my head and peering through my veil and the curtain of flowers hanging in front of my face, I rested my eyes on the bridegroom. He was clad in a black wool suit, a black fez on his head and a garland of red and white roses around his neck. He appeared to me at that moment like the hero of a Sharat Chandra Chatyapadhyay novel.

"I see a moon," I said.

The crowd around me broke into laughter. In truth, what I saw was the Uddin of those days, the incredible sight of a man who defied definition. The next moment, my fingers were shoved around the garland of red and white roses at my neck, lifting the garland over my head and placing it around my husband's neck. I had seen the face and exchanged flower garlands, but no words had been spoken.

My sister's Bengali friends in Ottawa had decorated our bridal room. In place of the usual yellow and orange marigolds used to decorate bridal rooms in Bangladesh, red and white roses lined the four-poster bridal bed. Loose rose petals had been scattered on top of the bedcover. The twin garlands we had exchanged earlier hung from the arm of a chair. On the first night of our life together, Uddin told me the story of a professor who did not give his wife a single moment of his time.

"If the professor were leaving the country to go on a foreign tour, the wife would come to know at the last moment that her husband was going abroad," he said.

I laughed at the joke of such an eccentric personality, but I was puzzled. What did he mean to tell me such a story? What did he wish me to understand? Next, he recited a poem called "Din Sheshe" by the revolutionary poet Shahadat Hussain. The poem went like this:

> *In the midst of the jungle's dense garden*
> *The darkness has unraveled its braid*
> *In the birds' song fades silently*
> *the Alkananda, outburst of music.*
> *From the scenery, the painting vanishes.*
> *All forms and smells are washed out.*
> *Into this lap of cold slumber,*
> *lift up this tired traveler.*

As he spoke, he lit up one cigarette after another, blowing smoke in the dark. Putting out his third cigarette, he told me a story about a king who asked all the wise men of his kingdom to compose an epic poem describing human life. The wise men wrote volumes and volumes on the subject. The king asked them to condense the volumes into manageable proportions, so the wise men set to, shortening their story in successive revisions, until at the end the story read thus: "People have come to the world, they have suffered, and they have departed."

I understood that I had been given three riddles. If I could solve these, I would be able to understand what kind of man I had married, and what kind of life I was to share with him. I was too consternated to speak. I spent the night answering his questions in monosyllables, while thinking hard. In the small hours of the morning, as I was drifting off to sleep, he asked me to name one thing I desired.

"I need proper shoes for the winter," I said softly, before my eyes closed from exhaustion.

In the darkness, I heard happy laughter.

Much later, I realized that the story Uddin had tried to tell me that night, through the accounts of the callous professor, the philosopher king, and the weary traveler, was about his own deep sadness in life.

The next day, Uddin's friends arranged a wedding reception for us at a local restaurant. My sister Shejo Apa dressed me in a pink handloom-silk sari and pinned my hair in a painful bun perched high on top of my head. Then she removed my glasses, so that I went to the party half-blind.

"Bhabi, you're looking nice." My husband's friends surrounded me.

"Bhabi, do you think you will be able to fill the large hole in Nasir's heart?" asked one man.

"That will take all the love in the world," said another. "Do you think you have all that love, Bhabi?"

"Bhabi, sit between us at the dinner table."

"No, Bhabi, sit next to me. Why sit next to Nasir? He doesn't have much to say!"

I blushed deeply, trying to think of an appropriate answer. I did not know if I was expected to reply. Was I being teased?

After dinner, Uddin disappeared into another smaller room. Looking around, I saw that all the men had vanished with him. I was left alone in the large dining hall among three or four other women. They were dressed in a similar fashion to me, in silk saris, carrying sequined purses, with heavy, dangling earrings and voluminous buns. I sat silently, studying the shoes of the other women.

"I am Ali Hussein's wife," one of them greeted me.

I smiled and nodded shyly.

"I pity you," she went on, looking at me with liquid eyes. "Imagine, what kind of man plays cards at his own wedding party?"

I stared at her. Was that what Uddin was doing? I was shocked.

My father never allowed cards in our house. None of my brothers-in-law played cards, which was considered a lowly activity in
our family. Should I feel insulted? I could not decide, but my eyes
filled with tears all the same.

"Listen," said the woman. "You will hear them. There!" She
pointed in the air.

I concentrated hard, pricking my ears. The sounds coming from
the other room grew louder. Soon I heard Uddin's ringing voice.

"Bhaiya, this is not fair!"

I had not known Uddin a day, but I recognized his voice. I
heard it distinctly rising. Then it exploded like a volcano.

"This is cheating!"

There were sounds of rushing feet. Uddin ran past where I was
sitting, flying like one possessed. His eyes were blood-red, and a
vertical frown marked the center of his high forehead. His friends
ran after him, calling him.

"Nasir!"

"Calm down!"

"It's only a game!"

Instead of slowing his pace, he reached the end of the hall and
pushed through the door into a private room, slamming the door
behind him and locking it. His friends gathered outside the door.

"Nasir, come out. Your new bride is waiting outside. What
will she think?"

Uddin did not emerge from the room for hours. I sat amidst
the consoling voices of strangers who explained to me in whispers
that everything was all right; Uddin was just young, sentimental,
excitable; I had married a real Bengali hero, an angry young man.
Indeed, indeed, indeed!

23. LOOT

Houston, April 2003

THE TV SHOWED THE looting of the museum in Baghdad. An Iraqi official based in the US (was it the ambassador?) was being interviewed, and he burst into tears. Watching the interview, Beena also started to bawl, loud, childish tears coming out of nowhere. Roberto was out of the apartment getting bread, eggs, and milk from Kroger.

Remembering that Roberto had instructed her to keep her eyes on the defense ("It's not going to write itself!" Roberto had joked), she turned off the TV and sat down at the dining table, staring at the computer screen open on her dissertation. The next moment, she opened another window on a report about the looting of the Iraqi museum. Someone had asked Donald Rumsfeld about the looting. Rumsfeld laughed. "The images you are seeing on television, you are seeing over and over and over," he said. "It's the same picture of some person walking out of some building with a vase, and you see it twenty times. And you think, my goodness, were there that many vases? Is it possible that there were that many vases in the whole country?"

Roberto walked in carrying canvas shopping bags, setting out bread, egg cartons, and clementines on the table. Beena rose and pulled him by the elbow toward her. Roberto gathered her in his arms. She turned his face toward her, studying its lean and triangular shape, with sunken cheeks, and slanted, narrow, yellow eyes.

"What's the matter?" He smiled down at her.

"Nothing. Just anxious."

"I'll take you to Italy," he said. "To meet my family. They live in the countryside." He mentioned a village on top of a hill.

"Promise?" she asked, clasping her hands at the back of his neck.

Roberto bent his head and brought his lips to hers. She closed her eyes. His mouth tasted soft and sweet. When had his face become burned in her mind? Had she really not noticed how close they had been, and how they could slip any moment into something more? When had she started to depend on him?

"Since when?" Salma had asked. When Beena had answered there had been nothing between them until a few weeks ago, Salma had scoffed. "You're lying!"

Beena had considered this. *Was* she lying? The long answer was this. When she had studied English Literature at Dhaka University, all the texts they had read in class had been romantic. Beowulf, Shakespeare, and the Romantic poets, always talking about romance. After classes, she read more books sitting at the British Council Library, English novels with more romance— *Pamela, Pride and Prejudice, Jane Eyre,* and *The French Lieutenant's Woman*—which formed her romantic view of the world. But her first romance had always been America. "My dream is to come to study in America!" she had written in her letters to her cousins in America. And now, here she was, living in her dreamland, the United States of America.

The phone rang.

"It's Salma," Roberto said.

Beena moved to the couch in the living room with the phone, turning on the TV as a calming effect.

"Beena, the preparations are coming along great for the

wedding. I have to discuss a few details with you." Salma's voice sounded bright and vibrant.

"Salma, did you get the names of the immigration lawyers?" Beena asked.

"Yes. Khaled gave me his lawyer's name. Khaled said he could walk you through the process. Should I give him your number?"

Beena hesitated.

"You know that Khaled is very fond of you. He can help you two."

"Wait, one sec."

The news had sprung up on Beena while she had been talking to Salma. The TV screen had filled with images of tanks and soldiers. She found the remote control and turned off the TV. The screen turned blank.

"Yes," she replied. "You can give him my number."

24. CASE STUDY

Ottawa, 1967-69

WE MOVED INTO A one-bedroom apartment on Sunnyside Avenue, a twenty-minute walk from the university. The bedroom and living room were divided by a cloth partition. There was a small kitchen. It was Uddin's habit to wake up in the morning, immediately have his breakfast of two eggs and a glass of tomato juice, then set off for the university.

"You are very self-sufficient," I remarked one day, rising to find him already in the kitchen. For days, I had tried unsuccessfully to catch him before he left for school. "You do not need me to cook breakfast for you!"

At this, he grinned. "I have learned how to cook from Dr. Ahmed," he said, showing me how to crack an egg on the kitchen counter and drop it in the frying pan with one swift motion of his hand.

After that, I did not try to interfere with his schedule. I was fast asleep when Uddin left the apartment. I waited impatiently for him all day. He would return at midnight and stomp his feet hard outside the door to kick off the snow. That sound alerted me that he was home. His Russian hat would be covered in snow. I shook off the white fluffs with great care and removed his long coat from his shoulders. Then I heated up the food I had cooked, boiled rice, daal, a fish curry, and we ate together. He read the newspaper with deep concentration for an hour or two. I sat in front of him, unseen. I wanted badly to listen to a story.

"What happened at the university today?" I asked.

"Hmm?" He never had the time to converse, to tell a single anecdote about his day.

One day, I found a photo of Uddin. In it, he was wearing a white shirt, laughing into the camera, his eyes creased with happiness. His tanned face and thick, coal-black hair were alight with joy. I snatched a pen from his desk and wrote on the white border of the photograph, stealing a line from a Rabindranath Tagore song, "Are you only a picture?"

As winter approached, the landscape of Ottawa became covered by a layer of snow. Everyone in Ottawa was bundled up. Even their ears were covered in earmuffs against frostbite. Someone had given Uddin a gray overcoat. I made it my life's project to urge this coat onto his shoulders to shield him from the inclement weather outside. I came to associate him with his overcoat. The long skirt drooped around his legs, lending him a forlorn look, a disappearing form in the snow, walking alone, determinedly. By now, I suspected that something was deeply wrong with him.

One day, Uddin called me from the university and told me to get ready. He was taking me to watch a movie. We wandered a street full of movie theaters, reading the billboards, until he finally chose a movie playing at one particular theater. After buying popcorn and drinks, we settled in our seats. Halfway through the movie, the main character's mother died on screen. I turned to offer Uddin some popcorn, but he pushed my hand away.

Later that night, after we had gone to sleep, I sat up in bed to find him crying in the dark.

"What's the matter?" I asked.

He turned on his side without replying.

We used to watch many movies together. The theaters used to show two movies for the price of one, and we had all the time and energy in the world to take advantage of this offer. After watching many movies, I had become aware that if anybody's mother died on the screen, Nasir Uddin became distraught.

"I am a psychologist," I began tentatively. "If there is some trauma, I can cure you."

At this, he sat up sharply and pushed his face forward. "What nonsense! Are you a small child that you think you can cure everything?"

"No," I said, shrinking back. "You are right. I cannot cure everything."

With time, I learned the story of Uddin's life. It appeared to me that he was still mourning the death of his mother. He had lost her at a young age, and this incident had left him traumatized. As a student of psychology, I was interested in analyzing all people. Uddin seemed to me a rare specimen, a man who baffled and eluded me. I began to study him closely.

CASE HISTORY: When his mother died of a snakebite, he blamed himself for her death. Later in life, he drove away his closest relatives and drew toward him strangers, trying to fill this guilt. He could love the world, but not those closest to him.

In the early days of our marriage, we used to play a long record on the gramophone. In the quiet melody of that song, we spun the memories of our life together. Nasir Uddin rambled off his philosophies to me. He used to tell me, "Come to people's aid, but do not expect anything from anyone or you shall be hurt."

I said, "I understand from your comments that your life is filled with sadness."

I had yet a while to wait before I would know the man. His

beauty amazed me, his absentmindedness pained me, and his utter neglect of his health saddened me. His love and generosity for all people made me proud, while his ignorance of all pragmatic things in life beggared me.

On the weekends, Uddin and I walked seven and a half miles to the open market downtown to buy lamb. He would stand in front of the shop and have the meat cut up as he liked.

As we walked home with our heavy load, I said idly, "I need to buy some winter shoes soon."

As soon as we reached home, Uddin called his friends on the phone and invited them to our home. I began to cook. At least ten to twelve friends came over. Uddin loved to feed people. It was one of his great pleasures to invite many people to his house to eat with him. He would tell me, you don't have to serve rich polao korma, just share with them whatever you have cooked, whatever food is at home. After dinner, the party split into two groups. Uddin played contract bridge, while I sat in the rummy players' group. He played with deep concentration, sucking on a cigarette and inhaling the smoke. When he played cards, he noticed little else. I played rummy at the other corner of the smoke-filled room, absent-mindedly arranging my cards in a clumsy fan, thinking it would be so nice if we could spend this evening together talking, just the two of us. Sometimes, the men forgot their game and became embroiled in an argument about religion or politics.

Uddin lost his temper at the mention of religion. "Those who pretend to be most religious are the ones who lie and steal the most."

"Come on. Surely, religion has positive influences. It gives people peace and purpose in life," his friends argued.

"All the evils of the world are committed in the name of religion!" Uddin retorted.

I discovered that he could not stand capitalists either. He thought that socialism was the best solution to all of society's problems. I joined in these conversations, arguing with his friends, who had also become my friends, but all the while I tried to make up my own mind, both about the issues and about the man I had married.

ANALYSIS: Perhaps he was suspicious of religion because he had seen his eldest uncle neglect his wife and children to go off to religious camps.

In August, Uddin and I visited Expo 1967 in Montreal. We wandered the magnificent stalls, holding hands and chatting. Coming to a display of home entertainment centers, Uddin stopped. I stared up at him lovingly. I knew that he had a deep love for music. It was his dream one day to have a musical sound system installed in his home.

He held out his hand to me. "Can you pass me your camera? I'd like to take some pictures."

Uddin had given me a Nikon S-2 camera as a gift for my birthday, but his love of photography was so great that he kept borrowing it to take pictures. I rummaged inside my bag, but I could not find the camera. I began to search frantically. I had seen the volcano erupt before.

"I forgot it at home," I said at last.

Uddin stared at me as if he couldn't believe what I was saying. He became apoplectic with anger, screaming garbled words. In the end, he left me standing alone and left the fair. For a long time, I walked on my own looking at the exhibits. I sat down on a bench and ate ice cream to compose myself. Then I boarded the monorail train out of the exposition grounds and rode the bus home on my own.

ANALYSIS: He cannot tolerate any neglect from me. He begins to scream like a mad man. He has communication problems. He becomes very excited when he wants to express himself. He needs my complete attention. It is impossible to relax with him.

By September, I realized that Uddin was a chain smoker. He always had a pipe or a cigarette in his mouth. His fingertips were stained. Our small flat was fogged with smoke.

"Please. Give up smoking," I pleaded with him.

But he did not pay heed. "If I smoke, I shall die. If I don't smoke, I shall still die," he said.

When I insisted, he said, "I shall quit tomorrow."

The next day he lit up another cigarette in front of me, staring absentmindedly into space, dropping ashes on the center table. Later, he developed asthma, diabetes, and glaucoma. With each new ailment, he smoked with more contentment, embracing the act of dying, as if he had been waiting all along for the cold sleepy lap of death.

By October, I realized that Uddin did not like to waste money. He never spent a cent on himself. He disliked wandering around in a store, window shopping. If he needed something, he would buy it quickly and leave without turning his eyes to any other tempting object on the shelves. But if he wanted to give anyone else a gift, he chose the best item possible, often the most expensive gift. He chose the gift himself. I had no part in the decision. He treated me with the same callousness with which he regarded himself. In the summer, I had earned some money from babysitting for a Canadian family. I expressed the desire to have a set of gold jewelry made from the money.

"If you give this money to my poor relatives and help them, that would be the best possible use of the sum," he said.

I agreed immediately to his proposition, to make him happy.

ANALYSIS: Perhaps he needs attention because all his life he experienced neglect.

Simply to get attention, he gave everything he had to people, to complete strangers. Yet I, his wife, had passed a year in Canada without proper winter shoes. I said to Uddin, "I need closed shoes. I have been watching the shoes of every woman in the capital city and I have a very good idea what I want."

Uddin laughed and proffered a joke. "A man will buy a thing for ten dollars instead of five dollars if he needs it. On the other hand, a woman will buy a thing for one dollar instead of five dollars which she does not need."

I did not smile. I did not find the joke funny at all. "That's not very nice, or true," I said, taking his arm and giving him a shove toward the door. "I need these shoes. This is a purchase you need not have any guilt about."

Uddin suggested that we should walk to the shopping center downtown. We walked for seven and a half miles in the cold. He showed me three or four shops, but he was not satisfied with anything he saw. We walked back and forth another three miles, deliberating the pros and cons and prices of many styles of shoes, but he still did not buy me a single pair. My feet began to ache. My eyes filled with tears. I said to myself, "I shall never again ask for anything from this man. It is true, to ask is to hurt."

"I know one more store," Uddin cried, hitting the palm of one hand with the knuckles of his other hand. "It is just five miles from here."

"I can't walk anymore." I lifted the edge of my sari to reveal a reddened heel.

Uddin considered this. "We can take the bus," he said.

The entire way on the bus, I did not speak to him. I thought, how could he profess to love the world and yet be so negligent toward those closest to him? I could not understand him at all. When we climbed down from the bus, darkness began to descend. The air was gray and cold. Uddin took my hand and led me through blustery blocks, past glittering shops with painted signs, until we stood in front of another glass-front store. A sign announced the name of the store: Freeman. A slanted mannequin in the window sported a pair of pink stilettos. Beside the shoed-up mannequin, tall leather boots, ankle boots lined with fur, sleek pumps, and shiny loafers with buckles stood arrayed neatly on glass shelves. I stared at this magnificent store-front display and sighed. A sign on the shop door read, SORRY, WE'RE CLOSED.

"Wait. Don't move. Stand there!" Uddin skipped away and aimed the camera at me. His face was hidden behind the camera. Only his voice floated to me. "Say cheese!"

I pushed back my tears and peered into the lens. Finally, I understood him. In the months that I had spent observing him and assessing him, he had already accepted me as his own, claiming for me the same treatment he bestowed on himself. I could see my future life, filled with endless disappointments, followed by repeated forgiveness. The darkness spread out in front of us, engulfing us.

"This one's for memories," he said. His tobacco-stained fingers gripped the camera as his tattered coat fluttered in the wind. "This way, we shall always remember the day that you wanted to buy a pair of shoes but could not do so!"

I nodded and smiled for the camera.

25. LATE NIGHT NEWS

Houston, 2003

LATE AT NIGHT, THE phone rang. Beena sprang from her bed to answer it. Roberto had taken to handing her his cellphone at night. She picked it up now from the bedside table, calming herself so that the right words would come out of her mouth. The eleven- or twelve-hour time difference between Houston and Dhaka had always meant that she was half asleep and irritated when she spoke to her parents, even if she had been thinking tenderly about them. It was her cousin Mukul Bhai, Rajani Phupu's son.

"Mukul Bhai! Are you working on my father's visa? Did he get permission from the government to travel yet?" she asked excitedly.

"Yes. I am working on it."

"Oh, good!" She searched her mind for questions to ask him about his family, trying to remember the names of his wife and children.

"Beena. Your father is in the hospital. He was weak from diarrhea. His sugar level dropped. He was exercising on the veranda when had a blackout. He fell and broke his right arm. The doctors at the hospital said he has multiple fractures. The bone is crushed."

Beena stood in her thin T-shirt. "Will they perform surgery?" she asked.

"Yes, he will need surgery. But first, they are trying to stabilize him. Now he is in the ICU. He is unconscious and they are monitoring him."

"He will be okay, right?" she asked in a soft voice.

"Yes, I hope so."

26. PRESSURE VESSELS

Ottawa, 1967

ONE DAY, WHILE WALKING across campus on my way to the department, I ran across my PhD advisor Dr. Bowes. The professor called me to come sit beside him on the grass. Pulling out a sandwich from a paper bag, he tore it in two and handed one half to me.

"It's very good, Uddin. If you don't take it, you'll regret it."

While I chewed, Dr. Bowes talked about the bright prospects of research at NRC and how badly he needed a bright student like me. He reminded me about the gloomy prospects for a researcher in Pakistan, with no equipment, funding, or appreciation. I said nothing, holding my lip between my forefinger and thumb, listening intently.

Dr. Bowes swallowed the last of his sandwich and twisted the brown bag in his hands. "What do you say? If you don't come to work for me, I won't recommend you for your PhD," he said jokingly.

"I intend to return to my country as soon as I finish my degree," I said. "If I have anything worth giving, I should give it to my country."

The professor had tried to convince me before to come work for him. He was very interested in my research. "Uddin, finish quickly. Then you can come to work for me," he would say. Dr. Bowes was the director of the structural division at the National Research Council of Canada. The NRC was short of well-trained researchers, especially in the structural division. Only a few years ago, after I completed my master's program, he said, "I am very impressed with your thesis. I would like you to work with me to complete your PhD." When I objected that my scholarship only covered my master's degree, he said, leave it to me. He used his own funds and obtained permission from both the Pakistan government and the Canadian government to extend my visa so that I could pursue a PhD.

As my graduation neared, Dr. Bowes began to insist more earnestly that I should come work for him. The research that Bowes found so impressive involved a new numerical method to calculate the deformation caused by stresses at the junctions of axisymmetric shells. Pressure vessels are axisymmetric shells. Most pressure vessels are thin cylinders fitted with spherical, ellipsoidal, or conical ends. The junction where the cylindrical body and the end meet is the most critical region of the vessel, where it is most vulnerable to stresses. In those days, people calculated these stresses manually. The results that they obtained were approximate and very unreliable. Using a new method for integration of highly nonlinear differential equations called multi-segment method of integration, I was able to predict the stresses and deformations at the junctions of the pressure vessels much more accurately. If the vessel is thin, it will collapse instead of breaking under external pressure. This pressure, at which the vessel would collapse, is called the instability pressure. Using the same method, I also calculated the instability pressure of pressure vessels. These concepts are transferable to human life. Imagine stresses and pressures impinging on a shell, the human body or mind, at the critical junction of life, where someone's choices would be critical for their future. Let the choice be to go or to stay. Let the pressure be the promise of a job in Canada.

A few weeks before my defense, I finished typing my thesis and called my wife Rahela.

"Let's go celebrate," I said.

We ate dinner together at a restaurant, reminiscing about the happy times we'd spent in Ottawa. I chewed on chicken drumsticks and smoked my pipe, looking forward to going home, but Rahela was restless. Pursing her lips and looking out through the glass at the street with flower baskets hanging outside shop windows, she said, "If we only stayed a few more years, I could complete my PhD here."

"Are you mad? I am not prepared to extend our stay by one more second," I said.

This was not the first time Rahela had mentioned her desire to pursue a degree in Canada to me. She had dropped hints many times before about wanting to start her own PhD after I finished my studies, but I had remained deaf to her suggestions.

After dropping Rahela at home, I walked back to my office to put the finishing touches on my thesis, but I could not find it anywhere. I lost my mind. There was only one physical copy of the thesis, which I had to submit to the committee before my defense. I sat down in my chair with my head in my hands, wondering what to do. At some point I fell asleep sitting on the chair, drifting in and out of a feverish dream. I dreamt that my visa had run out, along with my scholarship and personal funds. I could not complete my PhD that year. My only option was to start working at the NRC, so I could stay on in Canada and buy time to rewrite my thesis. In my dream, I got used to the working life in Canada and the opportunity to carry on ground-breaking research, and then I decided I would never go back!

In the end, it never came to that. Gathering bits and pieces from old versions and from my professors, including Dr. Bowes himself, I was able to re-type my thesis. But in that moment, when

I had been sitting in my office considering how I could slip into a future without having chosen it, merely because of an accident, I had already decided that no matter of chance could change my decision. I was determined to return home, even if it took me twenty years to do so.

My wife Rahela had enjoyed our time in Ottawa. Being quite independent, she used to babysit for Canadian families to pass the time and walk around the shops on her own. She had also developed a habit of watching TV. Her favorite show was *I Dream of Jeannie*. The wives of the graduate students at the university had formed a club called "Pushing Him Through." The PHT club had many activities, including the issuing of certificates to women who had successfully pushed their partners through a degree. In the morning, Rahela attended all the PHT activities. In the evening, she glided into my office to carry me away to some place outside the university. If I still had work to do, she read in the library and waited for me. In the winter, we went to the cinema or a friend's house, but in the summer, we always visited a small mountain overlooking a river, at the intersection of two freeways. We drove up part of the way and then climbed on foot to the top. From where we sat, everything seemed to mingle. The sky, the water, and the valley became one. The mountain was covered with crabapple trees. Rahela liked nothing better than to pick the apples from the trees, dust them, and bite into them right there, saying, "If I had one wish granted in my life, it would be to own such a fruit tree from which I could pluck fruits to my heart's content."

After my PhD convocation, Rahela and I invited Dr. Bowes and his wife and their three young daughters to our home. Mrs. Bowes and Rahela got along very well. Rahela cooked Bengali food and helped the children dress in saris. During dinner, Bowes said that in his early life, he had worked as a professional engineer on the Canadian railway. At that time, he had designed a bridge in his hometown in Newfoundland, and also supervised its construction.

"Whenever I go home, Uddin, I run to this bridge, and I sit under it listening to the trains pass overhead," he said. "Do you know how proud I feel sitting there? I close my eyes and think about all the people crossing the bridge, seated as comfortably as if they were resting in their own living rooms. And I made this possible for them."

My pupils shone brightly. Dr. Bowes made me dream about what I would do for my country.

"I have a wish to see your country and do some research there, Uddin," Bowes said.

"You must stay with us then!" Rahela exclaimed. "You must come and see how we are doing."

I never gave Rahela an opportunity to get a Canadian degree. Nor did I ever give her in her lifetime a crab apple tree of the sort that she had craved, sitting on her favorite mountain in Canada. But when we returned to Bangladesh, she visited my village home. I took her to the fruit trees, and there she satisfied her dream again, biting into the smooth flesh of ripe mangos, the juice trickling down her knuckles. Then we were both reminded of that mountain top in Ottawa at the intersection of roads, sky, and water.

27. TO STAY OR TO GO

Houston, 2003

BEENA'S FATHER HAD BEEN stuck in the hospital for weeks.

"Should I go back?" she asked Roberto.

Roberto tried to comfort her. "Isn't it dangerous for you to go now? What if they don't let you back in, to defend your thesis?"

"You're right. My father wouldn't want me to jeopardize my defense. My mother wouldn't, either. That's how we were brought up. Our studies came first."

They worked day and night on their dissertations, going to the library together, checking out stacks of books and driving home with the books rattling in the backseat. Her dissertation, overdetermined, traced modernity in Bengal through anglophone novels. There was more scholarly work on the subject than the entire volume of translated works, but at least she had fought to add Bengali literature to her list.

It was a comfort to her to always be able to reach Rajani Phupu, whenever she called. Rajani Phupu said that Beena's father was still in the hospital, but his condition was now stable. The doctors had said his arm would mend with time. Beena had tried to call the doctors herself, but there was a twelve-hour time difference, and she could never stay awake till the doctors reported to work.

One day, Beena's cousin Mukul Bhai called at six in the morning, as Roberto and Beena were getting ready to go to campus.

"Beena! Wait. Let me hand the phone to Boro Mama."

Her father sounded weak, wheezing, collapsing into fits of coughing when he tried to speak, but his voice was upbeat. In answer to a shouted question from Beena, he said he was all right. "Thik Achi, Ammu!"

Straining her ears, she heard him say softly, in a hoarse voice, that he was "coming home."

"Oh, you're going to be released from the hospital soon? You're going to go home? I'll buy an airplane ticket, right after my defense, in a few weeks, and I'll come home to see you," she said brightly.

"No," he said, pausing for another coughing fit. Then he continued in a weak voice, "I meant, after they release me from the hospital, I'll make preparations to visit you. In Houston."

28. LONG FLIGHT

Dacca, 1971

THE TROUBLE BETWEEN EAST Pakistan and West Pakistan had been building for a long time. Even as a student in Canada, I had witnessed the hostility of the Pakistan High Commission in Ottawa against Bengalis. By the time I returned home, things were heating up. General elections were held in 1970. The Awami League party of East Pakistan, led by the Bengali leader Sheikh Mujibur Rahman, won an absolute majority in the Pakistan National Assembly in a landslide victory against the Pakistan People's Party led by Zulfikar Ali Bhutto. The election results clearly expressed the discontent of the people with the current political situation. But the Chief Martial Law Administrator of Pakistan Yahya Khan was not keen about having an East Pakistani party ruling the government, so he had refused to honor the election and inaugurate the new National Assembly. Tensions had been mounting between West Pakistan and East Pakistan since then, leading to intense political unrest, with strikes and demonstrations every day. On seventh March of 1971, Sheikh Mujib had declared that East Pakistan would fight for independence.

On the evening of March 25, my colleagues and I were

discussing the political situation of Pakistan while playing bridge at the engineering university teachers' club. We had just heard the news that President Yahya Khan had flown to Dacca in his private plane for diplomatic talks with the Bengali leader Sheikh Mujibur Rahman, and speculation was high as to what would happen next. All the teachers were having a heated discussion. I was arguing aggressively with my colleagues, holding my cigarette in my left hand, my good hand. My right arm was in a cast. I had broken the arm on a visit to Jhenidah during the Eid holidays. I had borrowed a bicycle from a relative in Jhenidah to ride to Dari Binni. There was no moon that night and the path was uneven, full of holes that were not known to me anymore. The bicycle had toppled, and I had been thrown off. To break the fall, I had extended my forearm. Returning to Dhaka, I had discovered that the bone had fractured near the wrist. The doctor at the Dhaka Medical College Hospital who had plastered the arm had said, "Let it remain this way for a month and a half. We shall open the cast then and see if the bone has joined." But the Hindu doctor had since fled the country, expecting trouble.

While we were talking in excited voices, another teacher Kanti Shaha showed up and upset everyone with some news, "There are rumors that the army is taking position in Dacca now, even as the meeting between General Yahya and Sheikh Mujib proceeds. The meeting is a farce. The army is rolling in with tanks, armored vehicles, and trucks full of ammunition!"

This news sobered the rest of us. Nobody felt like playing anymore. Without another word, we walked out of the club and went our separate ways. As we were leaving the club, Kanti said to me, "Don't you young PhD-holders have anything better to do than playing cards all day? I have a big complaint against all Bengali intellectuals. All they do is talk and play."

"What else am I not supposed to do because I have a PhD?" I joked.

Although these comments were exchanged lightly without

any malice intended, I felt bad. As I was heading back from the club to the teachers' quarters, a light breeze shook the canopy of jacaranda trees. The air was saturated with the smells of budding fruit blossoms. Soon, the Kalboshekhi storms would start, bringing pitch-black skies and relentless hail and rain. I moved with a heavy step, my shoulders curved forward, oblivious to the sweet breeze that grazed my cheeks. My mouth was twisted, and my forehead was wrinkled in a frown. I could feel a constant pain and itch under the cast on my right arm.

Hearing the grating of metal, I looked up. Some students were barricading the campus gates on the side of Dhaka Medical College by dragging miscellaneous objects, including metal-and-barb wire, rickshaw vans, tree branches, and rubber tires. Shadowy figures moved in the dark, clad in loose shirts, baggy pants, and sandals, shouting instructions to one another.

"What is happening?" I asked the students.

"Sir, the talks have failed. We expect the army to crack down tonight," the students said. "People all over Dacca are putting up barricades."

"What are you saying?" I cried sharply. "What can the army hope to achieve by this? The army is very foolish to think that it can control a whole people by military force."

I arrived at our flat in the teachers' quarters with my heart beating fast.

"You've come late again!" Rahela cried, opening the door. "You are always at the club playing cards with friends." She appeared to be very disturbed. Her sari was wrinkled, and her loose hair flew about her head. She looked at me through wide and frightened eyes. "I am feeling afraid. When I was returning from the library at Dacca University, I heard shouts and demonstrations."

I stared mutely at her, wondering how to break the news. The door to my brother Asif's room was closed. I had brought him to Dacca to study for his B.A, but he did not seem that interested in his studies. I followed Rahela to the bedroom where our infant daughter

slept in the middle of the vast bed, flanked by two long pillows, with
a smile on her lips, her legs splayed in a diamond shape and her arms
gathered above her head in a careless, confident posture.

I turned to Rahela. "The army is going to crack down
tonight," I whispered.

The baby stretched and let out a cry. Rahela rushed to the
milk powder tin on a table in the corner of the room. Pouring hot
water from a flask into a glass bottle, she mixed in two scoops of
powdered milk, her hands shaking.

"What do you think will happen now?" she asked.

"What else? All hell will break loose! We shall fight for independence!" I cried.

As I uttered these words, I felt invincible. A struggle for an
independent Bengal was inevitable now, win or lose. Soon afterward, we went to sleep with our child between us, my plastered
arm suspended close to my chest in its strong cast.

I did not sleep for long. Nobody in Dacca slept that night, or
for many nights afterward. In the middle of the night, we were
woken by gunshots and screams. The sounds seemed to be coming
from every direction. I sprang from the bed and ran to the back
veranda, which had a view of the student hostels. Rahela and Asif
joined me. All we could see were large, leaping flames in the dark
sky as Dacca burned. We stayed awake all night, waiting for the
dark night to end. Slowly, a spot began to lighten and spread across
the sky. As dawn broke, bands of people appeared in the alleys
below, moving quickly and quietly like shadows.

"I am going downstairs!" I shouted to Rahela.

"Don't go! If you go outside, you will get killed!" Rahela
cried. "Stop your brother!" she shouted to Asif.

I ran down the stairs to Kanti Shaha's flat on the ground floor
and called his name outside his door. Everyone was surely awake
now in every flat, but nobody dared to make a sound. After several
minutes, Kanti opened the door quietly and let me in. We stood
inside the door, talking in low voices.

"Do you know what is happening?" I asked.

"The army has taken over the city," Kanti said. "They have killed a lot of people. They are killing everybody they find on their way. They shot several teachers at Dacca University in their homes, and they killed the students at Jagannath Hall in a brushfire."

"How do you know this?" I asked.

"A student from the residential hall at Dacca University was passing through our campus. He was trying to escape Dacca by Jinjira, crossing the Buriganga River to the South. The student told us what he saw with his own eyes. He said Dacca is being razed to the ground."

I was astounded. If the student spoke the truth, then our own deaths could only be a few hours away. Kanti was shaking. His eyes were unnaturally large, and his pupils were dilated. Suddenly, I realized that Kanti was Hindu. At the hands of the Pakistan army, his situation would be more dire than mine.

I returned home and began to wait, keeping watch from the back veranda. Late in the day, Putuler Ma, the woman who came every morning from the neighboring slum to cook and clean, appeared at our door. She said that the slum where she lived with her husband had been set on fire, and their bamboo-walled home had burnt to the ground. The family was leaving for their village home.

All that day, we remained locked inside, watching Dacca burn.

In the afternoon, I cried, "I cannot stand it. I am going to the rooftop to see what is happening."

Rahela grabbed me by the shirt to prevent me from going, but I pulled free. I ran downstairs again to call Kanti and suggested that we climb to the roof to get a view of Dacca from the top. Kanti and I walked to the parapet and stared down at the road below. We could see soldiers running down the alleys. Dead bodies lay scattered on the road and in the field in front of Jagannath Hall. We started talking excitedly. The soldiers on the street looked up and fired at us. We fell to the ground on our hands and knees and

crawled back to the opening. Once we were downstairs, we began
to discuss what would happen now. Would we survive the day?
What had happened to Sheikh Mujib and the other Bengali politicians? Where were our relatives?

Dawn broke on March 27 and incredibly, we were still alive.
The sky over Dacca was still filled with black smoke and red flames.
In the morning, the army announced a curfew and the gunfire
seemed to cease. Some of the teachers gathered under the mango
tree in front of the teachers' residential buildings. A group of Dacca
University students were fleeing their residential halls, intending to
cross the Buriganga river to go to their village homes. They were
passing through the engineering university campus because it was
a safer passage than the open streets. We rapidly fired questions at
the escaping Dacca University students to find out what was going
on outside campus.

"Anyone providing resistance is being killed," the students
told us. They named Dacca University teachers in mathematics and statistics and the provost of Jagannath Hall who had been
carried away blindfolded from their homes in the teachers' residence buildings.

When I returned home, Rahela was preparing for the night.
She had pushed our daughter under the bed and ordered my
brother Asif to sleep under his bed in his room. She suggested to
me that I should pray with her, as that was the only way out of the
situation. Looking down, I noticed that she was holding a jainamaz
in her hands. I told her that I would not pray to anybody to save
us because I did not believe that anybody could.

The engineering university teachers were fleeing campus while
they had the chance.

"What will happen to Kanti?" I thought. "If the army cracks
down on our campus, he will be the first person the soldiers come
after."

I ran downstairs to his flat again to find Kanti and his wife in a state of shock.

"Nasir, what will we do?" Kanti's face was white with fear.

Kanti's wife Shormila Boudi, who was a teacher at Eden College, entered the drawing room wearing a cotton sari, her hair tied in a braid behind her back and a red teep on her forehead. She served us tea nervously. The spoons and china clattered in her hands.

Handing me a teacup, she began to plead with me. "They are making sure to kill anyone who is Hindu. If they find us here, they shall certainly kill my family. Please help us in any way you can."

"I can drive you to Sadar Ghat, Kanti!" I said. "From there, you can cross the Buriganga River and escape to your district." I was glad to have something to do. I owned a silver Toyota Corona that I had imported when returning from Canada. Kanti did not own a car.

"But how can you drive with your broken arm?" Kanti said, pointing to the grimy cast on my forearm.

"It's time to take this off," I assured him. "Six weeks have passed already. Wait for me." Before Kanti could stop me, I ran back up the stairs.

Rahela followed me to the small storeroom next to the kitchen, explaining to me that she had sorted it all out. We would be safe if we stayed inside and kept close to the ground, away from the windows. If the soldiers came, she would lock me and Asif in the storeroom, as the army was after able-bodied men. The smell of starch filled the air. Rahela had been cooking rice and daal. I began to rummage in a toolbox that I kept at home and pulled out a pair of scissors for cutting thin steel plates.

"*Ei!* What are you doing?" Rahela shrieked. She clapped her hand to her mouth and her eyebrows shot up above her spectacles.

"I am going to open this plaster and drive Kanti to Sadar Ghat!" I announced with glee. "Get ready. We can all take a boat to the other side of the river."

"Are you crazy? Your arm is broken."

"Do you want us to die then? Do you just want to wait here
and let the army come and kill us?" I said roughly. Pushing past
her, I sat down at the dining table with the scissors.

With Asif's help, I cut through the plaster smoothly. Finally,
my arm was free. But it hung limply in the air. The forearm dangled
like a pendulum from the fulcrum point of the fracture, halfway
between my wrist and elbow. The arm was completely useless!
The bone had not mended at all. I had peeled away the plaster,
only to reveal a weak and useless limb. I cried out in extreme pain.

"I told you!" Rahela shouted, shaking her head. "Any thinking
person would realize this. Even if the bone had mended, you
would need therapy before you could use it. Now what will I do?
Where will I find a doctor?"

My face darkened with pain, but I did not utter a word. For
a moment, I sat still trying to take control of the pain. Then I ran
down to Kanti's flat again.

"Kanti, look what I have done," I said. "My hand is completely
useless. I can be of no use to you now. You must escape immediately any way you can."

"Don't worry about me," Kanti said. "I shall see what I can
do. But you must go away also. Think of your daughter."

I climbed the stairs with difficulty back to our flat. Then I lay
my broken arm carefully on the bed and rested my body on top
and began to smoke one cigarette after another, staring up at the
ceiling as I waited for our deaths. I felt powerless to save my family.

In the afternoon, Rahela's sister Shejo Apa and her husband
Dr. Ahmed, who lived on campus, appeared at our door with their
two small daughters.

"We can't stay here," Dr. Ahmed said, twirling his mustache.
"The university area is the most dangerous place in Dacca. The
Pakistan Army is targeting all the teachers and intellectuals first. It
is only a matter of time before they come for us at the engineering
university."

He suggested that we should move to Rahela's eldest sister

Boro Apa's house in Dhanmondi. Nobody knew if Dhanmondi was safer, but the idea was that everyone should be together. I liked the idea. Both families piled into Dr. Ahmed's battered Volkswagen and headed out of the campus with Dr. Ahmed at the wheel. As soon as we were out of the gates, we saw an army truck parked on the street piled high with dead bodies stacked one on top of the other. Some soldiers stood beside the truck, stopping any cars that passed and asking the driver at gunpoint to run errands for the army. A soldier noticed the Volkswagen and motioned to Dr. Ahmed to stop. Inside the car, Rahela and her sister began to pray loudly. The children began to cry. Dr. Ahmed slowed the car, moving it to where the soldier pointed. The soldier approached the car and stooped, leaning at the window in a leisurely manner. At that moment, Dr. Ahmed stepped on the accelerator and sped off into the dead city. So began our long flight.

29. AN OPPORTUNITY TO REBUILD

Houston, 2003

"THANK YOU SO MUCH for meeting me," Beena said.

"My pleasure." Khaled nodded, smiling.

They sat on metal chairs on the balcony of a coffee shop in Montrose that Beena had suggested, facing a side street. Cars buzzed by them on the street.

"Where is…?"

"Roberto."

"Yes, Roberto."

"He couldn't make it. He had some work to do at the lab."

There was still some daylight left, the sun just visible between buildings, hovering above the horizon. The clouds overhead were fiery orange and purple. Beena wore a full-sleeved, long dress over pants to be modest in front of Khaled. She noticed that his face was clean shaven and smooth, setting off his clean, good looks. Gripping the wide coffee cup with both hands, he lifted the cup to his lips. His eyelashes fell on his cheeks as he took a sip. There was a careful aspect to his movements that told Beena that everything about the coffee shop was new to him, the chipped ceramic cup, the noisy atmosphere, and being so close to the street.

"Salma said you can help with processing my immigration," Beena said.

"I know two lawyers. They are both good, but I went with one." He smiled at her as he spoke, gazing at her with his large, black eyes, as he had at the beginning of the evening at Salma's party.

"How long did it take you?"

"Three years."

"Three years!"

"It's not a problem. Once you file, you're in status." His eyes narrowed. "What's wrong?"

"My father."

"Oh! Sir can come and stay with you. When he applies to the US embassy in Dhaka, he gets a five-year visa with multiple entry. You can take him to Canada every six months."

She nodded, gulping down her latte. The hot liquid scalded her tongue.

"I recommend going with Richard Powers. He takes his fees in installments and he knows what he is doing. He has a lot of clients, so he may be a little difficult to get, but if he takes you on, you're in good hands."

He went on speaking in a rich, smooth voice. He was very helpful, she had to admit. She said thank you several times, smiling at him gratefully.

At last, when he had given her all the information, and she had asked all the questions, he leaned back in his chair, planted his legs apart, and locked his hands behind his head. "You look very pretty. Your features are very Bengali. Especially the wide, black eyes. But your hair is not very Bengali. Curls like that are rare. Usually, Bengali women have tight curls, close together, but yours are ringlets."

"Oh." She lowered her eyes and stared at the rim of her cup, not sure how to take his remark.

"Sorry. Was that not a proper thing to say?"

"No. It's fine. This is really nice, to be out," she went on, flashing her eyebrows, to show that she was grateful for his help. "Most of the time these days, I feel like I'm inside a dark cave, grieving."

"Grieving is normal," he said, smiling kindly.

"Thank you."

Talking about it helped, but not talking with the same person. When she showed any sign of sadness, Roberto took her in his arms and covered her with kisses, silencing her.

"The female students at Dhaka University were considered beauties among us BUET students." Khaled looked at her, making eye contact, and parted his lips. Then his face assumed a timid expression again. "Now you are really annoyed."

Beena laughed. "That may have been true of one or two women in my class. They were fashionable and glamorous, but not me. I was a nondescript person. I was very plain looking, but I had big thoughts. I just went to university on the bus and came back on the bus. I was a front bencher. Guys didn't notice me."

"That can't be true. What did you look like?"

"I wore these long, loose shalwar kameez. The pants were loose and long and the kameez were huge, one-size-fits all. Do you remember the style? Very funny to look at now!" She laughed. "I had bangs like Princess Diana, and my hair was puffy, shoulder length."

"I remember that hair!" he exclaimed. "What did women have to do to get that hair?"

"It was my natural hair. I had a lot of volume back then," she bragged, basking in his attention.

"Are you sure that no boys liked you?"

"I told you, I was a front bencher. All my friends laughed at me. I was so simple. I didn't have any fun. I didn't even wear any makeup. In the summer, I carried an umbrella to avoid the sun's rays. Everybody teased me about my umbrella. One day, I didn't have the umbrella with me, and my friends saw me from afar and started crying in unison, *Beena! where is your umbrella?* We used to sit under a big tree near the statue in front of the arts building. Probably, it was a banyan tree."

He was still looking at her.

"After classes, I used to go to the British Council and read one book after another. Almost every day, I went to the British Council to read novels. Not any useful books. I was a bookworm for storybooks."

"How did you come to study English?"

"My father wanted me to study English."

"Oh? That's surprising, since he was a man of science."

They both laughed at this remark, gazing at each other's faces. There was an energy between them that made her feel disoriented and guilty.

"My father had a keen interest in literature and mathematics. But he was poor, so he couldn't study something he liked. He thought that only those who have money can study literature, so he told me it was his biggest wish that his daughter should study literature."

"But you liked it?"

"Yes, although I wanted to study environmental science initially. I even had a scholarship to go to Australia to study environmental science, but my parents wouldn't let me go. But later on, I came to love English literature. I think we were very privileged at Dhaka University. We got to study for free, and we had the best teachers. Their lectures are still stuck in my head. Mashiur Sir taught us Beowulf for three months straight!" She started laughing in a delighted voice at this memory.

He nodded approvingly.

"We studied Chaucer, the Renaissance poets, *The Duchess of Malfi*, the five greatest Romantic poets, Jane Austen. Dryden. We used to say Dryden is dry." She giggled. "John Stuart Mill. And then the French authors. Flaubert's *Madame Bovary*. And twentieth century. Doris Lessing. Classical texts, Greek tragedy. Homer, Sophocles, Aeschylus."

"Your brother got his PhD in the States?"

"Yes." Beena nodded.

"What was his research in?"

"New numerical and computation methods?" She spoke slowly, pronouncing the words in an unsure way, then laughed and shook her head. "Sorry, I don't know exactly what that is."

"I can explain it to you if you like," he said, smiling.

Suddenly, her eyes contracted and filled with tears.

He made a movement as if to cover her hand to console her. "Sorry."

She smiled through her tears and blinked, taking the napkin he handed her from the table. "No, it's okay. We were very close. He came to see me all the time, and we could talk about anything. It's crazy to think that he is gone. I don't even believe that it's real, you know?"

"Only mortality has a probability of hundred percent," he said.

"What?"

"Everybody dies."

"Huh, yes, that's true."

She let her eyes run over him, the long, lean neck, broad shoulders, and toned arms, resting on his soft lips. He was dressed in a blue Polo shirt with a white logo, looking as if he had just showered, a sharp contrast to the grime and dust of the city.

"And you? What is your thesis on?"

She made a face, stretching the corners of her mouth and showing clenched teeth. "I'm so deep in it, reading a hundred books and trying to write at the same time, that most days I can't see it clearly myself! Uh. It's about Bengali modernity, gleaned from British and Indian anglophone literature."

"Hmm."

"It's okay if you don't understand."

Again, they both laughed. She lifted her cup involuntarily, tilting her head to take a sip, hiding her warm face behind the cup.

"What is modernity?"

"Uh. The age of reason. Bengali modernity would be rationality. Secularism. I'm looking at Bengali writers who wrote about life with detached objectivity. With, with a sort of rationalism.

Their writing showed the conflict between rationality and modernity on the one hand and traditional values on the other."

"So, not Tagore?"

"Yes, Tagore. He has been well translated."

Suddenly, Khaled beat the air with his hands and coughed.

"Are you okay?"

"A lot of smoke," he said, staring at the road with tears in his eyes. "This place is not in the best of locations, is it?"

A traffic jam on the street next to them had created a long line of idling cars a few feet from where Beena and Khaled sat on the balcony. The smoke was coming from a few of the older vehicles. As they stared out at the line of cars, he frowned, pulling his lips back.

"Sorry!" She glanced at him, registering his aversion to the city. Something turned in her.

"No, it's okay," he said, with red eyes. "So, you lived in Iraq?"

"Yes, Mosul. It feels terrible with the war going on. I can't even watch the news."

"Yes." Turning away from the traffic at last, he bent his head and gave her his attention. "But don't despair. It may be good, in the long run."

"How?" Her eyes flew open in surprise.

"The war will provide an opportunity to rebuild the country. Just one example. My company could rebuild Iraq's oil infrastructure. So many possibilities have opened up for the future of Iraq's oil now. We have a great deal of expertise in engineering and construction that we can provide them. Trust me, it will be better for the Iraqi people in the long run."

"How would you help exactly?" she asked, leaning an elbow on the table, taking care to speak demurely. He had helped her.

He furrowed the tips of his eyebrows. "We have the connections, and we have the business. We could supply the equipment to fight fires in oil fields. We could ramp up their oil production. We have the relationship with other governments to help with oil sales."

Beena lifted her cup, drank the liquid to the bottom, and put it down, looking away. She reached for her bag and looked at her watch, checking the time against the bus schedule.

"I have to get back," she said, rising. "But thank you very much for the contacts of the two lawyers. You've helped a lot."

"Sure," he said, rising with her, standing tall with his hands at his waist. "Call me if you need anything more. Any kind of help. Can I give you a lift?"

"No, I like taking the bus," she said, as he followed her out to the street. "Thank you for the offer." She fled, walking away from him as fast as her legs would carry her.

30. THE LAST INTELLECTUAL THOUGHT

Dacca, 1971

WE DROVE THROUGH EMPTY streets guarded by the Pakistani military with hard eyes like stone. Now and then, a lone car packed with fleeing people raced toward its destination, seeking shelter in a relative's home like us, perhaps.

Turning from Fuller Road, we crossed in front of New Market, where the military had torn down the boat signs of the Awami League, crushing the models with all their fury. Covering the short distance on Mirpur Road, we reached Boro Apa's house in Dhanmondi without further incident. I was not sure that Boro Apa's house was safer than the university campus, but with my relatives around me, I felt happy. There was no doubt that we would eventually die, but at least we would die together.

We had made our beds on the floor, pushing sheets and pillows under the beds, leaving the actual beds empty. When night fell, I sat on the floor beside the sleeping forms of my wife and daughter and concentrated on ignoring the pain in my arm. The only way I could overlook the pain was to smoke cigarettes, sitting in the dark, surrounded by the sleeping forms of my family. Late at night, we were woken by loud knocks on the door. Boro Apa pushed the children under the bed. My infant daughter screamed. The women and older children trembled, holding their breaths. Boro Apa went to the door. We heard the sound of heavy boots.

"Is there anyone in this house who served in the army?" a voice asked cordially in Urdu.

"No," Boro Apa replied, speaking Urdu. "In this house, we all believe in Pakistan, and nothing else."

"Good."

The boots continued to move through the house.

"Are there any young men in the house?" another voice barked.

"I am a widow and I only have three small boys. There is no one else here."

Rahela grabbed my arm as I exhaled smoke through my mouth. I was surprised at my wish to live, even if it was for just one more minute.

"Should I do something?" I whispered uncertainly to Rahela.

"What can you do?" she hissed back. She pulled back my good arm, as if to hold me fast and prevent me from rising to my feet. "Your arm is broken. You have to live for me and for your child."

I puffed silently on the cigarette, holding it downward, and concentrated on the future. We heard the soldiers leaving. The door shut on the dark house. I could not sleep the rest of the night, listening to the sounds of gunshots and human screams.

In the morning, we sat at the dining table eating omelets cooked from the eggs of Boro Apa's hens. She had divided the fried omelets into smaller rectangles to feed the large party. When the doorbell rang, we looked at one another. Who could it be? Was the army back for us?

Rahela's younger brother Helal pushed his way inside. His round face and big ears shone brightly. His thick hair stood on end, and he looked almost dashing in his dark sunglasses, coming in from the sun. We were happy to know he was alive. He was a young medical student, exactly the group the Pakistan Army were after.

"Come with me," he said. "Dhanmondi is not safe. We have to move to Banani. The diplomatic missions and the foreigners are there, so the army will think twice before killing people in that neighborhood."

Again, the fear of death drove us out in search of shelter. We piled into Dr. Ahmed's car and sped through the streets of Dhanmondi and up Airport Road toward Banani. Boro Apa and her family followed in another car that Helal had brought with him. The whole city was deserted, guarded by armed soldiers. Slums and police stations had been razed to the ground. The open markets that sat on the road were nowhere to be seen. Nobody bought or sold anything. There was no sign of commerce. Dead bodies lay everywhere, and the stench of rotting flesh filled the air. Crows perched on open garbage bins, pecking at human flesh.

After dropping us, Helal left on his motorcycle. He reappeared a few hours later with a bag of rice and a sack of potatoes he had purchased from a passing peddler. From him, we found out that people were selling their wares secretly, standing in alleys.

In the evening, we gathered to eat rice and mashed potato. My sisters-in-law laughed at my madness in taking off my cast.

"Is you brain filled with cow dung?" they asked.

"Please do something for your brother-in-law," Rahela begged Helal. "His pain is unbearable."

The next day, Helal drove me to Dacca Medical College on the back of his motorcycle. The hospital was empty. The doctors and staff had fled. We picked up some painkillers, other medications, and whatever supplies we could find in the cabinets. Returning home, Helal bandaged my arm and fashioned a cast with bamboo splints. I drugged myself with the painkillers we had brought. Now I felt no sensation at all, but the absence of sensation was worse than the pain. I thought that if I could not feel anymore, then my spirit had surely died.

Every night, gunshots filled the air. I thought that the army must be smashing every building in Dacca city. We expected to be picked up at any moment and carried away to be shot and thrown into a mass grave or tortured and hanged in the army barracks. I had always thought that I did not care much about my life, but now that I faced the possibility of death, I was amazed at the human instinct for survival. The large house in Banani filled with the running feet of children and their shrieks and cries, and the worried discussions of the adults. We had no news of Rahela's two sisters whose husbands were in the Pakistan Army, stationed in Lahore.

In the evening, we gathered to listen to the secret Independent Bangla radio station. Through the Shadhin Bangladesh Betar Kendra's broadcast, we found out that Maulana Bhashani had left for India and an all-party consultative committee had been formed, with Tajuddin Ahmed, Khondokar Mustaque, Moni Singh, Muzaffar Ahmed, and Monoranjan Dhar. In April, Bhashani delivered a statement to the world asking them to come to our aid. "The people of East Bengal, in this moment of crisis, pose a burning question to humanity. Will this great and just struggle be allowed to be crushed forever?" Later I learned that Bhashani sent telegrams to the heads of states of the Soviet Union, Britain, France, USA, Yugoslavia, and Egypt, to Chairman Mao in China, and to the UN secretary general and the Arab league secretary. But not every country wanted to help Bangladesh. Because of the Cold War, the US and China were allied with Pakistan and supplying modern weapons to the Pakistan Armed Forces.

Slowly, through Helal, the news of the outside world began to trickle into our cocoon. The army had taken over Dacca. A nationwide curfew had been declared. Dacca was empty and silent. Those who had not died were more silent even than the dead.

Everyone in the house gathered to pray five times a day. My sisters-in-law were unhappy that I was not praying. They were afraid that I might anger Allah and bring danger on their heads. People were sneaking into mosques in thousands to pray. There had never been so many people at the mosques before. It seemed to me that people remembered their God with new fervor suddenly. Fear drove these people to God. They must have been praying hard to God when they were afraid of losing everything.

For twenty days, eleven adults and ten children survived in the two-story house in Banani on rice and potatoes. The presence of foreigners in the neighborhood meant that we were safe. There were books in the house. There was quiet and solitude, so I should have been happy, but I found it unbearable to sit at home and wait. Many times, I felt my blood rising. I wanted to run out and face the certain death that waited for me outside.

Just when I felt I would go mad and that it was impossible to feel greater fear without taking my own life, Dacca returned to normal. Foreign journalists roamed the streets of Banani with cameras slung over their shoulders. When the government realized that the foreign journalists were arriving in the city to investigate the genocide, they wanted to show the world that everything was normal. The curfew was lifted. Radio Pakistan announced that people could come back to work. The universities and schools opened again.

We returned to a deserted campus. The mango tree in front of the teachers' residential buildings hung heavy with fruit. The smell of the ripe mangos filled the air. In other years, the tree would be shorn clean of its fruit before they ever ripened. This year, the mangos had matured in the absence of any such adversity. Slowly, all the teachers returned to campus. People went about their daily work, trying to live normal lives. The teachers no longer took part in heated conversations about politics. I walked to the university, sat in my office, and tried to pretend that nothing had changed. I tried to follow the rules like everyone else, but I began to grow a strong hatred of myself.

In December, India officially went to war with Pakistan. Indian MiG-21 fighter jets entered the sky, chasing the Pakistani US-built fighter planes in dog fights. I rushed to the roof of our building to watch the planes. Rahela ran after me. I was lying flat on the roof when I heard Rahela behind me. The planes flew close above our heads, but Rahela was still standing. I jumped up and pulled her to the ground. We were both shaking. I felt angry and useless. We lay on the ground, watching the fight in the sky. Before our eyes, an Indian plane swooped and magnificently downed a Pakistani fighter. The war was being fought right above our heads. Victory was being won in front of our eyes.

I was sitting at home listening to the Independent Bangla broadcast. The Pakistan Army was losing the war at the borders and slowly retreating to Dacca. At noon, Dr. Ahmed knocked on our door.

"We have to leave campus," he said. "The Pakistani forces are leaving Dacca, but they are making sure to kill anyone they can on their way."

"I am not going anywhere. I want to face whatever comes," I said flatly.

"You don't understand." Dr. Ahmed started to explain again patiently, speaking in a low, sensible voice. "They are going to the teachers' homes at Dacca University, killing anyone who is outspoken, anyone who will be of use to a new nation. They want to make sure that even if we win the war, there will be no one left to lead the country."

"What is there to live for if I am always running?" I asked angrily.

"If not for your sake, then at least for the sake of your wife and daughter," Dr. Ahmed said.

"Yes, listen to Shejo Dulabhai," Rahela pleaded with me.

To their astonishment, I remained adamant. Turning my head, I stared out from the back veranda onto the ravaged city. Then I left them at the door and went to lie down on my bed.

There was something about me that my family did not know. My name was on the Pakistan Army's list of enemies. A month ago, the vice chancellor of the engineering university had handed me a letter from the authorities accusing me of violating the laws of the country. The charge against me was that I had insulted the local area commander. The letter referred to a recent incident at the university. All the university teachers had been issued identity cards. We were supposed to show these cards to the guard when entering any academic building. That year, I was tabulator of the annual examinations. I had been very busy during the exams, running back and forth between buildings. One day, when I walked home to eat lunch, a bearer came to fetch me and informed me that I must go to the department immediately. I hurried there, forgetting my ID card at home. The guard at the gate told me that he could not allow me to enter unless I showed him my card. This guard knew me very well. I passed him a hundred times a day. He had no reason to stop me. I lost my temper and shoved past him. A few days later, I received the letter from the vice chancellor with the charge against me. I did not tell anyone at home, but I consulted my senior professor Dr. Hashmat.

"What do you mean to do about this?" Dr. Hashmat asked.

"Nothing!" I replied.

"That will surely spell your death. You should not irritate the government now. If they take you away, they will surely execute you, as their rule is near the end. You must write an apology explaining the situation but blaming no one. Then you should go away from both your home and office. Get lost where no one can find you."

I wrote the apology and stopped going to my office. Since I could not leave home, I kept watch from the veranda for anyone approaching the building. Every cell in my body wanted to escape the prison I had built myself. I thought of the young people who had fled their homes without a thought to fight for our independence. They had crossed the border to India and trained in makeshift camps. Daily, the freedom fighters threw hand bombs near hotels and diplomatic missions, hoping to catch the attention of foreigners, to alert them that all was not well in East Pakistan. Others fought the Pakistan Army at the borders, taking back Bengal

town by town. The Pakistani government had shown the people
of Bangladesh what price people had to pay if they revolted, but
the freedom fighters had shown them what heights madness can
achieve. What if I were a village boy again, crossing from Jessore
to West Bengal, taking up arms to fight for my people, sleeping
fearlessly under the open sky?

In the afternoon, Professor Hashmat came to beg me to leave
campus. He asked me why I was acting in this way.

"I am tired of running, living like a coward, dying a thousand
deaths every night."

"Everyone else has left. Our three families are the only ones
left on campus," he said. "Listen to me. For the sake of your child,
come with us. I know everything about you. You must do this for
the sake of your wife and child."

So, I agreed to run again for the sake of my wife and daughter.
We planned to escape through Old Dacca, the neighborhood
behind the university campus. We would travel to Sadar Ghat, the
bank of the Buriganga river, and cross the river by boat to Jinjira.
From there, we would travel to any village where we could find
shelter. Dr. Ahmed, Asif, and I traveled on three separate rickshaws
with our luggage, while Professor Hashmat brought our families
in his car. As we weaved through the narrow alleys of old Dacca,
the ancient, narrow buildings with lattice-work balconies looked
down impassively on our flight. A brown cow appeared on the
road and refused to move, gazing at us through pensive, thick-
lashed eyes. The placidity of the animal appeared to me a laughable
contrast to our haste.

The rickshaws traveled faster than the car on the narrow road,
so the three of us reached Sadar Ghat first. Surveying the scene,
we saw that armed Pakistani soldiers were guarding the riverbank.
They were allowing the people to cross the river, but the atmosphere was tense. While waiting for Professor Hashmat's car, we
hired a boat and started ferrying our luggage across the Buriganga
river to Jinjira. The soldiers did not attempt to stop us. Everything

went well. From Jinjira, we could see that Dr. Hashmat had already arrived with the women and children. Dr. Ahmed and Asif stood guard over our belongings on the Jinjira side of the river, while I started back on the boat to bring our families.

When the boat reached the middle of the river, gunshots sounded in the air. Bullets whistled above my head. I swung my neck to see that the soldiers were shooting randomly with rifles and automatic guns. People on the Sadar Ghat bank started crying and running. The boatman who had been rowing me jumped into the water, leaving the boat floating aimlessly. I ducked inside the raised cover of the boat. There was nothing to do but wait. To live or to die was pure chance.

After several minutes, the bullets stopped. The river was calm again. The wooden boat buoyed musically as its hull displaced the river water. The boatman floated on the surface of the water, pulling the boat with one arm, straining his arm and shoulders. After some time, he climbed on board and began to row silently toward the riverbank. Sitting on the boat, I searched the Sadar Ghat riverbank for my wife and child and for Dr. Ahmed's and Dr. Hashmat's families, but I could not spot any of them. Neither could I see my brother and brother-in-law on the other side of the river. Both the riverbanks were deserted. I did not know if my family and friends were dead or alive.

"Oh, God. Why am I alive?" I thought.

After reaching Sadar Ghat, I asked the peddlers, tea shop owners, and the people who lived in the shanty houses if they had seen my family, but no one could tell me anything. After an hour of searching, I hailed a rickshaw and collapsed onto the passenger seat.

"Rickshaw-wallah, take me to the engineering campus!" I cried.

The young man wiped his forehead with a gamchha. He looked to be in his early twenties. His skin was the color of coal. He had a sharp, triangular face with large eyes.

"Where is your family?" I asked.

"Rajshahi," he answered laconically. After a pause, he added, "I don't know if they are dead or alive."

Hanging his gamchha around his neck, he mounted his cycle and began to pedal, straining his back and shoulders to carry me home.

31. DEFENSE

Houston, May 2003

DURING THE LAST WEEK of the semester, there was an incident in one of the classes Beena taught. She had shared an article with her class from *Z* magazine, one of the online news sources to which Lenin had introduced her. This article criticized the war in Iraq. Beena was working with the students on reading comprehension, leading the class through the text paragraph by paragraph. Now she asked the students to analyze the argument by writing down the thesis of the article, the claim of each paragraph, and the evidence presented to support each claim.

A pretty young woman named Rose with long, straw-colored hair and hooded eyes sat in the front row. She put down her pen and bit her lips, staring at Beena through red eyes and furrowed brows.

"Is everything okay, Rose?"

Rose shook her head violently. She ran her painted nails through her hair, then gathered it up with a scrunchy and spat out, "These are lies! All lies!"

Beena looked at her in surprise. Rose's face was contorted in an anguished expression.

"Sure. That's possible," Beena said slowly. "Those are the author's opinions. We're not reading the text as content. We are trying to analyze it as argument and engage with it. Perhaps we can respond to the text now. What are your thoughts, Rose?"

"I don't want to share my thoughts!" Rose shouted. Tears streaked her cheeks.

Beena stiffened. Her heart was racing. Tears on young women students' cheeks were frightening to all the student teachers. She ended the class ten minutes early. The students filed out slowly, but Rose stood with crossed arms, waiting. She was dressed in a beige peasant blouse and blue jeans, pretty and innocent.

When Beena began to gather her markers and textbook, Rose approached the teacher's desk. She was crying openly now, wiping away her tears with both hands.

"My boyfriend is there," she said. "He is eighteen. The sweetest boy you know. He and his friends are over there, giving their lives, and you say that this is an...unjust war!"

Just the past week, she said, hiccupping, she had received a letter from her boyfriend. In it, in shaky handwriting, he had written that he had held a gun to a young Iraqi boy's face. The boy was perhaps his age. An insurgent. They had both been trembling. He had never killed anyone before in his life. She started to shout at Beena, accusing Beena of endangering her boyfriend's life. Beena suggested that they walk to the English department office together.

The faculty supervisor Dr. Greta Bauer was busy in another meeting. They waited in front of her office, standing stiffly side by side. At last, Dr. Bauer opened the door and called them inside. Greta Bauer was Professor of British Romantic literature and one of the readers on Beena's PhD defense committee. She was almost six feet tall and lithe, with long, straggly hair that she called hippie hair. Usually, she piled it into an untidy bun and stuck a twig in it, with a bunch of leaves sticking out from the knot. Aside from her wild hair, Dr. Bauer dressed primly in long skirts and colorful blouses, bright orange and fuchsia pink, frilled at the neck.

Beena and Rose sat on the two chairs across from the professor's desk, positioning their bodies as far apart as possible. They did not look at each other. Beena explained Rose's objections while Rose cried, and Dr. Bauer listened with wide, frightened eyes, bounding about her office, picking up a small can and watering a plant on the windowsill. Her movements disconcerted Beena even more than Rose's tears. She had expected the professor to sit and face them. Finally, when Beena stopped speaking, Dr. Bauer asked Rose to apologize to Beena, and then she asked Beena to apologize to Rose.

"Perhaps you can write each other letters?" she suggested.

Beena and Rose looked at each other dubiously, united in their revulsion at the suggestion. Finally, Rose left with some tissues from Dr. Bauer's box, slamming the door behind her.

Immediately, Dr. Bauer abandoned her activities. "Sorry! That was rough. I hope you're holding up okay." She smiled at Beena, standing barefoot.

"Yes. Thanks for helping. I understood she was upset. I didn't know how to respond."

"Hey, there's a sit-in happening tomorrow to protest the war. Yeah, the protests haven't stopped. Do you want to go?"

"No!" Beena shook her head quickly.

Dr. Bauer squinted at her.

"I'm too busy!" Beena said, blushing. She craned her neck to look up at the tall professor. "Otherwise, I would go."

"Of course. I understand." Dr. Bauer nodded sympathetically. "You have a lot going on. You lost your mother and brother. And you have a defense coming up!"

Beena nodded. In truth, she was too frightened of the war. She couldn't process the information as objective facts. She felt too emotional.

A week later, Roberto's defense went smoothly. The professors on his panel loved him. Over the years, they had invited him into their homes and shared their personal lives with him. Roberto bought cheese and crackers and little purple grapes and laid them out on a table in the back. Lots of people turned up, crammed into the old classroom, talking and laughing. It was over by ten in the morning. Afterward, everyone left in a procession to eat at a Chinese restaurant, except Beena, because she was still preparing for her defense later the same day.

By afternoon, she was feeling jagged and shaky. She had told Roberto not to come. A defense was academic, like an exam. She couldn't be relaxed about it like Roberto. She was still shuffling her papers when the professors began to pile into the room.

She stood up nervously. "I'm just going to run out and get something from the vending machine!" she squeaked. She had not eaten anything all day, not even Roberto's crackers and cheese.

"Sure." Her supervisor nodded. This was Dr. Emily Meyers, who taught Victorian literature. She had written and published about the works of Dickens, Charlotte Brontë, and British colonial literature. Dr. Meyers was smart, with sharp blue eyes and ciga-rette-blackened teeth. She could often be seen smoking outside standing near the parking lot in the open air.

Beena headed out with a fistful of coins. At the vending machine, she had to borrow a quarter from another student. At last, she returned to the room with a bottle of water and a bag of peanuts.

"I heard about your mother and brother," Dr. Meyers said as Beena sat down. "I'm sorry for your loss."

Beena nodded.

"How are you coping?" Dr. Bauer gazed at her with wide eyes.

"My father had a fall recently. He broke his arm."

"Oh! Sorry to hear that," said Dr. Jones, Professor of postco-lonial studies.

"Thank you."

"I heard there's some news. You got married recently?" Dr. Tracy said, gazing slyly at Beena.

"Yes." Beena nodded. Her mouth dissolved in an embarrassed grin as the professors congratulated her.

"All right, let's start," Dr. Meyers said, making a movement with her wrist, flipping the stiff pages of photocopied paper. "Yes?"

"Yes!" Beena placed her fingertips on the table on either side of her dissertation, waiting for things to begin, the end of five years of hard work.

Dr. Bauer patted the manuscript in front of her. "This has heft."

The room broke into laughter. The air lightened.

"It's fascinating," began Dr. Jones. "Bengali modernity as a period in which a society adopted rationality over superstition."

"Yes."

Studying English Literature in Bangladesh, she had fallen in love with the English poets and writers of a faraway land, reciting Wordsworth and Shelley with fervent romanticism. But here, at an American university, she had moved away from the Romantic poets she loved to vast, boring tracts of Victorian prose, polemical essays dry in tone and full of practicality, and then, for her dissertation, making another about-turn, she had chosen to pursue her research in comparative literature, studying Bengali authors writing in colonial India. "Are you sure about this? Dr. Meyers had asked Beena several times when she had chosen a thesis, fixing her with sharp eyes. "It is very difficult to find a job with that kind of specialization." Dr. Meyers could be sharp tongued, but she had seemed genuinely concerned. During the oral defense, the professor had tried again to gently nudge Beena to change her focus, but Beena had not budged.

The professors were making comments, asking questions. The hour went by in a blur. Beena blushed, looking around at the smiling, admiring faces. For a year, writing the proposal and going through rounds of discussions, she had looked forward to chatting about this work, enjoying the moment.

"Do you have the bond paper for us to sign?" her supervisor was asking now.

"Oh, yes. I have it. I bought them at the bookstore earlier."

"Congratulations." Dr. Bauer smiled at her, twigs bouncing in her hair.

32. JACKALS

I HAD RETURNED HOME with savings from Canada, but after the war those funds were quickly exhausted. Despite Rahela's contributions from her lecturer position and her PhD fellowship at Dacca University, we ran into debt. Instead of helping my father financially, I became the recipient of rations from his agricultural fields. Asif carried sacks of rice, molasses, and lentils from Dari Binni. My plans to build a road to my village, bring electricity to the village houses, and raise funds for a proper school building had to be shelved as I struggled to keep my family alive.

The newly independent country sank into an unbearable situation. Illegal arms were everywhere. Powerful people looted the country and gunned down the people on the street. There was a full-blown famine. In the capital city, beggars could be seen rummaging in garbage heaps, fighting with crows for food. Several teachers at the engineering university left for jobs abroad. My brother-in-law Dr. Ahmed and his family left for England.

At this time, my PhD supervisor Bowes visited Bangladesh as a consultant to build ferro cement boats to replace the traditional wooden ones. A large number of boats were built under his supervision. When Bowes travelled all over Bangladesh to research the sizes and shapes of existing boats to design his prototype, I accompanied him as his guide, translator, and driver. I did this for my own pleasure, but when Bowes was leaving, he paid me for my services.

When I tried to refuse, he said, "Think of it this way, Uddin. I am entitled to money for my transport. I am just passing on that entitlement to you. Take it for your daughter. I am sure that one day she will conquer the world."

With my head bowed, I accepted the money out of dire need, but after Bowes left the country, even that money was gone. After our son Lenin was born, Rahela had to stop her PhD research again. Now we faced the worst of our troubles. Rahela could not breastfeed, so Lenin needed powdered milk for infants. No milk was available in the open market. I tried all possible sources without success. I even went to the general manager of Glaxo and the officers at the food ministry, but nobody could help. We tried to feed Lenin cow milk, but he vomited everything he was fed and became very ill. We could only watch helplessly as he perished by the day.

We lived on the second floor of our building. Professor. K.K. Huq and his family lived on the third floor. K. K. Huq and his wife visited one day with a red mobile for Lenin's crib. Lenin's body resembled a skeleton, with protruding ribs and pelvic bones, loose skin, and enormous eyes in a shriveled face. Seeing the baby, they gasped. I explained that we could not find milk for Lenin in the open market. Mrs. K.K. Huq promised to mention the issue to her son Erfan.

Erfan was a young man in his earlies twenties, but he was highly connected to some powerful people in the country. The night after Victory Day, Rahela had watched Erfan and his friends from her back veranda enter an empty flat with a line of blindfolded Biharis in tow. There had been screams all night, mixed with the cries of jackals from the road. The day after Mr. and Mrs. K.K. Huq's visit, thirty cans of Glaxo whole milk powder for infants were delivered to our home. When I realized that I had searched everywhere for milk that had been available in such plentiful quantities while my son had almost starved to death, I felt ill.

At night, lying beside our sleeping children, Rahela and I decided to leave the country. The law-and-order situation was uncertain. Our financial situation was worse. In the 1970s, Iraq was an oil-rich country offering foreigners lucrative positions at its universities and refineries. Before long, I obtained a teaching position at the University of Mosul. At one time, I had traveled to Canada for higher education, to fulfill an idealistic dream, but now I prepared to travel to Iraq for money. I was a family man with two children to feed. My country, liberated, was in shambles. I could do nothing for my country. I could only think practically. I needed to earn money.

33. SALMA'S PLANS

Houston, May 2003

RICHARD POWERS' OFFICE WAS deep and cavernous, with long windows. His secretary, a silver-haired, slim woman dressed in a green skirt suit, had opened the heavy curtains to reveal a foggy downtown skyline. Roberto and Beena sat across from a large desk overlaid with books and notepads. In a few minutes, the lawyer walked in, waddling a little. A man of wide girth and confidence, he was dressed in a grey suit and smelled of spices. His face was pink and cherubic, with twinkling blue eyes and a full head of wiry black hair.

"Don't worry about a thing," he said, swiveling his leather chair.

Beena half-expected him to bring out a cigar.

"I've got all the papers ready. Did you bring the documents I asked for? Good, good," he said, as Roberto handed over a clasped manilla envelope. "You leave it to me. There are a few more additional steps, with a…new marriage like this. You will need to both give separate interviews. And we need photos."

"Sure." Roberto leaned back in his chair and grinned at Beena. "This is fantastic. Thank you."

"I'll make this promise to you, young lady." Richard Powers now turned his keen eyes on Beena, holding her gaze. "By the time you are getting your dissertations bound, I will have this filed for you."

"Thank you! You're terrific." Beena smiled broadly to show him her admiration.

"It's an exciting time for you both," Richard Powers said, clasping his hands together and cracking his knuckles. Sunlight entering through the glass pane enveloped him in a warm, avuncular glow.

"Let's grab some Vietnamese sandwiches and drive to Hermann Park to celebrate. We're both getting our PhDs, and you're going to be a citizen," Roberto said as they came out of the lawyer's office.

At the park, they stood on the grass beside the lake and fed the ducks with crumbs from their baguettes, then started to walk on the concrete path, holding hands, taking the small footbridge over the water.

"We should plan our honeymoon."

"Where?"

"Where I would really like to take you, eventually, is Italy. But for now, I looked up a place in Louisiana. Lake Fausse Point. We can rent a cabin on the water . . ."

"Roberto! You thought about all this already?"

Below them, white paddle boats waited on the water to carry people across the small, misty lake. A little ahead, children lined the hill, preparing to roll down to the bottom on their sides.

"Do you want to do that?"

"What? Roll down the hill?"

"Why not?" Roberto laughed shyly, flinging back his hair, like a young boy.

"You first," Beena said.

"All right." Roberto trudged to the top of the hill and lay down horizontally, resting his head gingerly on the grass.

Beena smiled. Her cellphone began to ring (she now had a cellphone; Roberto's graduation present), and she flipped it open.

"Where are you? I was calling you." Salma sounded panicked.

"We were at the immigration lawyer's office."

"Oh, good. Listen. Shona wants to drop off food. What is Roberto's address?"

"I don't need any food. But thank you. Please thank her for me."

"Jahan Apa wants to invite you to her house."

"Salma, I can't go to a party now. My mother and brother died. I'm worried about my father."

"I'm worried about Uncle, too. Listen. We should have a prayer for Auntie. A milad or something. Let's do that."

When Beena demurred, Salma became insistent. "Okay, as you wish, but we have a lot to plan for the marriage ceremony. Let me come over. Tell me where Roberto lives. What is his address?"

34. LAND OF BOUNTY

Mosul, 1975-82

ONCE OUT OF BANGLADESH, Rahela and I found that the world
was full of baby food. We could buy all the things we needed.
Nobody was stocking anything in a dark corner. To reach Iraq, we
had to travel through Kuwait, where the shops overflowed with
merchandise. Rahela and I could not help staring. We stayed overnight at an airline hotel, where we were served an endless array of
delicacies. The food kept coming–dainty sandwiches, little trian-
gles of cheese wrapped in silver, and tart orange juice.

"Others in the world are not starving!" Rahela mused. "They
are served more than they need."

I was relieved that our son would not perish now.

From Kuwait, we flew to Baghdad, where we boarded another
plane to take us to Mosul. But in Baghdad, a terrible shock awaited
us. My four-year-old daughter Beena carried a large baby doll with
lifelike pink skin, blue eyes, and golden hair that I had brought back
for her from a study tour in Tokyo. Beena sat down next to an Arab
woman at Baghdad airport and struck up a conversation about her

doll. Although Beena did not understand any Arabic, the woman seemed to be saying that the doll was beautiful, jamila, and Beena was flattered and babbling back. I told Beena to get ready to board. We started walking toward the boarding gate. I carried our bags and official documents, and Rahela carried Lenin in her arms. At some point, we noticed that Beena was not behind us. We could not see her anywhere in sight. We were in a foreign country where we did not speak the language. How could we find our child? Children were lost every day in Dhaka, kidnapped, never to be found.

"Why did you not keep an eye on her?" I charged Rahela.

"The doll! She must have left the doll behind and gone back for it!" Rahela said.

I retraced my steps to the seating area and found Beena sitting on a chair, clutching her doll and crying. Once again, I had come close to being deprived of one of my children.

We had arrived in the country in the middle of the bitter winter. Lenin was six weeks old, bundled in a handknit red wool suit and a sky-blue wool blanket gifted to him by his aunt. Rahela hid him under her shawl, afraid of losing him again.

All the foreigners who had arrived recently in Mosul were accommodated at the best hotel in the city while they looked for housing. The children of some twenty families ran through the hotel corridors. We were served the best foods on sparkling crockery. A maid came to change the sheets every day. But the hotel was not centrally heated. I shut the doors and windows and lit the kerosene heater. The room filled with smoke but did not warm up. There were patches of dampness and chill in the air. Lenin, who had been weak from birth, fell ill within days. On our fifth night in Mosul, he ran a high fever. All night, Rahela and I washed his forehead with damp cloths. I smoked one cigarette after another, stubbing out the ends, until the tables and carpet of the hotel room were covered with discarded butts.

In the middle of the night, Lenin started to have trouble breathing. By dawn, his body became icy cold. The color drained from his lips to his limbs, turning them blue. I clutched my head in my hands. I had fled my country to save my children, but now my son was dying in front of my eyes.

In the morning, I rode the bus to the university to seek help. The only person I had come to know a little was the head of the department Dr. Saadi, a round-faced Iraqi man in his forties with large, sparkling hazel eyes, long eyelashes, and a bushy mustache, always immaculately dressed in pale suits with a folded handkerchief in his breast pocket. I ran to his office and explained my son's situation. Dr. Saadi came out with me immediately and drove me to the chamber of Dr. Thabit, a giant of a man with a pale, chubby face and hairy arms, a sharp nose, and large eyes covered by steel-rimmed glasses. Dr. Thabit was kind enough to visit Lenin at the hotel.

After examining him, Dr. Thabit said that Lenin appeared to have a lung infection. He gave Lenin an injection and a liquid medicine to be taken at intervals. Slowly, Lenin started to improve. His color returned. He stared at us with wide eyes and appeared to laugh. For the first time, we discovered that he was a beautiful baby, with large eyes and thick, black hair.

Wherever I had worked in my life, I had stirred trouble, but in Iraq, I decided not to open my mouth or challenge anything I disliked. I needed to keep my job to feed my family. However, despite my efforts, I soon ran into trouble. One day, Dr. Saadi called me to his office and told me that a student leader had complained about me, saying that I did not teach from the book.

"What is the explanation of this?" Dr. Saadi twirled his mustache and glowered at me.

"The student leader is correct," I replied. "I don't teach materials directly from the book. I present things in my own way. I tell the students stories and jokes and give funny examples of concepts in the book. I think the best way to resolve this issue is to ask them directly how they feel about my teaching."

Dr. Saadi was kind enough to act according to my wishes. He asked me to meet him again in his office the following day. The next day, I found the professor seated at his neatly arranged desk writing something on a notepad. Seeing me, he beckoned me inside with a wave of his hand.

"Doctor Nasir, I spoke to the students."

I sat down across from him with a racing pulse, expecting the worst.

"They said they like your teaching, Doctor Nasir." Dr. Saadi's face opened in an amused smile. "They said they remember the material better through the stories." He informed me the students had told him that because of my teaching style they learned the most in my class.

Later, I came to know that the complaint had been instigated by the former teacher of the course, who had been angry that his course had been given to me. He had spied on me through the student leader, then advised the student leader to approach Dr. Saadi. I escaped trouble that time, but not for long.

Within a few days, Dr. Saadi called me into his office again and told me to close the door.

"Doctor Nasir, do you keep records of student grades in a bound register?"

"Yes," I replied.

"And do you keep the register open on your desk?"

"Yes," I replied again.

"If a student changed his marks, what would you do?"

Suddenly, I became aware of a horrible possibility. I replied slowly that in that case I would simply disregard the changed marks.

"Doctor Nasir, how would you know which marks have been changed?"

I thought quickly. Fortunately, I maintained a back-up copy of the marks at home to check my arithmetic operations. I promised

Dr. Saadi that I would check the register and report to him the following day. The next day, comparing the two sheets, I found out that indeed, two students had raised their marks in the register that I left in my office. I went back to Dr. Saadi the next day and reported my findings.

He did not appear to be happy with me. For several minutes, he did not speak, simply looking at me with a frown, his hands steepled under his chin. At last, he said, "I am satisfied with your report, but I am not happy with the way you manage your office affairs. Please, don't let me have to call you here again about this kind of problem."

I could only express my thanks and apologies. As I was leaving the office, Dr. Saadi called me back. "Doctor Nasir, be careful," he said in a low voice. "This place is full of the ears of the party."

I had arrived at the University of Mosul in the middle of the second term. I spent the remainder of the academic year trying to catch up. Eighty percent of the teachers at the university were foreigners from Egypt, Jordan, Palestine, Poland, Denmark, and the Indian subcontinent. The foreign teachers formed a tight community. We took Arabic lessons together, held Scrabble and bridge tournaments, went on sightseeing picnics, rented cottages in the foothills of the mountains in Kirkuk, Sulaymaniyah, and Arbil, held dinner parties, and watched English movies on a large outdoor screen on the lawn of the Cultural Center, sitting on lawn chairs and eating kebab, pickles, and khubz bread. We attended one another's religious ceremonies, Eid-ul-Fitr, Christmas, and Diwali, and cultural and national celebrations. Sometimes, we drove to a friend's house to play a game of Scrabble and ended up staying overnight, letting the children sleep on the floor, sprawled on Syrian mats.

After several months of searching, we found a suitable house in Zahoor, about twenty miles from the university. Visitors complained that it was too far, but we liked the house very much as it was ideal for raising kids and the rent was extremely reasonable. There were many empty rooms upstairs and downstairs where the children could play. We kept all the rooms empty with few furnishings, sleeping on the floor on cool Syrian mats. Rahela filled the room at the front of the house with English books she collected from other foreigners and anywhere else she could find them. Here, the children could get lost choosing whatever book they liked and reading according to their pleasure. The lawn had a periphery of rose trees that bloomed with many-colored roses in the spring. My children helped me clip the roses and make bouquets for their aunties. A grapevine covered the arch over the driveway. There were orange trees, pear trees, and a tree bearing a plump and fleshy fruit called safarjal. It has a dusty jacket and a big seed in the middle. I have not seen this fruit anywhere else in the world. It is a sour fruit, yet delicious.

A year after we arrived in Mosul, our second son and youngest child was born. Rahela and I were searching for baby names, so I asked Dr. Saadi to recommend some names. Dr. Saadi suggested that we take a walk around campus.

As we circled the campus lined with flower beds, butterflies flitting in the hot air, Dr. Saadi said to me, "For you to choose a good name, first I shall have to tell you the history of Iraq, so that you understand well the meaning of the name you choose."

Having a natural curiosity to learn about all subjects, I agreed that this was a good idea.

"Before the Ba'ath Party came to power, the communist party was very strong in Iraq," Dr. Saadi began, planting his sleek black shoes on the ground one step at a time. I was used to walking fast and energetically, but now I walked alongside the Iraqi professor, matching his leisurely steps. "The year 1958 marked the height of the golden period of prosperity for the Iraqi people. The nationalists and the communists all opposed the Hashemite government, especially after it signed the Baghdad pact, a military alliance intended to secure the oil wealth of Iraq and keep the communists at bay. After a revolution in 1958, the monarchists and puppets of the British empire were overthrown, and Iraq became a Republic. The nationalist and social reformer Abdul-Karim Qasim was put in power. The leftists in Iraq achieved a lot for the poor people at this time. Agrarian reform restricted land ownership, high taxes were imposed on the rich, and education was guaranteed for all the people."

"That sounds like an ideal state," I said.

"But soon all that came to an end." Dr. Saadi continued with glistening eyes. "There was conflict between Egypt's Nasser and the Ba'ath Party on the one hand and the communists on the other. Qasim was neither a Ba'athist nor a communist. He was afraid of each faction. Unfortunately, all these political parties could not learn to coexist. In 1959, the Ba'ath Party attempted a coup. Months later, the current vice president Saddam Hussein, then a young member of the Ba'ath Party, carried out an assassination attempt on Qasim. By 1963, the Ba'ath Party were finally successful. They carried out a coup and removed Qasim from power. Qasim was executed. Thousands of Iraqi leftists were killed by the Ba'ath Party at this time. Others left the country and now live in exile. It is thought that the American intelligence gave the Ba'ath Party the names and addresses of the leftists who were killed. How else could the Ba'ath government find out all their names so easily?"

I nodded slowly, still perplexed, thinking Dr. Saadi was now going to offer me the list of names of the murdered people as possible names for my son.

"We leftists despise Saddam Hussein," Dr. Saadi continued in a sad tone of voice. "The country is not in a good state. Saddam Hussein has imprisoned, tortured, and killed many of my personal friends, Doctor Nasir. The Iraqi people are waiting for a day when we can live freely again."

"I had no idea!" I cried out in extreme surprise, thinking how happy Rahela and I had been to be living in a country without want or poverty. In all our time in Mosul, we had not seen a single beggar asking for alms.

"Doctor Nasir," Dr. Saadi said briskly, as we turned around and headed back toward our department, "you may name your son Fahd or Qasim after our fearless leftist leaders who fought for the people. Or you may name him Zaki, after the romantic revolutionary who returned from exile in London in 1968 to fight the right-wing Ba'athist government. They executed this handsome young man in a brutal operation. Or you may name him after the revolutionary Iraqi poets, Saadi Youssef or Mudhaffar-al-Nawab or Badr Shakir al-Sayyab."

I nodded vigorously, wondering which name to choose. In the end, Rahela and I decided to name our son Kazi after the Bengali poet Kazi Nazrul Islam, as we did not want him to meet the fate of the leftist leaders Dr. Saadi had described. The Iraqi women who birthed him and wrapped his body in white cloth gasped at his fat body, rippling limbs, large head, and fair skin, saying that he was a true baby of Mosul, a Muslawiya. The day Kazi was born, Lenin was one year, six months, and twenty-six days old. This small seniority in age gave Lenin a tremendous power over Kazi, who never accepted anything in the world unless it was confirmed by his Bhaiya. If I said to Kazi, 'The sun is a star,' Kazi immediately replied that he would ask Bhaiya about it. He never came to me to learn anything. He always went to his older brother, his Bhaiya.

At last, I was happy that I had created a secure environment for my children. They had all the fruits they could eat and all the space to play. Lenin, who had been so ill when we had arrived in Mosul, grew fatter by the day. He was a beautiful baby whom the Iraqis stopped on the street to kiss and pinch. We spent our afternoons planting vegetables in the garden and playing Ludo on the lawn, sitting on lawn chairs with crossed hatches. The garden yielded so many fruits that we had trouble disposing of them. Rahela prepared jam out of the fruits and packed them in jars to gift friends. The children played with the neighborhood Iraqi kids. We had many neighbors and friends from the Indian subcontinent, Poland, Finland, Egypt, Denmark, and Palestine.

The university opened a school for the children of all the foreigners working in Mosul. The name of the school was Al-Mustansa-
riya, which means simply "school" in Arabic. Although the university had solved the problem of schooling, it remained a problem
for our family. When the school opened, Beena was five years old.
She could not speak Arabic. The school bus came only as far as the
university campus, so I had to drive my daughter to the nearest
bus stop. We developed a ritual in the morning. I rose and lit the
kerosene heater and woke Beena in the dark. She made straight for
the heater, dancing up and down to keep warm. In the kitchen, I
made her gulp down a glass of milk and a sandwich of samn bread
(a loaf in the shape of a fish) with syrup. Rahela and the boys were
still asleep when Beena and I left the house. I dropped Beena at a
crowded public bus stop under a crown of date palm as the sky lightened overhead. I had to leave immediately to catch an early morning
class. In the evening, I picked my daughter up from the bus stop
long after the school bus had dropped her off. I could see her from
a distance, waiting on the dark street, standing alone in the cold air.
We could survive the ordeal only by having faith in strangers.

The Mosul summer was three and a half months long. During the
day, it was so hot that we stayed inside the house. Iraqi houses are
cooled by water coolers. The children sat in front of the water duct,
eating juicy watermelon. The cool, blowing air slowed down time
to a single instant, sweet despite the surrounding bitterness. In the
evening, we drove out to the nearby mountains or the riverbank
of the Tigris, where Lenin and Kazi collected pebbles of all colors,
filling their pockets. For the following few days, these pebbles
were their most valuable possessions in the world and could not be
lost under any circumstance.

One evening, we drove to the city to buy new shoes for Kazi.
Afterward, we purchased a whole chicken roasted on a spit in
the street, along with the dry bread khubz and olive pickles—the

children's favorite meal—and carried the warm paper bags down to the bank of the Tigris river. We planned to pass the evening by the cool atmosphere of the river. Iraq was a desert country, so the air was dry no matter how high the temperature. The dry air evaporated the river water at a high rate, making the surrounding air cool and pleasant. We parked the car high on the road, took the food out of the backseat, and proceeded down the hill towards the riverbank. The children ran ahead of us and reached the water in a rush.

"Stop!" I shouted at the top of my lungs, mad with panic.

Kazi stopped one step short of the waters of the Tigris. "Why?" he asked. "Will the water get dirty from my shoes?"

35. ROBERTO HAS GUESTS

Houston, May 2003

"THE AMERICAN SOLDIERS ARE so brave. They're sacrificing themselves to rescue the people of Iraq," Salma said, staring at the TV screen.

It was Salma's husband Ronny who had asked for the TV to be turned on, after a few minutes of extreme discomfort during which he had been squirming and making grunting noises.

"Yes. They must be frightened young men going off to war," Roberto said. He was sitting in a relaxed posture. "Who knows what the war will do to them? Deaths, injuries, PTSD, that is how every war destroys young men."

"I follow the news too, like you. As soon as I come home, I turn on CNN!" Salma spoke to Roberto in an over-friendly voice, flashing him a smile with teeth. She had taken care with her dress—a glamorous purple silk shirt over grey slacks with high-heeled sandals—and put on heavy makeup.

Beside her, Ronny sat stiffly with his shoulders drawn forward. His cheeks were blanched and drawn in. He did not look at Roberto, much less talk to him, as if he had never met a foreigner before. Roberto smiled pleasantly at his guests, but Beena thought that his face looked strained.

The party had turned up at Roberto's apartment early on Saturday morning. Beena had been expecting Salma and Ronny, but she was surprised to see the third person, the tall, stooped figure who stood behind them, smiling. Now Beena felt Khaled's eyes move over her face. She felt embarrassed about the way she had confided in him and flirted with him, saying that no one at Dhaka University had given her a second glance.

Beena and Roberto sat side-by-side on the loveseat, arms crossed, self-consciously spaced apart. The other three shared the sofa, their perfumes filling the air. When she wasn't looking at the TV screen, Salma eyed Beena and Roberto through slit eyes. Ronny, in his discomfort, had picked up the remote control, asked Roberto for quick instructions, and now controlled the TV.

An embedded journalist showed the inside of a marine battalion. Laughing young men showed the journalist their gear. A voice-over said the marines had felt that the diplomatic efforts were just a distraction from their mission to march on Baghdad. Ronny turned up the volume, leaning back against the sofa, his body relaxed now. The video footage showed young men with keen faces cleaning their guns and rolling their tanks through the desert, then their spam cans, gas masks, and bibles. A map of Iraq with arrows painted across the country showed a full-scale invasion, fast and deep. The screen cut to the emotional story of the family members of one young marine and then another who had married his high-school sweetheart in a rushed wedding when he had learned that he was being deployed to Iraq.

Khaled turned to Roberto. "So, you're a scientist too?"

"Yes, I am a PhD student in engineering. You're all engineers, too, right?" Roberto said.

"Yeah. I work at H–," Khaled said.

Ronny, whose eyes were still fixed on the shiny tanks and new war technology, laughed suddenly. "I wonder if Iraq will become a hardship zone now, for companies."

Khaled turned to him. "If I get a posting there, I will certainly accept. I would like to help."

"Allah, Khaled, that's such a wonderful thing to do for that country, such a great contribution," said Salma. "We are so proud of you. You know, both Ronny's parents and Beena's parents lived in Iraq."

"They made their money there," Beena said.

Ronny lifted his head and screwed his eyes, as if he was displeased with what she had said.

"What's the oil and gas prospect in Bangladesh?" Roberto asked.

"Bangladesh has a lot of gas!" Khaled boasted. "Many multinational companies are interested to explore and develop our gas. We will be self-sufficient in a few years and start exporting. Fracking is also important."

"Fracking? Isn't that dangerous? I thought Bangladesh is sitting on a fault line. Isn't there risk of an earthquake? And what if we run out of gas by exporting it all?" Beena asked, echoing Lenin. Her brother's smiling eyes blazed inside her head.

"No, no," Khaled said, shaking his head and smiling. "It's perfectly safe."

The loud voice on the screen proclaimed that two marines had been killed.

They broke their conversation to stare at the images of the two smiling young men. Salma cried, "Aah," in a voice of sympathy. The news went on about the soldiers, their families, and a funeral service.

"I wonder how many Iraqis have died?" Beena said.

"Beena, take me to your room. We have to fit you for the blouse." Salma pulled out a bright red Benarasee sari and threw it on Beena's lap. "How is it?" she asked, pointing at the heavy material embroidered with gold thread looped like spreading flowers.

"It's beautiful!" Beena said. "But it's your wedding sari. I might ruin it."

"Don't be silly," Salma said. "When do I ever wear it? It's too heavy to wear to any party."

"Would the blouse fit me?" Beena asked Salma.

"My dear, I am an expert tailor. You try it on. Then I'll fix it. Let's see." Salma held the blouse against Beena's chest. "Not here, though, in front of the men!" She giggled, gazing at Khaled from under her thickened eyelashes. "Let's go. Where is your room?" A look in her eye showed that this was a meaningful question.

"Good," said Ronny, sighing, "now we can watch the news in peace without all the chattering."

Beena stood up and walked with Salma to Roberto's bedroom.

"So, this is your room?" Salma said, looking around keenly at the walls and the windows, and then at the bed that Beena now shared with Roberto. "Try on the blouse." She handed over the folded material.

"It fits! But the sleeves are too tight, don't you think?" The exquisite, short-capped sleeves gripped Beena's upper arms.

"This blouse is from when I was twenty years old. It doesn't even fit me anymore. I'll take it out. Let's see, half an inch should do it," Salma said, speaking in Bengali, making soft, caressing sounds.

"Thanks!" Beena said.

"And here." Salma rummaged in her purple bag and yanked out a velvet box, pulling out a long gold necklace, a Sita Har, with embedded pink stones. The pendant fell plumply against Beena's chest.

"It's beautiful."

"Wear it without guilt. It's not real gold. Just imitation."

Beena's own mother's gold was in a locker in Dhaka, meant for her, preserved for her, waiting to adorn her at her wedding, and yet she would be married without gold.

"And earrings to match. There." Salma held two trapezoid structures of filigree gold earrings near Beena's ears.

They stood in front of Roberto's standing mirror, admiring the earrings.

"He's nice," Salma said. "I never knew what kind of man you liked. I was surprised."

"Why?"

"I always thought you would like someone Bengali."

Beena took off the earrings. Salma slipped them back in tissue and handed the box to Beena. A maroon velvet box, the kind they gave out at gold shops in Bangladesh, it made Beena nostalgic for home.

"You know, Khaled still likes you." Salma looked at Beena slyly in the mirror and gave a little giggle.

"Why did you bring him? It's really awkward."

"He wanted to come. He cares about you. It was *his* idea that we throw you a wedding reception. The date is set. Next Saturday night at my house. Beautify your groom for the occasion!"

36. USTAD TAMATA

Mosul, 1975-82

WHEN WE FIRST ARRIVED in Mosul, we traveled everywhere by bus. When I put my hand in my pocket to pay the fare, the bus driver informed me that someone had paid for me already.

"Who?" I asked, looking around.

The bus driver shrugged his shoulders.

The same thing happened at the stationary shop at the university. The shopkeeper informed me, "No need, the pencil has already been paid for." I guessed that my students had paid for me. One of them was always there, wherever I went. I thought they must have instructed every shopkeeper in the city not to accept any payment from me. I could not avoid Iraqi hospitality anywhere I went. Often on long road trips, we would stop at a village home to use the toilet. We could never come out of a home without being fed and honored like guests.

Over time, Dr. Saadi became a close friend to me and my family. He arranged the medical services for my children, took care of all our official work, and obtained food items for us that were in shortage in the market. At the beginning of our stay in Iraq, consumer items were in short supply. People had money, but there was not much to buy in the market. Eggs, chicken, lamb, beef, tomatoes, onion, and potatoes had to be imported from other countries. The government distributed these items through designated shops. When an item became available for sale, a long line formed outside the shop. If Rahela and I spotted a line forming, we joined the queue quickly, not knowing what we would find once we reached the front. If a desirable food item was being sold, we bought as much as we were allowed and distributed it among friends.

With time, large department stores opened in the city and became surfeited with cartons of fleshy dates, juicy watermelons, whole chickens, ducks, and goats, Lego sets, battery-operated dolls and other imported toys, children's books in English, washing machines, hair curlers, color TV sets, two-in-one stereos, and electric gadgets of every kind. Education was free through university. The gypsies and Bedouins wore gold around their throats and dangling from their ears. Old men sat at the streetside shops drinking sweet tea from tiny glasses. In sharp contrast to my country, Iraq felt like the safest place in the world. Nobody stole anything, nothing was in shortage, and there was no crime. It was the best place to raise our children.

When it was becoming cumbersome to travel on the bus with three children, I thought that I needed to buy a car. Cars were very costly in Iraq because of the heavy duty imposed on imports, but cheap imported vehicles were readily available for purchase at the duty-free markets in Damascus and Kuwait. Foreigners could purchase a car in another country as long as they did not sell the vehicle in Iraq. They had to take their car with them when they left Iraq or donate it to a junkyard.

Another Bangladeshi teacher Dr. Shah also wanted to buy a car. We traveled together to Damascus by bus, passing through Turkey and Aleppo. In Damascus, we each bought a Peugeot. Mine was white and Dr. Shah's was grey. In appearance, my car seemed to be in better shape than Dr. Shah's. It was a newer model with a better-looking body, and the engine seemed to be in good condition. That evening, we started our return journey from Damascus in our new cars. We reached the Iraqi check post the next morning, but we had to wait a long time at the Iraqi border to get the cars registered. It was already dark when we received our papers and started on our journey to Mosul in heavy rain.

As I was driving, leaning on the steering wheel in low visibility, a truck coming from the opposite direction smashed into the Peugeot. The impact felt immense, like a bomb going off. The car came to a sudden stop. My body was flung forward. My chest hit the steering wheel and my head crashed against the windscreen. I sat for a few minutes trying to take stock of the damage. I was unsure if I was still alive or if I had cracked my ribs, or if I still had a face. After a few minutes, I saw that I was miraculously unharmed. I got out of the car. The impact had buckled the front and cracked the front glass. The truck driver came to check on me, trembling, begging for forgiveness. After clearing out the broken shards with my fingers, I got back inside and drove the rest of the distance without a windshield, with the cold wind blowing inside. I could only be thankful that I had escaped with my life.

I reached home late at night. Parking in the driveway under the covered arch, I switched on the veranda light to examine the extent of the damage from the collision. What I found out was not palatable. The car had many defects, apart from the damage it had suffered in the accident. The bottom was corroded and there were holes under the floor carpeting.

The next morning, I drove the Peugeot to a garage and asked for an estimate to replace the bottom of the body. The quote I was given was almost fifty percent of the car's original price. I was shocked. I didn't know what to do. At that time, Iraq was fast becoming a rich country. Labor was scarce and expensive. The joke in the foreigners' community was that if you took a broken item to a mechanic for repairs, he would invariably tell you to throw it away and get a new one.

It so happened that Dr. Saadi was having some construction work done at his house. His driveway was packed with steel wire nets, cement, and other construction materials. I had once asked the Iraqi professor what proportion of sand and cement he had used in the mortar. Dr. Saadi had answered that he was using as much cement as possible. I had asked him why he did not use the recommended ratio.

"Cement is very cheap in Iraq, but sand is costly," Dr. Saadi had replied.

"How is that possible?" I had asked.

Dr. Saadi had explained that cement was manufactured in government factories and supplied to construction sites by government transport at very low cost, whereas one had to gather the sand from the bottom of the Tigris River, hiring local labor to do so, which made sand very costly for construction.

Taking this information into account, I devised a plan to repair my car cheaply. I requested Dr. Saadi give me some wire-net, cement, and sand. He readily agreed to make a gift of these materials to me. After work, I drove my car to Dr. Saadi's house and removed the seats and floor carpeting, cleaned the corrosion as much as I could, painted the cleaned surface with a red oxide coating, and spread two layers of steel net on the bottom like wall-to-wall carpeting. Next, I applied a sand-cement mortar to the wire net. I left the car at Dr. Saadi's house, and he gave me a lift home. The next evening, I accompanied Dr. Saadi to his house again, fixed the car seats and carpeting back in place, and drove away. I drove the car for eight years without trouble, up and down Iraq.

Once we had a car, we lost no opportunity to travel across Iraq. We started our journey in the early morning with the bluish-purple sky overhead, driving past vast green fields with grazing lamb and Bedouin tents blowing in the wind. The Peugeot was an ideal transport for sightseeing. The children ate their meals sitting in the car. The front and back seats could be flattened, making suitable beds for them. There was a sunroof through which they could

look out, standing on their toes, gazing at the clash of colors in the
dawn sky as we set off on a trip.

We visited Kerbala, Najaf, Kufa, Kut, and Babylon, the Shatt-
al-Arab, Nineveh, Kirkuk, and Duhok, and the two rivers of Iraq,
the Furat and the Tigris. Every time I beheld a ruin, a mosque, the
burial ground of a prophet, Adam's tree, or the hanging gardens
of Babylon, I gasped with wonder. This once great country had
become poor, and now it was becoming rich again through oil,
giving foreigners jobs in its oil refineries, roads and highways, and
the universities.

The national museum in Baghdad was filled with the rich trea-
sures of the ancient civilization of Mesopotamia, and the national
library in Baghdad held the largest collection of ancient books
dating back to the Ottoman Empire. In Babylon, on the bank of
the Euphrates river, we gazed at the tower of Babylon, the seat
of King Hammurabi, the maker of the first laws on tablets. Sadly,
these tablets had been looted and are now in the Louvre Museum
in Paris, while the grand Ishtar gate with its glazed tile work of
lions, bulls, and dragons is now housed in a museum in Berlin. In
Kerbala, we saw the battlefield where the battle of Kerbala was
fought and visited the shrine and burial site of Hussein, the son
of Ali and the grandson of Prophet Muhammad. In Nineveh, we
wandered through the ruins of an empty palace. Labels explained
that the artifacts had been carried away to British museums. The
wind blew hard as Beena wandered through the doorways, imag-
ining a king, a queen, her dressing table, and makeup.

It was in Basra that I fell in love with Iraq. When I first saw
the Shatt-al-Arab, the Arabian Gulf, I realized that all along I had
been afraid Iraq would swallow one of my children, but now the
opposite was happening. I swallowed up the blue Shatt-al-Arab, its
vast waters rolling into the distance, pouring into the Arabian Sea,
as far as the eye could see.

My students were perplexed by my behavior. They complained that I was careless about my attire and that I was the most ill-dressed teacher at the university. They said that every other teacher at the university wore a tie, but I never used one. The other teachers wore tailored suits, but I only wore the same dusty, checked wool jacket every day, on top of faded turtlenecks, with my long hair falling over the back of my neck. Further, I came to class with my hair flying, and flecks of ash on my skin and clothes. The students themselves were extremely well dressed. The male students wore shirts with long collars, stylish jackets, and curly hair styles. The women wore their hair cut and styled and dressed in blouses with tie knots, long skirts, and black, polished, high-heeled shoes.

One day, the students in my second-year thermodynamics class walked up to me together and presented me a paper box in colorful wrapping.

"What is this?" I asked.

"It is a gift for you, as you are liked by all of us." They opened the box themselves and showed me the twelve ties inside. "Every other teacher wears a tie to class. We would like you also to come to our classes wearing a tie."

Secretly, I had a low opinion of the well-dressed man. I used to think that only people who had no worth inside wore nice clothes to show off their superficial exterior. I felt insulted, but I tried not to show the students my hurt feelings.

"I am very pleased, as I like any gift given with affection," I said. "But you can only change my philosophy on ties by argument, not by giving me ties. I will take one tie from the box to accept your love." I selected one tie. "I shall wear it to class only if you can prove to me that wearing a tie will improve anything. Other-wise not. I would rather tell you a story. If you hear it, you will never ask me to wear a tie again."

I told them the story of Shaikh Saadi of Shirazi, a Persian philos-opher of the thirteenth century who studied at the University of Baghdad. One day, Saadi was invited to his native land of Shirazi by

the Persian ruler Atabak Abubakr to dine with him, but when Saadi
tried to enter the palace, he was denied entry because he was dressed
in rags. Saadi walked to the market and bought expensive clothes.
Then he returned to the palace gate to keep his appointment with
the ruler. When the food was served, Saadi did not eat any items.
Instead, he stuffed all the delicacies in the pockets of his clothes.

"What are you doing?" The Salghurid ruler cried in astonishment.

Saadi replied, "Your Highness, I was not allowed to enter the
palace without these clothes. Only these clothes allowed me access,
so I am feeding the ones for which all this honor is intended."

After finishing the story, I said to the students, "Let me be
your teacher without a tie. Don't dress me up like a Shaikh Saadi."

Soon after this incident, my Egyptian colleague informed me
one day that my students referred to me as Ustad Tamata, which
meant Tomato Teacher. The teacher wanted to know if I knew
why I was thus addressed. I felt very insulted.

In the next class, I asked the students, "Have I been nicknamed
Ustad Tamata by you or not?"

They said yes, indeed, they had given me this nickname.

I was furious. "How did I earn it?" I asked.

They explained, "The tomato is a vegetable that goes with every
curry in Iraq, and you are a teacher who teaches us every subject."

I calmed down and felt very happy. It was true that I taught
all the subjects, taking on any extra courses. I loved teaching. I
had also partaken of tomato curry, dipping the samn bread in it,
sitting on a cool mat among fine cushions at an Iraqi neighbor's
or colleague's house in the cool evening air. Sometimes an Iraqi
family sent kubeh stuffed with tomatoes or dolma cooked in the
aroma of rice and tomatoes cocooned in grape leaves. A student's
mother arrived at our house with klecha, date sweets, or pastry
covered with sugar dust. In spite of myself, I had fallen in love with
my teaching job at the University of Mosul, the people I had met,
and the food I had eaten.

37. HARSH TERRAIN

Philadelphia, 1998

"WAIT. I THINK I saw one." Lenin stopped near one of the tables set out on the sidewalk.

The man sitting behind the table smiled at Lenin, revealing a golden upper tooth. He wore a crocheted rastacap. Loud Reggae music played on a stereo system behind him. Lenin bent to look at the watches arrayed on the man's table.

"Lenin! These are cheap!" Beena flicked her bangs and blew air through her mouth. Her breath came out as smoke in the cold November air of Philadelphia.

This incident was only the latest in a long line of frustrations during her visit to her brother. Her handsome brother, with his angular face, square jaw, and long eyelashes, was practically unrecognizable in his new appearance as a graduate student. He seemed to be habitually dressed in baggy jeans and shiny, synthetic clothes with loud patterns. Every time they had gone out, he had dressed like that.

Earlier that day, Beena had dragged Lenin to Filene's Basement and bought him two pairs of dress pants, two buttoned shirts, and a ribbed V-neck sweater.

"I'll never get the chance to wear such a nice sweater," Lenin had protested.

In response, she had added on a parka jacket from L. L. Bean, making him try it on in the dressing room.

"There, much better," she had said, when he had come out to show her the ensemble.

"Now for the next step, getting rid of your ugly glasses and wristwatch."

But this was where she had hit a wall. The sharp nose pads of Lenin's metal-frame glasses had made incisions on either side of his nose. The bridge of the glasses had split in two, and he had taped it with Scotch tape. Still, he would not part with the glasses. He also wore a ladies' wristwatch with a silver chain-link and a round-shaped face that had belonged to their mother. He bragged that he had been proudly wearing it for four years. He would not replace the watch either. "Why won't you cooperate?" she cried in frustration.

Now she thought Lenin had picked up the watch to please her.

"Brother," the man said. "You want these? These are ladies' watches!"

"See?" Beena said triumphantly.

She had to drag him away by the arm. When they had walked a block up the street, out of earshot of the street vendor, she said, "Are you mad? Buying watches from the street? I'll buy you a proper watch."

"Ah, where will you get the money? You're spending too much," Lenin said.

They were on their way to a Bangladeshi grocery store, where Lenin planned to buy a few things to cook a Bengali dinner. Beena slipped her arm through his as they began to walk uphill. Her feet were cold in thin socks and canvas sneakers. The one thing that impressed her about Philadelphia was the cold air, so new and surprising. It had not snowed while she had been visiting, but in a corner of one of the streets, she had spotted a heap of dirty black slush and smiled. There were a lot of homeless people on

the sidewalk, dressed in tattered layers, walking slowly, or curled
up near a grate. Their long coats and gaunt faces stood out sharply
against the bleak, foggy atmosphere. This one aspect of American
life had surprised Beena. She had never properly understood the
separation of races, but now seeing the wealthy white college
students and the poor black residents of the city so visually separate
in this beautiful landscape of upscale shops with bright awnings
and rows of brick houses with balustrades and windows peeking
from catacomb basements, she felt sick. In Houston also, where
she had just arrived, taking the public bus to school, she had gazed
in amazement at the poor, black children who boarded the bus
wearing threadbare sweaters on a cold day, shivering. As the bus
neared the university campus, the neighborhoods became barren,
with empty lots of scarred walls and strewn trash and shanty houses
barricaded by grilled windows and doors.

"So you see, it's very worrying because we are not at all
responding to climate change even as the science is clear," Lenin
said, continuing an earlier conversation, opening his mouth dramat-
ically in the pose of giving a lecture. "The governments won't
do anything about climate change because all they care about is
protecting capitalist interests. The worst effects of climate change
will fall on low lying areas. Bangladesh will be under water."

Beena felt that Lenin only wanted to talk about abstract ideas.
Not once had he asked Beena about her life. It made her sad that
he didn't really care about what was going on with her. She made
a restless movement with her shoulders. Why did they have to talk
about such distant topics when she wanted to complain about how
lonely she was, or how her mother kept giving her number to
strange men in the hopes of getting her married?

"The Third World War will be about resources like water and
food, brought on by climate change. Natural disasters will wipe
out habitats." Lenin gestured with his fingers to underscore his
arrogantly uttered opinions.

"I don't understand," she said, not wanting to understand.

Her brother's life, too, seemed so alien to Beena. He had given her an extended tour of all the places that were important to him on campus, the dreary David Rittenhouse Laboratory building with pipes running overhead through the halls like the annals of a haunted house, and another building, where he took organic chemistry, with bottles that held aborted fetuses, the library where he studied, and the computer lab. That was it, his whole life in a nutshell on this sunny campus with laughing, beautiful people dressed in gorgeous clothes calling out to one another in passing on Locust Walk or sitting luxuriously on the green. Not once had she seen one of these people call out to her brother.

At the Bangladeshi store, Lenin picked up Basmati rice, masur daal, and frozen rui fish imported from Bangladesh.

"Don't buy fish," Beena warned Lenin. "Neither of us knows how to cook it. You don't even have the right spices."

"Why? What do we need?" he asked, turning around to look at her.

"I don't know!"

"Don't worry. It will taste good. Oh! I almost forgot." He ran back to the shelves and reappeared holding a glass jar. "Mango pickles!" he grinned.

They spoke in Bengali with the shopkeeper, who said he had worked in the Middle East before coming to America.

"Where?" Lenin asked.

"Iraq. Life was good. But then after the sanctions in 1990, they could not sell their oil and there was no food in the country. Children were dying of malnutrition. I came here then. Illegally at first, but now, *mashallah*, I have started my papers."

"Well, at least they removed the UN inspectors now," Lenin said. "The crisis seems to have been averted."

The shopkeeper looked at him blankly.

"They were looking for chemical weapons," Lenin explained. "But they didn't find anything. And now the inspectors have left Iraq."

The shopkeeper nodded. "Bhaiya, please take a free Bangla-deshi newspaper from me. You must be missing home."

They walked back with their arms wrapped together for warmth, clutching the heavy plastic bags in their cold, stinging hands. At the apartment, Beena washed Lenin's roommate Nilim's dishes in the sink while Lenin dumped the frozen fish under hot water, dried the pieces by shaking them a bit, and plonked them on the frying pan on top of cold oil. The half-thawed fish sizzled as the water mixed with the oil. The frying pan exploded, spraying hot oil in every direction. Lenin sprang back with a cry.

"Did you burn yourself?" Beena cried angrily, running to fetch ice from the refrigerator.

Lenin and Nilim had elected not to turn the heating on, to save on their electricity bill. Instead, they heated the apartment by turning on the gas oven and leaving the door open. Beena had been dressed in her puffy jacket the entire time they had been inside.

"Can't you get gas poisoning like that?"

"Really?" said Lenin.

"I don't know. You're the scientist."

As Lenin turned the fish around in the pan, Beena cut onions and garlic (this was all they had in the way of spices besides the bottle of curry powder), glancing at Lenin from time to time. Her stomach growled with hunger. She was not optimistic about his cooking.

"You'll see. It will turn out good," Lenin assured her, gazing at the contents of the pan as if scanning a science experiment. His tanned, shiny face glowed in the light of the stove flame.

At least here, leaning against the glass door of the closed oven, they were warm.

"Anyway, back to what I was saying. Just at the moment when we have a global problem to take care of together, we cannot. A few companies will have all the power over governments, over everything, and they will do everything in their power to protect their interests. Governments will work only to protect the interests of the companies," He spoke with his eyes closed and lips expanded, in a haughty, confident voice.

"*Oof.* Doom and gloom. Can we not talk about politics?"

He laughed sheepishly. "Okay, I will stop."

The meal was terrible, a crude mockery of the food they had grown up eating. The fish tasted flat. The curry powder had not penetrated its surface. Lenin had not fried the onions sufficiently before throwing in the fish and dousing the whole concoction with water. The effect was a cold, watery ocean of distinct, separate tastes—raw turmeric, raw onions, and then the pasty flakes of fish. Beena piled more rice onto her plate to cover the watery fish. She had cooked the daal herself, but it was too salty.

"Oh! The *achar!*" Lenin cried, springing from his chair with a gleam in his eyes. "Perhaps the mango pickle will make it taste better."

They could not open the bottle. The metal cap had been sealed too tightly.

"Use the flame from the stove," Beena suggested.

Brother and sister concentrated on the task. As Beena instructed him, Lenin held the bottle horizontally above a burner, rotating the glass slowly. Still, the metal cap would not open when Lenin twisted it. He took the bottle and began to hit the neck against the small, square dining table. The glass shattered with a cry and a sinking sound of escaping gas. Lenin picked out the large pieces of glass, then lifted his head, smiling at Beena.

"There, I got it open!"

"It has glass in it," she said with muted anger. "We can't eat it. It's spoiled."

"Are you sure? There were only a few large pieces, and I think I got them all." He held up the broken glass bottle with its jagged rim. The room reeked of mustard and cumin.

"Yeah," Beena said. "I don't want to swallow glass."

"Okay." Lenin threw the bottle into the trashcan and returned to his chair.

She felt bad for yelling at him, for being annoyed with him, especially because the night before he had been telling her that their father wasn't happy about him being a poor PhD student in mathematics. Their father had called Lenin to say that his students were all working for big companies and earning a lot of money; couldn't Lenin do something like that? "I didn't expect him to say that, especially him, knowing how he lived his own life," Lenin had said, with confusion in his eyes.

"So anyway," Lenin started again, sitting down. "Any world news you see, anything you read in the papers, you should look at it in the light of its consequence for climate change."

"*Oof!*" she cried, shivering uncontrollably in her jacket, running her fingers through cold rice. "Can we stop talking about geopolitics for once? I can't think about such abstract things when there is so much going on in my life."

Lenin gave a timid laugh. "All right. What do you want to talk about?"

"I don't know. My courses. What I think of Houston."

"Okay," he said, leaning forward and pushing up his taped glasses with two fingers. "Tell me."

38. AT THE BOTTOM OF THE RIVER TIGRIS

Mosul, 1975-82

THE DUST OF THE desert never settles. Just as Iraq grew from a country of Bedouin nomads herding camels, donkeys, and sheep to a modern land of bounty, soon that moment was taken over also. Summer returned, and the air became hot and heavy. The sky grew thick with rumors. The Ba'ath party became more hard-lined. Dr. Saadi lost his job to a Ba'ath Party member who was many years junior to him, because the Ba'ath Party government desired his appointment. Saddam Hussein declared himself absolute ruler of Iraq. My students became dark faced and disheartened. They met secretly in street-side shops under the cover of dark to sip bitter coffee in tiny cups, discussing the revolutionaries who had been imprisoned, tortured, and hanged, and those who had fled to other Arab countries or Europe. They whispered to me that people on the left were being disappeared daily, including some decent people inside the party.

Then, things took a turn for the worse. The Shatt-al-Arab was in dispute. Shockingly, trouble started with Iran, at first merely as exchanged insults and satirical cartoons of the Iranian ruler Ayatollah Khomeini dancing madly on TV. I asked the students, "What is

the conflict?" They said that the Iranian leader had instigated Shia
rebellion against Saddam Hussein and there was dispute over terri-
tories. The fervor kept mounting, and in September, before our
shocked eyes, a war started, with Washington supporting Saddam
Hussein, and Libya, Syria, and Israel supporting Khomeini.

The country where we had been living in peace for so
many years changed before our eyes. Food became scarce, and
many items were rationed. Rahela stood in long lines to collect
whatever food was being given out on ration. As petrol became
scarce, the government ruled that cars with even numbered license
plates were allowed on the road on one day, while cars with odd
numbered license plates were allowed to drive on the alternate day.
The markets thickened with the Popular Army, formed by civilian
volunteers signing up to fight against Iran.

"Don't you think this war is a mistake?" I asked the Iraqi
students. "Even if Iraq defeats Iran, what will come of it? Both
countries will be strained by the cost of fighting a war."

"Don't worry," the students assured me with big smiles. "The
war will be over in a few days."

The male students, young men with bright eyes and tufted dark
hair, started joining the army and going off to war. In a photograph
taken with me before the war, they are standing tall with their
chests out, stylish, holding cigarettes at an upward angle in their
hands, looking modern and intellectual.

We moved to a flat in Babultope, in the city, close to the children's school, public transportation, and the markets. The children
were cramped for space in the flat, caught in the anxiety of the
grown-ups. Rahela and I decided we had to leave. Eight years
had passed since we arrived in Iraq. Several coups had taken place
in Bangladesh in the interim years. The prime minister Sheikh
Mujib had been assassinated, followed by several unstable years
and multiple changes of government. Recently, President Zia, the
latest in a long line of leaders, had also been assassinated. Rahela
and I tried to make plans while we ate dinner.

Lenin kept interrupting us. "Abba, Amma! There is nothing to be afraid of in war. We shall die when God wishes us to."

Rahela was irritated by the interruptions. Realizing that the children were vying for attention, I told them to watch the Polish cartoons on TV in the drawing room. Just after they left, a high-pitch siren sounded outside. The drawing room was next to the front street, with windows facing the street. Lenin started to scream at the top of his lungs. Rahela and I rushed to the drawing room and picked up the children, dragging them away from the open windows. For the next few hours, we hid in the inner corridor of the building till the air-raid siren subsided.

After that day, we began to prepare to leave. Beena had dreams in which we almost reached Bangladesh but couldn't. Bangladesh was like a dreamland to my children, so fantastic that they couldn't believe we could actually go there. My youngest son Kazi pestered me with questions about the mechanics of traveling home.

"Abba, is Bangladesh in the sky?"

"Why do you say that?"

"Because Bangladeshis come here from the sky, and they fly off into the sky."

Kazi was referring to the fact that when other Bangladeshi families returned to Bangladesh, we went to the airport to see them off. Kazi had watched the planes fly into the sky. I smiled at my son's conviction, feeling satisfied that we would get home in no time.

Once again, Rahela stood in line at department stores. This time, we bought luxury items to carry home—trousers that arrived in cartons from China, dinnerware, gold jewelry, Georgette saris, and show-piece Iraqi dolls dressed in traditional clothes. I bought a maroon brocade material and foam to make a sofa. We piled everything into our suitcases, determined to leave nothing behind. But our travel plans soon became complicated.

When the first bombs fell on Mosul, the airport in Mosul shut down. Baghdad Airport was also closed. The only way to leave the country was to take a bus to Kuwait and board a PIA flight from there. Most of my foreign colleagues had left already or were scrambling to get out. The Americans and Europeans had fled the country long ago, rescued by their foreign missions. Only the unfortunate citizens of the Indian subcontinent remained.

One day, I went to collect my three children from school. Loud ululations could be heard in the house next to the school. The son of the house, a young man who had served as a pilot in the war, had been killed when his plane had been shot down. Now, hundreds of family members gathered at the house as the dead body was carried in. From the road, I could see the fallen soldier's family sobbing uncontrollably.

I took my three children out of the school and began walking toward the parked car. Suddenly, air-raid sirens began to sound above our heads. All around us, parents and schoolchildren jumped out of their cars and ducked low on the road. In a few seconds, planes swooped over our heads, accompanied by the loud cracking of anti-aircraft guns from the ground. My children covered their eyes and ears with their hands, crouching on the ground. Then I thought I heard the sound of a bomb falling. The explosion was louder than anything that could be imagined.

"Quick!"

Before the planes could come back, my children and I flew to the safety of a neighboring house. An old couple with lined faces opened their door and ushered us in, leading us to an inner court-yard that was open to the sky. They fed us water and date cookies and calmed the shaking children. Speaking in a mixture of Arabic and broken English, they told us that their three sons had gone off to fight in the war against Iran. They had no idea about their sons' whereabouts. Later, I learned that a military base had been bombed that day.

A few days later, we faced a big setback. The teenaged boy who came to exchange our empty gas cylinders ran away with them. The cylinders were rationed by the government. Each family was awarded two gas cylinders. It was not possible to simply walk into a market and buy another one. Without a gas cylinder, we could not cook. Seeing no other alternative, I lodged a complaint with the police. The next day, two mustachioed policemen brought back the cylinders and the young man who had taken them, holding him between them.

"Is he the one who stole your gas?" one of the police officers asked me in English.

I peered into the boy's face and recognized him immediately. He had a mischievous, youthful face, with red cheeks and curly hair, and dark blue eyes the shade of the water of the Tigris. He had made an impression on me because his eyes were hollow and stark against his otherwise plump face.

"Can you ask him why he stole the cylinders?" I asked the officers.

One of the officers spoke rapidly with the boy, who answered feebly in a shaking voice.

The officer turned to me. "He says he was going to sell them. His family is poor. He has five younger brothers and sisters to feed."

I pleaded with the police to let the boy go, but the policemen said that this was impossible. I had to come down to the station with them and promise in writing that I was withdrawing my complaint. I drove to the police station and asked them to drop the charges. After many formalities, the young man was released. Before I left the station, I had to promise the police never to complain again if I was only going to withdraw my accusation.

Dr. Saadi asked me to come to his house to discuss a personal matter. We sat in his living room paneled with rich wood and filled with bookshelves and fine cushions. Dr. Saadi served me bitter coffee in a delicate cup without handles and broached the subject for which he had summoned me. His younger brother, a pilot, had gone missing in action in the war. Dr. Saadi's family did not know if his brother's plane had been shot down, if he was still alive or dead, or if he was a prisoner of war in Iran. Dr. Saadi wanted me to try and find out about his brother's whereabouts from outside Iraq, by writing to the foreign missions.

"When will this war end?" I asked, feeling bad that I was escaping unhurt while leaving my Iraqi colleagues and neighbors behind.

Dr. Saadi informed me that there were some people in the government desperately trying for a ceasefire with Iran.

"You said earlier one time that so many people on the left have left the country. Will you not leave?" I asked.

Dr. Saadi laughed with a sad smile and ran his fingers through his thick hair. "This is my land, Doctor Nasir, no matter what happens. I have given up my politics and my dreams. I am content to be able to kiss the soil of my country." He shifted his position on the sofa. "The world will never allow there to be peace in Iraq because this land is too important to the region. The Iraqi people will never be left alone to determine their dreams without interference from the international powers."

I nodded sadly.

"But no matter. Remember the history of Iraq, as I told you? The city of Babylon has existed for four thousand years. We had Assyrian kings, Abbasid caliphs, and Ottoman rule. Then the British came to rule us, but the Iraqis rose against the monarchy. In every period, the people fought for their freedom, no matter how grim their situation became, and no matter what jackals betrayed them. Our spirits will live on, no matter what happens in the future."

"It is the same way in my homeland," I said excitedly. "When the people of Bangladesh were being massacred by the Pakistani State, Bangladesh was simply a calculation in the Cold War game of the international community. It seems that the ordinary people everywhere struggle for better lives, but the politicians and international bodies see them only as pawns."

In May, I took my family to Baghdad to buy new airplane tickets for our passage out of Iraq. I was successful in buying the tickets on the first day, on a flight leaving in June from Kuwait Airport. We were staying with some Bangladeshi friends in the city. That evening, to celebrate, we drove to a park in Baghdad, parking the cars beside a small pond. We enjoyed a small picnic sitting on a Syrian mat, laying out cucumber sandwiches, roast chicken, sheesh kebab, and pickles, reminiscing about home and looking forward to leaving. My three children ran freely among the swings and slides. Still, a war was going on, and we did not want to risk an air raid, so we piled into our cars before dark, preparing to leave.

A car rammed the Peugeot from behind. I swore and got out of the car to examine the damage. The Peugeot's body was dented badly. The children were in the backseat. After checking quickly that they were all right, I left my family and drove off in our friend's car, chasing the other car, which had backed up and sped off. I was determined not to let the culprit get away. We flagged down the car about a kilometer from the park and forced the driver to go to the police station with us. To my surprise, the driver was drunk and contrite. The police asked me for an estimated cost of the damages in dinar. I named a sum. The police obliged the other driver to pay me the full sum. When I returned to the park in my friend's car, Rahela was screaming. Our youngest child Kazi had died of an internal hemorrhage. He looked spotless on the outside. I started to hit my head against the car's body, screaming soundlessly.

Rahela and I buried our youngest child Kazi in Mosul. I lifted the surprisingly light box containing my son's body and descended into the dirt hole. I howled like a child and had to be carried away by my friends. I thought that my son had been swallowed up by the Tigris River, to rest in peace at its bottom forever, frozen in time.

A month later, we finally started our journey to Bangladesh with heavy suitcases and boxes tied with rope. From Mosul, we rode a bus to Baghdad, where we boarded another bus to carry us to the Iraqi border with Kuwait. In Baghdad, we were surprised to find beggars banging their alms cups against the windows of the bus. Our fellow travelers were mostly South Asians—laborers from India, Bangladesh, and Pakistan with big eyes and frightened expressions. In disjointed voices, they told us about their harrowing journeys out of the different parts of the country.

In the evening, the Iraqi bus reached the border with Kuwait and dropped us in the middle of nowhere. That night, we slept in an open field under the Iraqi sky. The next morning, we rose with the sun and hauled our luggage to the Kuwaiti checkpoint. After the Kuwaiti officials verified our papers, we boarded another bus that carried us to the Kuwaiti airport. Finally, after several days of travel, we were on a plane to Bangladesh.

Once I was in Bangladesh, I tried to trace the whereabouts of Dr. Saadi's brother through various international agencies, but I was not successful in my efforts. In the end, I could not help Dr. Saadi in the one favor that the Iraqi professor had asked of me, in return for all the kindnesses he had shown my family.

In leaving Iraq, I left many parts of me behind. Long into old age, I woke up screaming from my sleep. The frowning face of my son Kazi, standing in the sun in a plump safari suit, accused me of leaving him behind. Kazi used to always be an angry child, full of frowns and commands. Rahela and I used to admire the boy's confidence. But now my son turned his angry face toward me, standing in the sun with a forlorn expression, shielding his eyes with a small, fat hand.

39. GOLDEN BENGAL

Dhaka, 1982

As soon as the plane touched down in Dhaka, the passengers started clapping and crying, *Sonar Bangla!* Was this it, Golden Bengal? Beena and Lenin exchanged secret greetings in Arabic as their parents waited nervously at the airport customs inspection. They used Arabic as their defense, to shield themselves from the confusion all around them. The building was hot and airless, even with giant fans groaning overhead. The customs officials were equally heated in their deliberations. They took apart the family's luggage bag by bag, tugging their mustaches and shaking their heads, to say there was a big problem. Rahela's brother-in-law Chhoto Dulabhai (Chhoto Khalu to Beena and Lenin) had come to fetch them, resplendent in a golden safari suit and exuding the scent of a masculine aftershave lotion. He told Beena and Lenin to be quiet.

"No, no, can't bring this. And not this," the customs officials were saying.

"Have you brought any cigarettes?" one of the officials asked finally, peering into Nasir Uddin's face.

Nasir Uddin stared back blankly. Beena watched the blankness transform into a slow, incredulous understanding, as a cigarette box was passed from one hand to another. They were finally allowed to collect their luggage.

Throngs of people waited outside the airport, their noses and palms pressed against the dirty glass windows. The air was hot and sticky. As they walked toward Chhoto Khalu's car, a group of porters swarmed them, trying to lift their suitcases and carry them away.

"Sir, need help? Let me take the luggage! Give me!"

"Move!" Chhoto Khalu barked. He shouted to two men he had brought from home. The two male servants dressed in orange uniform came running and picked up the suitcases, taking them from Nasir Uddin's hands.

When they had almost reached the car, a dark, bare-chested boy with stick limbs and a distended stomach flung himself in their path, springing a plate. "Sir, give me one Taka. Any currency. Sir, I did not eat," he cried in a singsong voice.

Beena's uncle grabbed the boy by the shoulders and shoved him. "Go! Rascal! Can't you work? It's people like you who have brought Bangladesh to this state."

The boy ran away. Beena climbed quickly into the car before her uncle could shout at her also.

The house in Banani had many rooms filled with teak wood furniture. Bookcases held every kind of book imaginable, from Bengali novels to English paperback mysteries. Fruit trees lined the periphery, brushing the boundary wall, bearing fruits they had never eaten before, mangos, guava, purple jum, and, the children's favorite, the ata fruit with a crocodile skin outside and delicate, white flesh inside. They were served their meals at a long, teak-wood dining table covered with an embroidered tablecloth. The food was more sophisticated than anything Beena had ever tasted— white rice cooked in ghee, white chicken in a sugary, yogurt sauce, and ilish fish cooked in mustard sauce. In the afternoon, they relaxed in the drawing room, leaning back against sofa cushions with crocheted covers, while tea was wheeled in on a metal and wood trolley and served on quarter plates with embroidered napkins. Whenever she wanted something, Beena's aunt pressed a bell and a servant appeared in a neat, orange-colored uniform.

Beena was aware that her aunt's house was only a temporary shelter. The sun was always beating down outside. Beena and Lenin stood on the roof under the overpowering fragrance of the Hasna Hena flower, the night-blooming jasmine that called forth snakes, each holding a segment of the ata fruit, paring off its crocodile skin and sucking on the succulent white flesh inside. Their father and uncle sat on the roof in lawn chairs, talking in low voices.

"Dulabhai," Nasir Uddin said, "I want to teach, and I want to farm for fish, ducks, and chicken. The farm will work as both a poultry farm and a fishpond. The fish will feed on the excrement of the ducks." In Mosul, he had collected books on the subject and written copious notes in his journal.

Chhoto Dulabhai, Chhoto Khalu to Beena and Lenin, laughed loudly. "Welcome to Golden Bengal, the land of golden dreams," he said. "You won't be able to achieve any of these things. You have no idea how to deal with the corruption and bureaucracy of this place."

When Nasir Uddin went to report to work at the engineering university, his dream burst in his face. The university did not want him back. His former colleagues and friends, who were now deans and department heads, pointed to various technical problems, saying he had not reported to the university at the end of his leave period. The same thing happened to Rahela at the psychology department of Dhaka University. They would not let her back in her old position as a lecturer.

Dr. Shah, who had returned to Bangladesh the year before Nasir Uddin, came to tea in Banani one day. "It's like this now. Everything is political. They are jealous of anyone who returns from abroad," he said.

"I acquired my education solely to teach at the engineering university," Nasir Uddin said. "I always believed that I belonged to the engineering university. What shall I do now?"

"*Aarre*, we all had to go through this. There is no one at the university specialized in your discipline. Everybody knows the university needs you. This is just the ritual, the fight you have to fight."

A month later, they moved to a rented house in Lake Circus, Kalabagan and came to see the Bangladesh outside Banani, as a harsher, stickier place. To reach the house from the main road, they had to pass through a maze of alleys heaped high with decomposing garbage, holding their noses so that they would not inhale the smell of bloody meat, a dead crow, and discarded food. The four of them piled on top of one another on a single rickshaw, trying not to fall out, while the rickshaw puller tried not to break his sweaty back. Where the paved road ended, they climbed down and walked another mile on a brick path, past a line of crowded, bamboo-walled cottages with tin roofs that had been rented out to poor families. A lone brick house girded by a grilled veranda sat in the middle of a field, set far back from the road. A pond ran beside the house, skirted by a tangle of bushes. Beyond the pond lay more shanty huts—in worse condition than the tin-roof cottages leading to the house. Rickshaw pullers, domestic servants, and factory workers lived in these homes.

The hired men who had pulled their belongings on van-carts all the way from Banani deposited their luggage and the furniture donated by Rahela's sister Chhoto Apa in front of the house and left.

Lenin tore through the empty rooms, shouting. "Yaaaaa!"

There was nothing to be happy about, so Beena caught him and smacked him above his ear. He began to wail, and Beena crossed her arms with satisfaction. The walls, ceilings, and floors of the house crawled with scorpions, spiders, cockroaches, and ants. In the evening, bats flew in, screeching blindly around the drawing room. At first, they did not own a refrigerator, so after the night's meal, Rahela simply plonked the pot of leftover rice on the kitchen counter, heating up the same food the next day. The grains were red and hard, a different variety of rice than Beena was used to. Once, Beena found insects crawling through the rice on her plate.

"Amma!" she shouted frantically. "There are insects here!"

"Where? Where?" Rahela cried, squinting through her glasses.

Although Beena could see the insects clearly, turned on their sides or happily climbing a mound of daal, they seemed to escape her mother's eyes.

Rahela hired a chhuta bua, a maid who came in to work during the day and left at nightfall for her home in the slums. Her name was Marinar Ma, meaning the mother of Marina, although she had several other children as well. She arrived from the slum like a rocket, her short, hard body tightly wound in a cotton sari with the edge pulled around her head and a naked baby hanging at her waist, and moved at great speed through the house, cutting fish, grinding spices, washing clothes, and sweeping floors, sending up dust balls in the air. Sometimes she set the child down on the floor, but at other times she simply shifted him about her body. Beena hated having a maid in the house. Once she found the maid's daughter Marina playing with Lenin, building a tower with the Lego blocks they had bought from catalogs in Iraq and had shipped to Bangladesh. Marina was about the same age as Lenin, a thin girl with a dark face filled with large eyes. Beena scolded the girl and told her to run off. Marina looked at her with frightened eyes and fled the room.

Beena turned on Lenin. "Why were you playing with a dirty girl like that? You don't want to become dirty also, do you?" She made him wash his hands in the bathroom.

Beena and Lenin were admitted to an English Medium school for rich kids in Dhanmondi. Rahela went to fetch them after school. As they walked on the road, looking for a rickshaw to take them home at a reasonable fare, Lenin wandered into the tin-shed shops on the roadside, asking to buy potato chips and a bottle of Coca Cola.

"You fool! Don't you understand that we have no money! Abba doesn't have a job!" Beena dragged Lenin out of the shop by his wrists, while he cried and kicked. "Right, Amma?"

Rahela pursed her lips and said nothing.

Reaching the gate of their home, they spotted the distant

figure of Nasir Uddin sitting on a chair on the veranda, staring out
at the field of tall grass. He sat on this veranda all day and night,
smoking Boss cigarettes, a local brand, and cutting out job adver-
tisements from newspapers. Sometimes, his friends came to visit
and argued with him. Intense negotiations seemed to be going on.

"You are a full professor," Dr. Shah said. "You should not
join as an ad hoc lecturer. That's worse than an insult. Look, the
university is very short of teachers, especially in your discipline,
but they are deliberately not advertising the senior positions just
to tease you."

"Then, to show them, I shall apply for the ad hoc position,"
Nasir Uddin said.

Beena stood in her school socks and listened to the men until
her mother called her inside to bathe.

All of Nasir Uddin's projects, the fish farm, the poultry farm, and
the intercity bus service, came to nothing. Perhaps he realized that he
didn't have the smarts to do business in the country. All he could do,
the only way he could offer himself, was through his teaching.

One evening, when the colony of bats that perched on the
trees outside swooped and soared in the dark air, Nasir Uddin's
nephew Mukul arrived at the house. Beena watched him sitting
in the drawing room with his head down. He was a stout young
man in his twenties, with a thick, black mustache and bushy black
eyebrows filling most of his face. He had traveled all day from
Jessore by bus and by ferry. Beena gathered that he had come at
Nasir Uddin's command. Nasir Uddin's sister Rajani had been
complaining about the family's costs. She wanted her eldest son
Mukul to start earning money for the family instead of going to
university. Nasir Uddin wanted to give Mukul One Lakh taka to
provide for his university education as well as the family's financial
needs. As Mukul waited alone in the drawing room clasping his
hands in his lap, Beena's parents argued in angry whispers in the
bedroom, standing in front of the locked steel almirah where they
kept all the savings they had brought from Iraq.

Rahela barred the door of the almirah, crying, "You can't give away our money like that! You don't have a job. You have two small children to provide for!"

"He will make good use of the money." Nasir Uddin was adamant. "He will go to college. I could not educate my brother. My sisters were married early. It is my hope that at least my sisters' children should get an education."

They argued in raised voices while Mukul Bhai squirmed on the sofa, scrunching his eyebrows and mustache. Going back and forth between the bedroom and the drawing room, Beena realized that her cousin could hear her parents' words as well as she could.

Months later, reports arrived from the village that Mukul Bhai had used the money to start a pharmacy business. He had not sought admission to a university or handed the money to his parents.

Lenin stayed out all day playing with the rough-looking boys who lived in the tin-roof cottages, climbing trees or playing football in the swampy field in front of the slum. At nightfall, he ran inside the house covered in mud and sweat, with scrapes on his legs, deliriously happy. One day, there was a dispute about a game, and one of the boys threw a stone at Lenin, cutting him above his right eye, narrowly missing the eye. Beena pulled her brother inside the house, burst open the door of the imported refrigerator, and pressed a fistful of ice to his forehead. Then she dragged him by the arm as he cried and struggled and produced him in front of their parents in the drawing room.

"They are dangerous boys!" she cried in an impassioned voice. "He shouldn't play with them. Look at what they have done. They will kill him one day!"

Lenin freed his arms from her grip, crying, "You are nobody to me. Those boys are my friends!"

Their parents were watching *Charlie's Angels* on television. To Beena's surprise, they said nothing. Beena ran to the bedroom and locked the door. Holding her cheeks, she cried till her ribs hurt, afraid that she was losing her brother to the slum children. She hated this country.

Beena and Lenin had started school in October, at the end of the semester and only a month before the final exams. Neither Beena nor Lenin knew how to read and write Bengali. They didn't understand anything else taught in class either. Lenin was placed in class three, a year above his grade level in Mosul. At the end of the year, in December, Beena and her mother rode a rickshaw to school to collect Beena's and Lenin's year-end results. On the way home, they sat silently on the rickshaw, bearing the report cards, their faces drawn. Beena's rank was nineteen in a class of twenty-three. She had several Ds on her report card. Lenin had failed class three. As they slumped down from the rickshaw onto the dusty road, a lady who lived at the mouth of the road in the only other brick house called out to her mother.

"My son came first in his class! How did your children do?" The lady's face glowed with pride.

"Ah, they did well! Beena came fifth and Lenin stood tenth in his class," Rahela said brightly.

Beena glanced at her mother, stunned by the dire lies.

"Good, good," the lady said. "All our children are doing well."

They hurried home and slipped inside quickly.

"How did I do?" Lenin came running in his brown legs, with a stupid, eager look on his face.

With grave faces, they delivered the bad news. Lenin didn't seem too bothered. A few minutes later, his friends came to fetch him to play, calling for him. Lenin stood on the veranda, looking out with big eyes, his thin hands clutching the railing, talking with them.

Beena ran out to the veranda and announced to his friends, "He failed!"

She watched her brother freeze, as if he had just understood the import of the report card. His face crumpled. Nasir Uddin rushed out of the house to the veranda, lifted Lenin in his arms, and carried him to the dining table.

"It's all right," he said, cradling Lenin.

Lenin laid his head on Nasir Uddin's shoulder, his legs spilling over his father's arms, and sobbed himself to sleep. Rahela stroked his hair while Beena stood at a distance with folded arms, watching them with big, guilty eyes, like a villain.

A few days later, Lenin went bathing in the pond beside their house with his friends, despite Beena's attempts to scare him with tales of leeches that would drag him to the bottom and suck the blood out of him. She had also tried to warn her mother that Lenin might drown, but Rahela had merely said that the water was shallow. To Beena, her parents seemed too distracted to notice or care about what happened to them. That night, Lenin developed a high fever. All night, he beat his ears, screaming. Nasir Uddin carried him around the bedroom, soothing him.

"Shut up!" Beena covered her ears with her pillow, trying to sleep.

In the morning, Lenin was carried away to the hospital by ambulance. Their parents accompanied him, leaving Beena at home. In the evening, Nasir Uddin returned home alone. Rahela had stayed behind with Lenin at the hospital. He sank down on the sofa and stared at the blank TV screen with exhausted eyes.

"How is he?" Beena asked.

"His inner ear is clogged," Nasir Uddin said. "To release the pressure, they have to make a hole in his ear drum."

"Will he be okay?"

Her father did not reply. He frowned and smoked one cigarette after another, stubbing out the half-finished cigarettes in the ashtray. Finally, he said, "He may not hear again."

"I'll be nice to him," Beena promised. "I won't be mean again." Then she said what she really meant to say, offering a solution. "Abba, we have been having an awful time since we came here. Why don't we leave?"

Nasir Uddin looked at her with wild eyes and said, "No! I will not do that! If I run away now, why did I come back from Canada in the first place?"

"I don't know." Beena shrugged her shoulders.

"Listen. I left my country for Iraq once, thinking to escape poverty by going away to a better country, but look what happened to Iraq. It became destroyed in a war overnight. When I was in Iraq, I asked myself, why am I in Iraq? The answer was, because of the behavior of the people in authority in my country. They gave me the impression that the country belongs to them. When I realized that this was my reason for leaving my country, I understood that I had made a mistake."

Beena didn't hear what else he had to say because she fell asleep.

One evening, Beena and Lenin were sitting at the dining table with Rahela, working laboriously on their Bengali homework, when they heard howling noises outside. When they opened the door, they found two black cats sitting on their doorstep, outside the grill of the veranda, crying in the rain.

"It is bad luck to see a black cat," Rahela said. "I hope your father is all right."

After that, Beena couldn't concentrate on her books. She waited for her father to return home. The engineering university hadn't responded to Nasir Uddin's application for the ad hoc position. He was always out, either interviewing for jobs or seeking advice from friends. When he was at home, he sat on the veranda, staring with blazing eyes at the tall grass and smoking.

When it was time to go to bed and he still hadn't returned, Beena said, "Is he dead?"

"Go to sleep!" Rahela said sharply.

The doorbell rang, a faint sound in the downpour. Beena and Lenin ran out to the veranda as Rahela unlocked the metal door. Nasir Uddin stepped inside. His hair and clothes were damp from the rain.

"Where were you?" Rahela screamed.

"I did not get the position," he said quietly and walked past her.

"Khalamma, may I leave now that sir is here?" Marinar Ma stood with the edge of her cotton sari pulled above her head.

"Yes, thank you for staying. Go home to your children," Rahela said.

Marinar Ma packed some leftover food in a bundle, slipped on her rubber sandals, and left quickly. But as soon as they had locked the grilled door of the veranda and come inside, locking the house door behind them, they heard screams outside. They ran back out to the veranda.

Marinar Ma was banging on the metal bolt of the grilled veranda. "Khalamma! There's a poisonous snake outside!"

Beena stared out at the dark field.

Rahela began to scream. "A snake killed your grandmother!"

Nasir Uddin emerged from the house and turned on the veranda light. As they watched from the veranda, he stepped down into the dark expanse of greenery and picked up a stick. Beena could see the snake now, quite close to the steps. Its gray body lay in ribbons in the grass and its head was raised off the ground.

"Is it poisonous?" Rahela asked. She had been raised in the city and did not know much about snakes.

As she spoke, the snake's head shot forward and struck at Nasir Uddin's shin. In the same moment, Nasir Uddin started to beat the snake with the stick. They watched wordlessly as he appeared to strike the snake several times, although they were not able to see clearly, looking from the light into the dark.

"It's dead," Nasir Uddin said, putting down the stick and straightening his back, panting.

A few days later, the engineering university advertised another position. Nasir Uddin applied for this position also. Once again, he made triplicate copies of every document, arraying the papers on the dining table. Rahela returned from her routine trip to the psychology department at Dhaka University.

"They will never let me in!" she cried. "I gave up my job to go to Iraq. I gave up my PhD research. I could do nothing with my life."

"It's okay, Amma." Lenin wiped her face. "You can teach at our school."

Rahela smiled at Lenin through her tears, pulling him to her and hugging him tightly as Beena stood and watched.

One day, Rahela's sister in Banani invited them for dinner. They walked through the alleys of Lake Circus, past little shops, the cycle rickshaws tinkling their bells, and overflowing garbage bins, almost to Mirpur Road before they convinced an autorickshaw to go for forty taka. They climbed aboard, Beena, Lenin, and their mother tangling themselves to fit in the back seat while Nasir Uddin sat in the front with the autorickshaw driver. The driver revved up his engine and the baby-taxi throttled down Mirpur Road, coughing black smoke.

In Banani, they ate chicken korma, polao with little raisins, tomato chutney, and succulent pieces of fried rui fish, delicacies that a person could live for as they plodded through a lifetime's daily fare of worm-infested rice. Food like this made everything bearable, even their long walk through the rotten alleys of Kalabagan, the bumpy ride to Banani that had thrown them to the ceiling of the autorickshaw, even the noxious fumes on the road. Beena ate her fill and asked for more. That night, her aunt sent them back in her Toyota car with her chauffeur. The driver was afraid to take the car too far, so he dropped them where the alley narrowed. They climbed out and started to walk, negotiating their way between cycle rickshaws, a herd of cows, and a man on a bicycle.

"We are out of eggs," Rahela said.

They stopped at a small, thatched-shed confectionary that sold eggs hanging from a wire basket in front. Nasir Uddin bought four of the small and smelly deshi chicken eggs, the local kind that were so overpowering that Beena would not eat them. He picked up Lenin, who was sleepy and slumping against his legs, and they started to walk home. A full moon floated overhead, flitting between clouds. Filmy music from a roadside shop carried in the air, punctuated by the sweet sound of rickshaw bells. Added to that was the pleasure of their full stomachs and the lingering taste of the superior food of Banani.

A car honked behind them. "Can't you get out of the way? Make way for the cars of the road!" someone shouted.

Nasir Uddin turned around angrily.

Dr. Shah laughed from behind the wheel. "Hello, hello," he said. "How does it feel not to own a car?"

Dr. Shah walked home with them and sat on the veranda overlooking the lawn. Nasir Uddin and Dr. Shah spoke intensely in low voices. Rahela put Beena and Lenin in bed, but Beena could not sleep. Soon, there was the honk of another car on the road. Footsteps sounded on the stone steps and the doorbell rang.

Beena sat upright in bed. "More guests!" she cried. "What a happy day."

Lenin was fast asleep. Beena tiptoed to the drawing room, which had only two pieces of furniture, a divan and a coffee table lent by her aunt in Banani. Her father's friends sat around him, talking in low voices. Her mother brought in tea for everyone and laughed at a joke.

"You'll join as a lecturer, but it will be no time before you are a full professor again," Dr. Shah said.

"You just have to sign this contract," another friend said. "It simply stipulates that you have to agree to certain special conditions."

Dr. Shah produced the contract out of his breast pocket and laid it on top of the center table. Nasir Uddin clasped the proffered pen and signed the document. When he had finished, his friends cheered and clapped. Nasir Uddin remained seated, his head bowed in submission, accepting the terms on which his country wanted him back. Then he gave himself up to his friends for embraces.

40. THE ETERNAL ASSOCIATE

Dhaka, 1982-95

THE ENGINEERING UNIVERSITY WAS in dire need of senior teachers in my discipline, but to avoid me the university authorities advertised for a lecturer, a position for which a person of my qualifications and experience would be mad to apply. So I applied.

When the engineering university authorities realized that they could not stop me from applying for a teaching post no matter how incompatible the requirements were with my qualifications, they saw no reason not to advertise for assistant professors. So next, I became an applicant for the position of assistant professor in mechanical engineering. I received a letter of invitation asking me to face the selection board for the position of assistant professor, disregarding my application for the position of lecturer.

As I lathered and shaved that day, cutting my face in several places, I sang the poem "Ideal Boy" by Kusumkumari Das. I felt very happy because nobody could stop me now.

Most of the board members were junior to me and from outside my field. They asked me several long-winded questions but could not find any way to disqualify me. The university authorities were still trying to stop me from entering the university.

According to Dr. Shah, who attended the syndicate meetings, their hope was twofold. One, I would not humiliate myself by pursuing this low-ranking post. And two, they would be able to stop my appointment on the grounds that there would be a breakdown in discipline in the department if they hired me. There was much talk of my volatile nature. The syndicate met many times after my interview in September, but they kept any decision about my appointment pending till they could find a suitable obstacle. At the same time, the department authorities were worried that the syndicate might, in fact, hire me, so they were trying to close every avenue to my appointment. A number of syndicate members and senior teachers in the department told me that I should simply give up the idea of working at the engineering university.

When I was finally appointed, the university authorities forced me to sign a bond promising that I would never claim any benefit in return for my earlier service to the university and that I would be careful to maintain harmony in the department. At first, I thought my bond to the university would put an end to the animosity between my bosses and myself, but soon I realized I was wrong in this expectation.

On the first day of my appointment, I turned up at the registrar's office wearing a white shirt with a pen in my pocket. The pen had leaked into the shirt, streaking it blue. I handed my joining report to the registrar. As the appointment letter had been issued by the registrar, I assumed I should submit the joining report to him. But as soon as I entered the dusty office that had been assigned to me, a note was delivered to me from the head of the mechanical engineering department, reminding me that I should have reported to the department first and submitted my joining report to the head of the department instead of the registrar. In the letter, the head of the department demanded that I amend my mistake immediately. Otherwise, my appointment would be cancelled. I threw the note in the waste-paper basket and left the campus that day, with the joining report still in the registrar's office, but the next day I retrieved it and reported to the Head of Mechanical Engineering.

I had also thought that once I started teaching, I would be given the appropriate post suiting my teaching experience, putting an end to the bitterness of the hiring episode. Again, I was proved wrong. Several times, the head of the department called me into his office to remind me that the authorities would not consider my past service and experience. Only my fresh experience would be counted, and the onward ranks of associate professor and professor would be offered to me only after I had gathered the requisite experience from the date of my new appointment. When I heard that, I decided that I would spend the rest of my life as an assistant professor.

So, when a vacancy for the post of associate professor was advertised three years later, I did not apply. The registrar was my close friend. He knew of my decision and was trying to find a way around it. Without telling me, he recovered a copy of my earlier application for the post of assistant professor and submitted it for the new advertisement on my behalf.

When I was called for an interview for the post of associate professor, I went to the registrar and said, "How is this? I never applied for the position!"

The registrar said, "You had better keep silent about it if you consider me your friend."

I did not dare to defy the registrar's love for me. And so I became an associate professor.

Years later, when the authorities thought that I had gained sufficient fresh experience as an associate professor to become a professor, they advertised the post of professor for me. This time, I was adamant that I would never apply for the position. I would hold back simply as a matter of principle, to protest the university's narrow-minded politics. The post of professor was advertised repeatedly but I did not apply for it, defying my friends and well-wishers, including the new vice chancellor Dr. Shah. Ultimately, I was forced to become an applicant for professor by my family members. Their argument was that my refusal to become a professor was no longer my issue only. It was their issue also. They wanted to be the children and wife of a professor.

When the syndicate met to approve my appointment for the post of professor, an outside member present at the meeting asked why, with so much experience, I had been promoted to professor so late. Everybody was silent.

41. MAD MAN

Jhenidah, 1995

IT WOULD TAKE THE steamer an hour to cross the Padma River. At first, Beena and her father sat outside on the deck above the giant waterwheels with the spray of the river water on their faces. When the heat became overbearing, they moved inside the shaded cabin. Small ferry boys with earnest brown faces passed through the cabin with their wares hanging from their necks and arms, crying in loud voices, china badam, khobor kagoj! Nasir Uddin bought the small Jessore bananas called sobri kola, green coconuts full of fresh water, peanuts roasted in sand with salt and red pepper, and a copy of *Jaijaidin*.

Beena wore glasses like her father, but unlike him, who seemed entirely used to them, polishing them roughly with a towel or a shirt, peering at the world through the dirt stains and the fogged glass lenses, she never used hers. She had just finished her honors degree at Dhaka University, where she had discovered that beautiful women did not wear glasses.

"Your glasses are so dirty," Beena said in disgust, catching her reflection in her father's thick-rimmed spectacles. "It's a wonder you can see anything through them!" Realizing that she had just hurled all her insecurities about her own looks at him, she was immediately sorry and held out her hand to receive the peanuts in the small paper-cone bag that he had been badgering her to try.

Beena's three friends at university were bookworms like her. They ate up Shakespeare's sonnets and all his plays, and all the Romantic poetry in their courses, calling out lines from English poems during casual conversation and analyzing their every-day experiences through the eyes of the English literature they studied, but they missed out on everything else about being a university student. Only recently, during their master's degrees, had they started to apply lipstick, buy fashionable shalwar kameez sets at the new boutiques, shampoo the oil out of their hair, style them in layered cuts at the beauty salon, and venture out to TSC, the Dhaka University teacher student center teeming with campus life, to listen to Bengali poetry recitations.

They had already started planning how to go to America, the land of the TV series *MacGyver* and *Charlie's Angels*, and the music icons Bruce Springsteen (the Boss!), Jon Bon Jovi, and Michael Jackson. Beena's university friends thought that marriage was the ticket to America. The most desirable boys to marry, holding the highest prospect of going abroad, were the engineers next door.

One day, on the pretext of visiting Beena's schoolfriend Salma, who was a student at the engineering university, the four friends walked the length of Fuller Road to the neighboring campus. Standing under the shade of the krishnachura trees, framed by a canopy of flaming red flowers, they smoothed their hair and stared at the young men in open-neck shirts with rolled-up sleeves walking in the sun surveying the land with measuring tools. Suddenly, Beena realized that she didn't want to marry someone who would go to America to pursue their passions. She wanted to go to America to pursue her own dreams. Soon after that, Salma and Beena began to gather information on how to apply to graduate programs in America, collecting GRE and TOEFL books and faded, Xeroxed copies of practice exams from all the senior bhai and apa already on their way to the States.

Beena and her father were traveling to Beena's uncle Asif Chacha's home in Jhenidah, where all her father's siblings would gather to discuss how her grandfather's property should be divided. It was her grandfather's wish, or perhaps his children's wish, to sort out their inheritance before he died. Her father had invited her to come with him, describing the occasion to her as a happy family reunion. Only her mother had hinted darkly about the ugly business to be conducted.

"Why do you only say negative things about my father's family?" Beena had frowned. "You look down on them because they are villagers."

"Beena, I am only saying." Rahela had crossed her plump arms defensively. "Your father is not a practical man. He does not know how the world works. Just keep an eye on him."

Now Nasir Uddin turned to Beena and smiled. His attention was more sharply focused on her now that her brother Lenin had gone abroad to study in the States. "Your Dada will be very happy to see you," he said, speaking of Beena's grandfather.

Beena nodded awkwardly. The few times Dada had visited their flat on the university campus in Dhaka, he had slept on the narrow divan in the dining room where they ate and watched TV. During the day, he rolled up the bedclothes and the mosquito net and sat on the divan, his long back bowed, following their movements with his eyes, waiting silently for one of them to talk to him.

"*Esho, Ma*, come here," he called to Beena gently in a gravelly voice.

But Beena felt too shy to sit near him or speak to him.

"Ammu, Abbu, talk to your Dada," Nasir Uddin requested Beena and Lenin in a melodramatic, choked voice. "Look how he sits there all day, waiting to talk to you. Think about how far he comes to see you. I am heartbroken that you don't speak to your grandfather."

Nasir Uddin himself never spoke to his father. If he spoke

to him at all, it was to scold him in an angry voice, with a deep frown on his forehead. "*Uh-huh*, what are you doing? Don't touch the daal spoon with the hand that you are eating with. That hand is dirty." He acted as if he himself were a guest in his wife's city home, and to fit in the social circle of the city, he had to sever his ties with his relatives from his village home.

Now as Beena made the same journey as her grandfather, enduring the chaotic bus stop in Gabtoli, the hours in traffic jam on the Dhaka-Aricha Highway, and the long wait at the river ghat to board the ferry, she marveled that her grandfather, an old man, had undertaken this arduous journey at all. She imagined him now, disembarking the bus at the crowded terminal at Gabtoli, hailing a rickshaw to the engineering university campus. He would appear at their flat, bending his tall frame and the top of his round, bald head to step through the doorframe and smile at them with crooked teeth, his long, weather-beaten face glowing with happiness.

As soon as Dada sat down on the divan in the dining room, Rahela pulled a chair opposite the old man and started to scold him, accusing him of depriving the children of his first wife, reminding him how his second wife had mistreated the children of his first wife, and complaining about how the children of his second wife were trying to steal all their father's lands. Dada listened with his head bowed. After Rahela had gone on for a long time, he rose abruptly and said he was going downstairs. Who knows where he went? Perhaps he walked with long strides on the dusty city streets, taking in with wide eyes this strange city that was now his son's home. When her father returned home from the university, her grandfather would not be there.

When the steamer touched land in Khulna, hawkers climbed aboard and angled their way through the second-class and third-class cabins carrying chicken, fish, and mangoes on their heads, crying out the names of the items they were selling. Standing on deck, Beena watched the coolies balance the passengers' heavy suitcases on their heads, their necks throbbing under the weight of their loads. She was touched by the solidity of these men's burdens, who appeared to her to resemble the heroic men of Beowulf, sailors and warriors of another time. Oh, how she wished to belong to something so solidly! She was glad that she was going home to visit her father's family, who loved her but from whom she had been kept apart by her mother's snobbery. She had visited her father's village only a few times as a child. Each time, upon returning to Dhaka, Rahela had complained to her sisters about the long journey, the unclean water, and the poisonous snakes.

Asif Chacha's house was located at the center of Jhenidah town. Nasir Uddin had bought the land, supervised the construction of the house, and planted fruit trees along the boundary wall, but he could not live in the house because he had to work in the capital city. Asif Chacha greeted Beena and Nasir Uddin and led them inside to a room where her grandfather lay in bed. He'd had a high fever for the past three days. Nasir Uddin walked to the bed and sat down beside his father, hanging his head. His eyes were shiny behind his black glasses. Dada raised a thin, trembling hand to stroke his eldest son's cheek. Two sad faces gazed at each other. Beena felt glad that she had accompanied her father to witness such tenderness.

The old man's body looked shriveled and withered. He had been a strong, youthful man when Beena had last seen him, his age betrayed only by his white beard and a ring of white hair on his balding head. Beena had heard that in his youth he stood above six feet in his flat leather shoes. When he rode his cycle or walked on the mud paths with a straight back under the golden sun, people used to say he was a very handsome man. The emaciated figure lying on top of the bed, almost at one with the bedframe, still carried a nose that was high and straight. The eyes blazed fiercely, and the forehead was broad and strong. Seeing her handsome Dada, Beena was reminded again of the beauty of her father's side of the family.

"Beena, your Chachi has been waiting for you," Asif Chacha said. "She has been so excited that you are coming. Go look what things she has cooked for you!"

Asif Chacha shepherded Beena to the kitchen, which was open to the outside air. Her aunt perched on a low wooden stool, kneeling above a clay stove frying sweet pitha. Seeing Beena, Chachi rose to her feet and darted forward, hanging her arms around Beena's neck and crying loudly.

"*Ma*, you've grown so much." Chachi stood back and ran her eyes over Beena's dusty figure. "Ah, how long I haven't seen you, *Shona*!" With each speech, she dropped a new endearment.

Beena smiled and pulled a low wooden stool to sit down beside her aunt near the fire, tasting a pitha that Chachi handed to her from the tip of a metal ladle. Soon, her father's "own" sisters Kodom Phupu and Rajani Phupu arrived. While Rajani Phupu had a narrow, sunburnt face with a lean body, Kodom Phupu's face was pale and light, untouched by the sun. They both wore light cotton saris pulled loosely around their bodies, exuding the odor of talcum powder mixed with cooking spices. Her aunts took her face in both hands and kissed her on her cheeks, splashing them with tears. Then they embraced her hard to their chests. Pressed thus against their bodies, Beena felt the years of their hard lives filled with sorrows and disappointments.

Rajani Phupu sighed, running her hands over Beena's shoulders and back, recounting the tragic family history, the death of Beena's grandmother Dadi, and how the family was torn apart after that. "*O, Ma*. After our mother died, your father had to go far to earn money to support the family. Without a mother, he became isolated from his family."

Beena was overcome with emotion. As her aunts cried, her eyes moistened.

"*O, Shona*, you look just like your grandmother." Kodom Phupu held Beena's face in both hands.

Beena grinned. Tears of embarrassment sprang from her eyes. Her two aunts began to tell her all the latest ploys of their half-brothers and half-sisters, their *shoth bhai bon*. It was the husbands of the two half-sisters who were the most dangerous, they said. Both of these men had been seizing their father's lands, forging his signature to show fake sales.

"Beena, you will see with your own eyes, when they arrive. They will come here and fight about land even as our father is dying," Kodom Phupu said.

Later in the afternoon, after they had eaten a lunch of oily khichuri and goat curry with various fried vegetables, Nasir Uddin's half brothers and sisters began to arrive with their families. The air inside the house became tense and electric. The two younger aunts Dina Phupu and Lina Phupu entered the house cheerfully, wearing colorful silk saris. They stormed into the bedroom, where Beena had been resting with Rajani Phupu, Kadam Phupu, and Chachi, lying on a high bed with long pillows stuffed under their bellies, and tore Beena away from her "own" aunts to the open air outside. Standing under the sun, they peered at her face.

"How simple the girl is," said Dina Phupu in a caressing voice. "Her clothes are so plain, even though she is from the city."

Dina Phupu was a schoolteacher, slender and slight, with a thick braid that reached her hips. Crying and dabbing her eyes with the edge of her sari, she told Beena the story of her mother's recent death. Lina Phupu was shorter, rounder, and fairer than her sister. As her sister spoke, Lina Phupu sobbed loudly, rubbing Beena's hands together. Beena tried to console her, clutching her fingers tightly.

"*O, Shona*, nobody loves his family like your father does. But look how Kodom Apa and Rajani Apa and Asif Bhai are fighting like this over land as our father is dying," Lina Phupu said.

Suddenly, Beena felt short of air. Saying that she was going to fetch a glass of water, she pulled her arm free and fled inside the house. After wandering from room to room, she found the room in which her grandfather lay. Nasir Uddin still sat on the bed beside Dada. The room had filled with the menfolk of the relatives who had come to see her grandfather. More chairs and stools had been brought in, but many more people were standing around Dada's bed. Beena slipped in the back, relieved to have found her father.

Someone pulled Nasir Uddin to one side and spoke to him rapidly in a hushed voice. Beena moved closer to listen. The man was telling her father how Asif Chacha and Kodom Phupu's sons had behaved badly with him about the land he was managing, how they were always insinuating that he was going to steal the land, completely baseless lies! Beena realized that this was her father's half-brother, Haroon Chacha. He looked exactly like Nasir Uddin and Asif Chacha, with sunken eyes in a narrow, sullen face.

"Do you deny that you always meant to steal my father's lands?" Asif Chacha bore down on Haroon Chacha with his hands at his waist. "Don't tell stories, or I can too."

Nasir Uddin tried to calm both parties, saying to Asif Chacha, "Uh-huh."

But they paid him no heed. They began to shout at each other, appealing to Nasir Uddin. Nasir Uddin listened to them with his head bowed, cleaning his glasses with a finger. The dispute mounted until the room became divided into two parties shouting at one another, with fists raised in the air. Beena's grandfather was stretched out on the bedsheet, lying almost motionless. Once, he opened his eyes and made a long, moaning sound, as if to protest. Beena thought that he must be in great pain hearing all the fighting and shouting voices around him. Now her legs began to shake. It dawned on her that everyone else, other than her father, knew exactly why they had gathered. This was no reunion. Even Beena's mother, back in Dhaka, could guess everyone's intention, but her father was blind. Even now, he tried to bring his siblings together.

"Uhh! Can't we all live together in peace?" Nasir Uddin cried in an angry stutter. He flapped his arms in the air, indicating all the people in the room. His voice became almost hopeful and pleading. "At least, for the sake of this old man, let us all get along."

At first, her father sounded sensible to Beena's ears, and she took pleasure in his words, but when no one would listen to him, his voice began to mount. He began to shout, making incomprehensible sounds. Beena could not stand it any longer. She left the room.

Several of her cousins had accompanied their parents to the house in Jhenidah. Girls and boys of all ages, dressed in printed frocks and shirts, swung from the fruit trees or played football on the grass. Beena stood under a coconut tree, watching their lively play. Presently, Chachi came out of the house with a plate of rice-flour ruti and spicy goat meat. Beena received the proffered plate and sat down on a low stool, tearing the hot ruti with her fingers. Indeed, the chaaler ruti aar khashir mangsho that came to them from Jessore every year during Eid had no parallel. After every Eid holiday, Asif Chacha arrived at their doorstep carrying the delicacies with him all the way from Jhenidah, along with rice from their agricultural fields, date molasses in various solid and molten forms, sugar cane, and sobri kola, the sweet, tiny bananas of Jessore. When Dada visited, he would bring various pitha, bhapa pitha, kola pitha, and chitoi pitha, made from ground rice, molasses, coconut, and milk.

As she ate Chachi's food now, Beena tried to pretend that she was somewhere else. As long as she remained outside, she could not hear the raised voices. The air was peaceful, with a light breeze stirring the leaves on the trees. She watched the sun sink below the horizon, its light leaving each leaf on each tree until the atmosphere became completely dark. Kodom Phupu, Rajani Phupu, and Chachi walked outside and sat down on wooden stools in a circle around Beena, discussing the preparation of the evening meal. Beena felt happy and quite partisan among her father's own siblings. She and her father were staying the night at a rest house in Jhenidah. She couldn't wait for the evening to end. Soon, they would be safely ensconced in their room and then, after a good night's sleep, they would fly back home to Dhaka.

Kodom Phupu asked Beena if she could oil her hair, which she said looked red and uncared for. Beena nodded. Kodom Phupu began to rub oil into her scalp and tug her hair into a braid when they were startled by a cry that parted the air. A figure came running out of the house, shouting maniacally, followed by a crowd.

"I want to die! I shall die today and show you all!"

Beena saw that the man was her father. Her eyes widened with fear. Nasir Uddin ran across the yard past Beena with unseeing eyes. In another moment, before she could react, he shot out of the gate onto the road. Several men ran after him.

Seeing Rajani Phupu's son Mukul entering through the gate, Beena ran up to him, crying frantically. "Mukul Bhai! Save my father!"

"What happened?" he asked. "I just arrived from my factory in Khulna."

"I don't know," Beena cried desperately. "I don't know what is happening!" For the first time, she was speaking intently with the cousin who was almost a stranger to her.

"Stay here," he said.

To her surprise, he walked off in the opposite direction from her father, leaving her standing alone on the road, at the tail end of a throng of running and shouting men. At the head of this line was her father, far in the distance, a dark point disappearing into the night.

In a few minutes, Mukul Bhai reappeared, sitting in the passenger seat of a jeep driven by a chauffeur. "Get in!" he shouted to her.

Beena climbed in the back and settled on the new leather seat. The jeep glided along the road at a low speed, following the dark figure running in the middle of the road between cycle rickshaws and private cars.

"Mama! It's Mukul. Climb in," Mukul Bhai rolled down his window and called to his uncle in a rich, soothing voice as the car crawled alongside Nasir Uddin.

"Stop, Abba!" Beena joined her voice to her cousin's. "Abba!"

Mukul Bhai instructed his driver to cut the engine. Beena jumped out of the car and started to run behind her father, shouting to him. When she came abreast of him, she saw that his eyes were unfocused. He was shouting nonsense and sweating profusely.

"Stop, Abba! Or I shall jump under a car myself!" she cried in a desperate voice.

As she said this, he fell to the road. Perhaps he had let himself fall when she had made him aware of her predicament. Mukul bhai and the chauffeur appeared on the road beside Beena and lifted her father, supporting him under his arms, and pushed him deftly into the backseat of Mukul Bhai's car. Beena climbed in beside her father. His eyes were bare, exposing sunken sockets. Suddenly, it dawned on her why she could see his naked eyes.

"He lost his glasses!" She jumped back out onto the road as the engine started. Looking frantically, she located the heavy, black, thick-rimmed spectacles, a dark spot on the road, but when she picked them up, she saw that the glass lenses had shattered. She climbed back inside with the frame in her hand.

Mukul Bhai was sitting upfront beside the driver. He turned around to face Nasir Uddin in the backseat. "Mama! Let's take you back to the rest house."

"No!" Nasir Uddin became agitated again. "I want to die today. Take me to Dari Binni. Take me to my village home. I want to see the end of this!"

Beena sat mutely as Mukul Bhai and her father negotiated. At last, they agreed that Mukul would drive them to the house of a relative who lived in Jhenidah, someone Beena did not know. By now, she was used to feeling lost. She understood that there were important people and events in her father's life about which she had no idea. Her father had always seemed unreachable to Beena, despite his obvious love for his family, as if there was some place inside him that was locked to them. Sometimes, he would sit in his room in his white undershirt, his brown arms rippling, sucking on a cigarette and blowing smoke into the air, crying out suddenly, "I have no one! I am all alone in the world." It seemed to her perfectly logical now that her father should appear to her as a stranger at times. What influence did all these people have on him?

She had a nervous sense that the danger had not passed. Her father was breathing heavily, and his eyes held a wild, vacant look. Touching his forehead, she cried out. "His body is hot!" Her own heart began to pump unnaturally, as she remembered that her mother had not wanted her father to come.

"Drive faster," Mukul Bhai instructed the driver.

After that, they drove silently for a long time. Eventually, they stopped at a brick house in a dark neighborhood crowded with trees. A middle-aged woman came to the door with the end of her sari pulled over her head. She gazed at them with widened eyes. When Mukul Bhai introduced the party, she stood back and let them in, switching on the lights in the drawing room and leaving them there with a hastily uttered excuse. Mukul Bhai told his driver to wait in the car in front of the house.

The brightly lit room was furnished with two bamboo-frame sofas. A low, round table was piled with Bengali magazines. A cheerful singer belted an old Bengali song on TV, gesturing with her fingers. On every finger, she wore a gemstone ring. In every frame of the video, the singer changed her sari. Beena began to feel better. She walked to the kitchen and filled a glass of water from the tap and brought it to her father, who sat blind without his glasses, blinking his eyes rapidly.

After they had waited some time, a man entered the room. Beena stared at the man who was supposed to be an important link in the night's story. By the looks of his dilated pupils and disheveled face, it was clear that he had already retired for the night and had been roused from his sleep. He was dressed in a short-sleeved, loose shirt and checked lungi of blue and white squares. His face was brown and lined, with bright eyes and dewy skin conveying good health and a well-lived life.

"Muazzem!" Nasir Uddin cried in an anguished voice.

"What news, Ketu?" Muazzem said. "I heard you were coming to Jhenidah. How is your father?"

Beena was used to the people in the city who spoke in smooth, urbane voices, but the people in Jhenidah spoke simply and mechanically, with a sweet melody to their accents.

"Abba is very sick. I want to take him with me to Dhaka. If he stays here, he will go mad," Nasir Uddin said.

"But how will you transport him there? He is very ill."

"Muazzem, I want to go to Dari Binni tonight," Nasir Uddin began again with renewed energy.

"Tonight? In the middle of the night?" Muazzem Chacha cried in a surprised voice. "Why, Ketu? What will you do there?"

At this question, Nasir Uddin's wildness subsided somewhat. He dropped his shoulders and relaxed his raised cheeks. The woman who had opened the door to them reentered the room with her head covered by the end of her cotton sari.

"How are you, *Miah Bhai*?" she asked.

"I am well. How are you, Bhabi?" Nasir Uddin spoke to the woman, evidently Muazzem Chacha's wife, in an almost lively voice.

"We are well." Bending low, she placed plates of hot chanachur and sweet pitha on top of the table.

Both her bright sari and the sight of food cheered Beena. She asked for another glass of water and a hand fan and received them promptly with thanks from a cheerful, young servant girl dressed in a printed pink frock. Standing in front of her father, Beena held the glass to his lips and forced him to drink from it while she fanned him.

Mukul Bhai explained to Muazzem Chacha what had transpired earlier in the evening. Although he had not been present, he had somehow gleaned the facts from others. "We met to discuss how my grandfather's property will be divided. All these people were surrounding Mama with their complaints against one another and fighting over land beside my grandfather's deathbed. Right, Beena? Finally, Mama broke down. He kept shouting, to just give my grandfather peace for one moment, to allow him to die in peace. Then, when no one would listen to him, he ran out."

"I will show them. I will show them all!" Nasir Uddin cried in a hoarse voice. "I will die tonight. Let me die. *Then* they will be happy." His body began to shake again. His eyes were white. "Fix a cart for me. I want to go to Dari Binni tonight. Take me to Dari Binni!" Nasir Uddin renewed his demand.

"What will you do in Dari Binni, Ketu?" Muazzem Chacha asked. "Hmm?"

The question seemed to stall the issue for the moment. Mukul Bhai picked up his cup and saucer and slurped his tea, clattering the two pieces of china together, and asked the young servant girl to carry a cup of tea to his driver, who was waiting in the jeep outside. Then he leapt to his feet, gesturing to Beena to meet him in a corner of the room, and consulted with her in whispers, standing against the wall.

"I could give him some medicine to sedate him. Then we can carry him to the hotel."

"No! There is no need!" Beena cried, her eyes flying open in fear.

"All right," he said. "As you wish."

Beena returned to the sofa with shaky limbs and sat down beside her father.

"Muazzem, this is my daughter Beena," Nasir Uddin said. "My only daughter and eldest child. Beena, this is my cousin Muazzem, the son of my father's sister. He was my best friend in childhood."

"Yes, that is true. We got up to some crazy mischiefs." Muazzem Chacha grinned.

The mood in the room changed slightly. Muazzem Chacha rose and passed around the quarter plates, piling each plate with chanachur and sweets. "When we were children, I visited Dari Binni regularly. We played all day with no care in the world. We played in the courtyard of that house in Dari Binni, chasing all the animals. We played in the orchard and in the river. There were days when we never got out of the water. But Ketu, it's not possible to go back to that time." Muazzem Chacha turned to Mukul. "The house is locked, isn't it? Who has the key?"

Mukul nodded and mumbled something about a caretaker who lived in another village.

Muazzem Chacha turned back to Nasir Uddin. "See? Even if you go back, there are no answers there. No way to return to the past."

"Why don't you wait till the morning, Mama?" Mukul Bhai suggested smoothly. "I will try to find out about the key in the meantime."

Muazzem Chacha called to his wife to make some lime juice for Nasir Uddin, with molasses and salt. Beena looked from one man to another. She was still living a pampered life. She had earned a scholarship to study environmental science in Australia, but her parents had stopped her from going. Had she gone abroad, she would have become an independent woman. Instead, she rode the university bus to Dhaka University, only a few kilometers from her home. If she was late coming home, her parents met her at the front door with anxious faces, asking a thousand questions. At home, she only had to eat the food prepared for her by the maids, who also washed and pressed her clothes and laid out her shoes for her in the morning. Now she felt truly like a child among adults, in the grips of a world she did not understand. Could these people help her father? She found it difficult to trust them, these men who were complete strangers to her.

"I just want to die," Nasir Uddin repeated in a weak voice.

Beena spun around to face him. "Abba, nothing will change if you die! No one will care."

The three men looked at her blankly. For a long moment, the silent room picked up the sound of the slowly rotating ceiling fan.

At last, her father nodded. "You're right, Ammu. The important thing is to be happy in life. I want you to remember that." He looked at her fiercely. "Pursue whatever you want. Whatever goal you have."

Now that she had his attention, she leaned forward and pressed her point. "Abba, let's go home."

Mukul seized the chance and sprang up from the sofa, setting the cup and saucer on the table. "Mama! Shall I drop you at the rest house? Rest there tonight, and I will pick you up and take you to the airport for your flight home tomorrow," he suggested smoothly.

42. A BOY WITH A DREAM

Nasir Uddin's Journals

BANGLADESH IS NOT AN ideal place for research. Research activities are not appreciated here. Moreover, necessary laboratory equipment and funds are not available, although the prospect is brighter now because of computers. We can now use our brains to solve science problems even if we are challenged in terms of funds and technology. I want to work on some engineering projects especially appropriate for Bangladesh. These are:

1. Permanent magnet motor-driven rickshaw. Here, the rickshaw will be driven by a motor run by battery. The battery is either charged by line-voltage or solar cells. Ordinary car battery can be used. Once the battery is charged, it can run the rickshaw for 4/5 days. If the roof of the rickshaw is covered by solar photovoltaic cells, the daily energy requirement for charging the battery can be met by the solar-cell roof. The rickshaw will be fitted with a brake energy saver. This gadget will store energy from braking and use it in re-starting. The energy will be stored inside mechanical springs.

Rickshaw pullers do not want to brake because they want to avoid restarting, which takes a lot of energy. If the rickshaw is fitted with a brake energy saver, then the driver will not hesitate to use the brake and would thus avoid traffic hazard. The rickshaw should also have a vibration energy saver. Because of rough roads in Bangladesh, the rickshaw vibrates up and down. The vibration gadget will constantly convert this up-and-down motion to forward motion.

We should remember that the rickshaw is an ideal transport for Bangladesh. It is low technology and easy to produce. The distances we move, most of the time, are only a few kilometers, well within the range of the rickshaw. It does not create pollution, it has small energy requirement, and it is best suited to our narrow roads. I also think that the relatively low speed of the rickshaw is the pace at which life should be lived.

2. A ride-up machine. People would use the machine to go up and down by pedaling, similar to the motion of riding a bicycle. The rider will sit on the machine and then will go up by pedaling. This machine could be used for reaching date trees for extraction of date-juice and in painting and construction of walls up to three stories high. When not in use, it will remain folded.

3. Floating city. In my thinking, water body is better than land body for human habitation. We may consider a rectangular metallic box floating in water as a floating city. Within the box, we have apartments, roads, shops, factories, and appropriate transports, everything we want. The main requirement for survival in the city is energy. Once we have this constant supply of energy, we can do anything we need to do. This energy will come from three sources:

    a.   Tides. Everywhere, water height goes up and down by about 8 feet at minimum due to tide. Thus, the floating city will also go up by a minimum of 8 feet. This potential energy of the city can be converted into electrical energy.

    b.   Waves. Everywhere, we have waves in the sea. We can

float an unlimited number of cylinders in the sea. Due to waves, these cylinders will go up and down. These up-and-down movements of the cylinders can be converted to continuous pull for rotating generator shafts and, hence, production of electricity.

c. Wind. In the sea, we get continuous steady winds. We can build windmills on the rooftop of our city to be run by the steady wind.

I spent several months standing over papers copied in triplicate, mailing documents back and forth to my friend Ali Hussein in Canada. While working on the project, I did not experience any hunger. I did not eat or sleep much. I had already published several papers on the improved rickshaw design. I had also built a model at the university workshop. Now, I had obtained a grant from the Government of Canada for research and development of the motorized rickshaw in Bangladesh. All that was needed was for the ERD, the branch of the government that approved projects, to accept the grant.

In the morning, as I shaved and cut myself, I sang my favorite rhyme, "The Ideal Boy" by Kusumkumari Das:

When will that boy be born on our land,
Who is not big in words, but in deed?
A smile on his lips, courage in his heart,
He has to make something of himself, that's his vow.

The three men and one lady at the ERD office laughed loudly. The fan rotated above their heads.

"An improved rickshaw!" they said to one another. Then they turned to me. "Professor, you are mad. The only way to improve the rickshaw is to get rid of it. It gets in the way. It causes traffic jam. This is the age of top-speed Pajero jeeps and jet planes! Are you so backward in technology at the engineering university? No wonder we are in such a pitiable state."

They fell over themselves laughing, but they offered me tea. When I assented, the ERD officials rang for the clerk and the clerk hollered to another boy who ran off to the kitchen. Presently, the clerk brought in tea and biscuits on a tray and set them down on the table, passing a cup to each of us. The lady official pointed out to me that my nails were black and long. I needed to clip them.

I thanked her and gulped down the sweet tea, which was very good. "But you see, more private buses and cars are not the solution to our transport needs. We don't need to follow other countries. We could have a different kind of transport system that is best suited to . . ."

Again, the ERD officials laughed loudly. Their merriment seemed sincere because tears streamed down their faces. The room was dusty, but the men were dressed in freshly laundered, crisp shirts and pressed trousers. The lady among them wore a blue silk sari. She pointed out to me that my pen had leaked into my shirt pocket and stained it. I thanked her for pointing this out.

"This is the age of development," said the ERD man sporting a French goatee. He had a smooth, cultured voice that matched his pale, smooth face. "We are a developing country. Our goal is to catch up to the West as quickly as possible. Isn't it so? Some days, I lie in bed and think when? When will we catch up to the West?"

"Right. Right you are." The ERD lady nodded her head solemnly.

"Listen, professor," said the ERD man with the long, white beard, "usually in this room we have foreigners from the World Bank and the UN, fools offering us millions of dollars for national projects. We are buying secondhand bridges and helicopters and airplanes, things we need in a hurry, so please, we have no time for this dreamy nonsense. Take your dreams elsewhere."

Then the lady came to the point. "The UN we just approved has provisions for a new computer lab for ERD. What will your project have to offer us?"

I frowned. My eyes burned with anger. I pushed back my chair and stood up. "I am speaking about our country and all you can think about is bribes!"

I took a rickshaw home and went to sleep, covering my face with my arm. Rahela woke me and gave me the news that I had won the national science award that year. I looked wildly at her.

"Yes," she said, smiling. "It is true."

Without saying anything, I turned on my side and faced the wall. I understood now that my projects would never come to anything. People would call me a dreamer in a land with more important things in consideration, million-dollar projects for some people to line their pockets. Really, I didn't understand the essence of life in this country and around the world, the thing that drove the world, the personal greed of the few and the powerful. I was just a dreamer and a fool. At least, I could go on dreaming under the cover of my sagging pillow.

One day, I rose from bed and found that I had won a gold medal for best teacher. As I climbed the steps to the podium to collect the medal, this award, of all awards, filled my eyes with tears. I felt very happy, for this reason: All my life, I had been fighting the university authorities. In the process, I had created a lot of enemies. People disliked that I got in the way of smooth trans- actions. But that day, I realized that being a fool, I had gathered a fool's following. All the time while I had been running after improved rickshaws and poultry farms in which the excrement of the poultry would nourish the fish pond, my dreams had seeped into a thousand minds.

In our land, dream is a dirty word. Everybody speaks of dreams. The father of the nation Sheikh Mujib dreamt of a golden Bengal, but after his death that dream is being materialized every day on the streets through the robbing of ordinary citizens. The donors discuss their dream policies in soft voices under soft lights, beau- tiful words flowing smoothly over their smooth tongues, while they lend money at high interest to the government to buy foreign goods from their own countries. The harsh reality is that the loan will have to be paid back some day in the future.

Meanwhile, in big buildings across the country, bigheaded people sit around donor tables and discuss how to achieve what the Western countries have achieved; how to do it quickly, how to leapfrog, and frog dance. They sit on heavy chairs, doing absolutely nothing, not shaking a tea leaf out of place, so that they can continue to stuff their own pockets. The tea and biscuits at these meetings are delicious, the kind that you dream about.

43. THE BELLY OF THE BEAST

Houston, May 2003

THE AROMA OF HIGH-CLASS Bengali food hit her nostrils—beef smeared with the tangy fruit satkora, a Sylheti delicacy, a milder Chicken korma swimming in a sweet sea of yogurt, molasses, and raisins, fried pomfrets, and three different kinds of vegetables, besides the customary fragrant polao. The kitchen shone in the warm electric light. The windows stood bright against the night sky.

"Roberto will love this," Beena said to Salma, peeking into the covered dishes.

"You naughty girl, you must have always been thinking about Roberto when you came to my parties. Why didn't you ever invite him?"

"Have you cooked Bengali food for your husband?" Shona asked.

"No. He likes to cook himself."

The women giggled. They looked lovely. Salma wore a peacock blue sari with a fat blue border. Everyone wore blue saris, to contrast with Beena's red bridal sari. Beena's face had been painted by Salma, and her hair had been piled by Shona into a tight bun at the back of her head. Mehjabeen had lent her transparent pink glass bangles to scatter among the fat gold bracelets on her arms. Now she stood inside the circle of the Bengali women, surrounded by them.

"You look beautiful, Beena," Jahan Apa said. "You should always wear saris. They suit you."

"The imam will come soon to conduct the marriage ceremony. Should we serve the food before he arrives?" Salma asked Shona. "Then he can start the ceremony immediately?"

"Wouldn't it be more respectful to complete the ceremony first, Salma Apu? What time does he arrive?"

"Beena, will your groom change his name?" Salma asked.

"Yes. He doesn't mind," Beena said.

"Have you chosen a name?" Shona asked.

"No! I thought any name would do?"

"Silly girl, you need to choose carefully. You don't want to give him a name like Majnu, which means crazy." Salma laughed. "Wait! I have a name book."

"Salma! Are you pregnant?" Jahan Apa shrieked.

Beena laughed along with everyone else. She was part of the group now. Shona placed a hand on Beena's shoulder, tears in her eyes from the joke. Beena wondered if Roberto was comfortable in the living room with the other men. She worried that he would be left out if they were speaking in Bengali. What if the party bored him? She would never be able to attend Salma's parties then.

Salma made a decision, checking the kitchen clock. "It's eight-thirty already. We need to serve the food. I'll tell the men to take the food first."

"Salma, we should also complete our Isha prayers first, before the ceremony," Jahan Apa said. "Do you have prayer mats?"

"I'll bring them." Salma headed to her bedroom to fetch bedsheets and jainamaz.

"I have to go to the bathroom," Beena said, excusing herself.

When she emerged from the bathroom, Khaled stood at the door, his tall frame angled, leaning his head against the door jamb.

"Sorry!"

"No, I'm sorry! I had no idea someone was inside," he said in an embarrassed voice, straightening. "How are you?" He was dressed in an electric blue silk punjabi for the occasion.

"I am well." Beena nodded shyly.

"Your husband is very nice. I was talking to him."

"Is he okay?" Beena asked.

"He's fine. He's really laid back. We explained some Bengali jokes to him already."

"Thanks." Beena turned to go.

"By the way, how is your father?"

"His arm is healing, and the doctors say it should be fine. They put screws in. He is getting therapy to use the arm. But he's scared . . ."

"Yes, that would affect him badly. He is so independent."

Beena realized that Khaled knew her father. He knew her home, the red brick building on the university campus. He had walked the same tree-lined path under the crow-covered trees, from the red staff quarters past the student hostels to the corner of Palashi Road. They found themselves talking about those crows.

"Wasn't there a small shop by the residential hall at the end of that path?" Beena told Khaled how her father secretly bought cigarettes from the tin-shed store for residential students. She had caught him there once. He had quickly dropped the cigarettes and pretended to buy the dwarf bananas hanging from a rope at the front of the store.

"Did you ever eat from the vendors in Palashi Bazar? My friends and I walked to Palashi Bazar at night to eat boiled eggs, cut in half by a thread, sprinkled with salt and black pepper crushed together, and served on a square piece of old newspaper!"

Beena grimaced. "That doesn't sound very appetizing."

"They were delicious!" Khaled insisted. "I still salivate sometimes thinking about those eggs. He licked his tongue in a comic gesture to drive home his words. "You look beautiful, Mrs. Roberto."

"I'll see you later." Beena nodded quickly, preparing to go.

Roberto had not seen her yet. Roberto would think her lovely too, but in a foreign way. He would probably just say "wow!" He would not know how to respond to her kohl-lined eyes, the golden tiara, or the spiralling red dot surrounded by white dots on her forehead. He might even ask, "What is that?"

"I bought you a book of poems when I was at the Bangladeshi grocery store," Khaled said, holding out a thin hardcover book.

It was only then that she realized that he had come looking for her.

"They are poems by Jibonananda Das. You have read his poems? At least, 'Lashkata Ghor?' I wasn't sure since you studied English Literature." He recited the lines.

"You know the lines by heart!" she cried in an excited voice.

"Yes!" He grinned, standing with bent elbows, hands at his waist, pleased with himself. "Don't you wonder about that? A man who has everything, every happiness. Then he kills himself."

"I think that's what I am like," Beena said. "I always have the urge to destroy anything too serene. I am suspicious of happiness!" As soon as she had uttered those words, she expected him to think her strange again.

But Khaled was laughing. "Yes, I realized that about you!" he said. "That's wonderful about you."

"Actually, my favourite poet is Kazi Nazrul Islam. I had a brother once who was named after him. He died young."

"Oh, I am sorry to hear that." His voice fell.

"No, don't be, it was a long time ago." As she said this, she felt that Lenin's and her mother's deaths were also a long time in the past. "Think about how revolutionary Kazi Nazrul Islam's poetry was. *Chol Chol Chol. Urdho gogone baaje madol. Nimne utola dhoroni-tol. Orun prater torun dol.* March, march, march! High in the sky the drum beats. Below, the ground is restless. The youth of a new dawn."

Khaled made a chortling sound in his throat. "You remind me of Kazi Nazrul Islam a bit. Wild and restless."

"Really?"

"Khaled, won't you eat?" Ronny had come looking for Khaled. He smiled when he saw Beena. "Beena, don't worry about your husband. He is wolfing down all the Bengali food! We are getting along splendidly."

The stars were out in profusion in the dark Katy sky, away from the city lights, a bouquet scattered by hand, as Roberto, newly renamed Selimul Huque, walked out of the house with his arm around the shoulders of his new bride.

"Don't those stars make you think how vast the universe is? And how inconsequential we are?" he said, as he showed Beena the constellations, the Ursa Major, Ursa Minor, and Orion, and the bright star Sirius.

"Spoken like a scientist," Beena mocked him in an amused voice.

Behind them, her friends stood in glittering saris and punjabis outside Salma's house, waving. An orange-bearded imam had married them. Sitting in separate rooms, they had repeated their vows after him. Then they had each signed the contract. After that, when they were reunited in the family living room, among all the guests, it had been all fun and teasing. Khaled had appeared with his SLR camera, clicking away, blinding them with his flash. Salma had arranged for fresh flower garlands of white and red roses, like the roses of Beena's childhood, like the roses of Iraq. Roberto and Beena had exchanged the garlands. Multiple hands had pushed sweets and a glass of milk between Roberto and Beena amidst shouts of laughter. Then someone had brought out a mirror. The Bengalis had instructed Roberto in English to look at Beena in the mirror.

"No, not directly, in the mirror. Remember, you have never seen your bride before, so take your first look through the glass and tell us what you see."

"Wow!" Roberto had said.

"Your friends are nice," Roberto said now, as he drove around the cul-de-sac. "Do you know what my name means?"

"I know it doesn't mean mad," Beena said. "They made sure of that!"

No, Roberto was not mad. She had separated herself from that destiny. Letting out a deep sigh, she settled back in the passenger seat. Her father would arrive in a week. Roberto had promised that they would all live happily together.

In the distance, she thought she saw a dark silhouette on the road, a young boy. "Be careful! There's a child!"

"No, there's nothing," Roberto said. "Believe me, I have very good eyesight."

She had to admit she needed glasses. Still, she couldn't shake the notion there was a figure standing up ahead. She kept staring with narrowed eyes as the car sped past the dark spot.

"A trick of the light perhaps," she said. Or perhaps a jackal. A ghost. A djinn.

44. REUNION

ONE DAY AFTER RETURNING from their honeymoon on Lake Fausse Pointe in Louisiana, Beena and Roberto drove to Continental airport to receive her father.

"Look, that's the H- campus! Khaled's company." Beena pointed out the window, then blushed, lest Roberto think that Khaled meant something more to her.

Roberto twisted his head to look. A large-sized compound jutted out on the freeway, guarded by a boundary wall the shade of desert sand. A large, squat brick-façade building soared above the wall, trailed by several smaller buildings. Peering inside the open arched gate, Beena could see pretty, sunny gardens, a fountain, and tree-shaded walkways, reminding her of the lines from Coleridge's poem about Kubla Khan's pleasure-dome.

"It looks intimidating," she said with a backward glance. Then her face changed. "I left my cellphone at home! How will my father communicate with me?"

"It's okay. He will come out of arrivals, and we will see him," Roberto said.

They waited at the arrivals area where her father would exit after passing through immigration and customs. Beena scanned the crowd looking for him.

"He's not going to eat properly on the flight. What if his sugar level falls?" she said to Roberto in a panic. "What if he wanders off somewhere and gets lost? He always gets things wrong."

"Beena, your father has traveled halfway around the world on his own. He can take care of himself," Roberto said.

She swung around and looked at Roberto then. Somewhere along the way, he had acquired form and become a solid presence beside her. If she turned away from him to look for her father, he would not vanish into thin air.

The arrivals area cleared. Only a few people still shuffled out. Families reunited with hugs and kisses. Beena turned away in disappointment. Roberto took her arm and led her to a back seat to wait.

"What time is it?"

Roberto consulted his watch. "It's two hours since the plane landed."

"I feel so angry with him!" she cried, gripping Roberto's arm. "All his life, he gave up everything for others. He made us all give up everything." She had been seized with sudden new feelings as soon as they had arrived at the airport.

Roberto nodded. "Let's take a walk and look around."

They stepped out of the area and immediately found Nasir Uddin standing at the lost baggage claim desk, dressed in a long grey woolen coat that hung loosely from his shrunken shoulders to his knees. He was speaking to the attendant, his eyes intense and shining.

"What is it? What are you doing here?" Beena asked, going up to him. "Where were you all this time?"

"Hello, Ammu," he said, turning and embracing her. His face was a skull, hollow and dark, but it broke into a smile now as he shook Roberto's hand. "Hello, Roberto."

"Hello. It's nice to meet you."

"How long have you been out?" Beena demanded in a raised voice.

"Oh. An hour. I tried to call on your cell phone using their phone." He indicated the phone on the desk.

"I left my phone at home! My God, you've been waiting for an hour!" Beena was near tears. She had failed even to receive her father on time at the airport. How could she take care of this man who had always been beyond her reach? "Did you take the wheelchair service?" she asked angrily.

"No, Ammu. What would I do with a wheelchair? Why depend on other people? I had fun walking. Roberto, I am very pleased to meet you. I feel very happy for the two of you. Wish you all the best."

"Thank you," Roberto said. "Is there a problem here?"

"One of my suitcases got lost. I am trying to file a report."

The sky was dark by the time they reached home. The air was saturated and too full to bear. Nasir Uddin had trouble getting out of the car. Roberto had to guide him, cradling his head so it wouldn't hit the roof of the car. His body was stiff, as if it did not know how to bend. Beena was shocked by his decline. In the guest room that was now her father's, the three of them opened the carry-on suitcase that had come through and tried to assess what was in the other suitcase that was lost.

"All my medicine," Nasir Uddin said, surveying the contents of the flat-open suitcase. He pulled out the small amount of medication he was carrying in his hand baggage, a loose assortment of boxes containing eye medicine for his glaucoma, ointments for the festering wounds on his feet, multicolored vitamins, Comprid for diabetes, inhalers for asthma, Oroxine for thyroid hormone, Neoceptin as antacid, milk of magnesia for constipation, and Flagyl for the days he had diarrhea.

Beena found him a towel and showed him the bathroom. Before leaving the house, she had sautéed salmon and tomatoes. Now she set these on the table. They had turned the A/C off before leaving, and the space had heated up. The whole apartment throbbed in her head as she waited for her father to step out of the bathroom. Suddenly, she felt they had too much heaviness to sort. Her mother and brother were gone. They could never be a whole family again.

She had sent Roberto downstairs to the garden below their apartment building to fetch fresh coriander. He returned now, stomping his boots.

"What is it?" Beena asked, seeing the shine in his eyes.

"I found a snake!"

"Is it poisonous?" she shrieked.

Roberto looked at her with a puzzled expression. "No, I don't think so. I threw it over with a stick deeper into the bushes so it could go away. It wasn't trying to do any harm."

Beena kept shaking her head, saying how dangerous snakes were, how they had killed her grandmother, how all Bengalis, including her friends in the suburbs who had built houses on cleared land, were afraid of finding snakes in their yards. Roberto laughed, saying snakes never meant any harm to people. The best thing to do, even if one found a poisonous snake, was to leave it be.

"All right, then. I'll trust you on that," she said in a light-hearted tone, then her voice darkened again. "Roberto, what will I do with this anger? I have so many questions to ask my father. I am filled with all these emotions!"

"He made decisions in his life, and he paid his dues. It's his life," Roberto said.

"My mother would have said that his need to keep going back to serve his country was unhealthy. He was always daydreaming about moving back to his village. She said it was regression, sliding backwards in life, that people behave that way when they are not emotionally mature and healthy. She called it neurotic behavior, this tendency to keep thinking about the past or to keep dreaming about the future, to expect to change the world. My mother used to say that my father was trying to fill some deep hole in his life."

"A hole!" Roberto said. "Your mother was the psychologist! Don't be so serious, or you'll spoil the visit."

There was a sharp noise from the bathroom of a heavy object falling.

"Abba! Are you Okay?"

Nasir Uddin emerged with a wet towel slung across his shoulder.

"Did you fall in the bathroom?"

"No."

"But you did!" Beena wailed.

Blood gushed from his face. Beena and Roberto rushed to pull out bandages and alcohol from the bathroom cabinet. They hovered over him as he sat on a kitchen chair, wiping the surface blood to search for the source of the wound. The blood took a long time to stave off. They gathered from him that he had slipped on the floor rug and fallen, striking his chin on the corner of the sink counter. For the first time, Beena had a sense of the danger of her father's visit. An accident like this was possible at any moment. She bit her lip and frowned, worrying that she and her father would be a burden to Roberto.

After her father was bandaged and Roberto had cleaned up the bathroom, the two of them stood in the living room, waiting for her instructions. Beena crossed her arms to calm herself. Face to face with her father at last, she found herself on the verge of exploding. It was her responsibility to protect him, yet she felt in no way capable of doing so.

"Let's eat."

Nasir Uddin and Roberto sat down at the dining table. Beena carried the bowl of daal to the table, followed by spinach cooked in a garlic and onion paste (she had taken the time to prepare the paste in a blender), tilapia fish fried in turmeric and salt, and steamed white rice. The salmon was the only non-Bengali dish. She had bought spices at the Bengali grocery store in Bellaire to cook a proper meal for her father.

"Okay!" She exhaled audibly. "Let's eat."

Roberto started with a clatter of forks. He offered the rice stiffly to Nasir Uddin but did not make any conversation. Everyone was awkward. She felt that everything had been spoiled by a deep well of sadness that rose from within her. She had no idea where it had come from or how to get rid of it. Before they could eat, Nasir Uddin broke down in tears. Beena sprang from her chair and embraced him around his neck. He clutched her wrists tightly and his stubbled cheeks grazed her face, covering her with sweaty tears.

"I have nobody in the world!" he cried. His eyes were small and frightened, and his lips trembled.

"But Abba, you've been saying that all your life, even with all of us around you," Beena said.

"What will I do all alone?"

"You can live with me. With us!"

Roberto nodded eagerly. Nasir Uddin shook his head.

"What? What do you mean no?"

Again, he shook his head.

"But…" Beena exploded. "You can barely stand." Letting go of him, she gestured angrily with her hands. "You can barely get out of the car. Who will take care of you?"

All her tenderness turned inexplicably to anger as she realized that her father was still going to be stubborn, that he still hadn't agreed to live with her. The questions that had receded in Louisiana returned with full force. Had it been a mistake to marry Roberto? Should she have returned home to take care of her father? She started to cry also.

When Nasir Uddin retired to his room for the night, a light still shone under his door. Roberto had shown him how to access the Bangladeshi newspapers online on Roberto's old laptop computer so that he could read the news headlines. The light made her smile as she sat on the living room couch, feeling calm and happy at last, taking pleasure in his pleasure from across a closed door.

In the middle of the night, she woke up and lay stiffly on the mattress, thinking of the day. Roberto snored gently beside her, his chest falling and rising softly. Beena had known Roberto five years, but she had not known that he snored. She wanted to speak to him as they used to when they had been friends. Now that he was so close, with their breaths on each other as they slept, he seemed inaccessible to her. With a slight whimper, Roberto turned on his side and faced away. Beena decided that she could not fall back asleep. It was as if she too had jetlag like her father. Dropping her feet on the carpet, she plodded to Roberto's desk and pulled out a yellow writing pad and a blue ballpoint pen from his desk drawer. Sitting down on his chair, she began to write in the dark.

I wonder what propelled my father through life to bring us all to such a fate. Was it worth the price? What vision did he pursue? What was it that drove him? What was it?

Then it came to her. It was lust. For life.

45. PROJECTS

Houston, July 2003

THE FIRST THING NASIR Uddin did after he arrived in Houston was to say to Roberto, "Roberto, can you take me to a dollar store? I have some urgent business there."

They drove around in Roberto's car until they found a 99 Cents store tucked away in a strip mall. Nasir Uddin bought needles and thread, pliers, a hammer, nails, screw drivers in different sizes, and sandpaper.

"Ah, thank you. Now I feel happy," he said. "I feel at home now."

In the one month he spent at his daughter's home, Nasir Uddin developed a routine for himself. In the morning, he walked in the sun to the Barnes & Noble bookstore a mile from his daughter's home and sat there the entire day, sipping tea from a paper cup and writing in a composition book. While staying with his daughter, he had suddenly found a new burst of energy. He was working on a mechanical engineering textbook, as he had never felt satisfied with the books he'd had to use as a teacher. The only problem was that he had broken his right arm, which was his dominant arm, and now his writing was lopsided and labored. He could only manage weak, illegible scribbles. The words ran together. His handwriting was small and cramped, slanting down the page. He had been losing function in his hands for a long time, but now the decline was drastic.

Sometimes, Roberto picked him up on his way home from the university. Back in the apartment, Nasir Uddin made tea by heating up a mug of tap water in the microwave oven with a teabag already inside the mug, humming a tune as he inserted the mug in the oven. He drank black tea without any sugar or sugar substitute. When the tea was done, he carried the mug (he had chosen a fat yellow mug with thick walls) like a prize in both hands to the dining table. Then he sat on a straight-back dining chair and sipped. His small, black eyes crinkled with pleasure. At first, he used to also light a Boss cigarette, a local brand from his country, but Beena had made that impossible by informing him that smoking was not allowed in the apartment.

"Didn't you have a stroke because of your smoking?" she had asked, looking balefully at the culprit stick in his hand. "Do you still think it is worthwhile to smoke?"

He had smiled helplessly at her, making small, chuckling sounds of defeat. Then he had replied meekly, to answer her question, "Yes. Still, I feel it is worth it."

One day, finding Beena in the kitchen making tea, he approached her. "Beena, I was thinking. When you move to Alabama with Roberto, you should look for a job for yourself, preferably in teaching. You should not give up your career."

Beena frowned, her hand paused on the cabinet door. "I just earned a PhD. I'm allowed to rest and make my own plans. I want to stay home and look after you."

"Yes, of course, you must do whatever you wish. Still, I'm just saying. Your career is important."

At dinner, which was pasta, Nasir Uddin twirled his fork helplessly, his fingers trembling, while Beena pestered him to sell his property in Bangladesh and move to Houston.

"I'll think about it," he said. "Too much change in life is not good for happiness. You'll notice, Ammu, whenever people's circumstances change too quickly, they are not able to adjust, and they feel unhappy."

"I don't mean right away," Beena said. "Let's say it will take five years. But you have to plan. You have to sell your property now. It'll take me five years to get my citizenship. Right, Roberto?"

Roberto nodded.

"My dream is to open a university in Bangladesh, from nursery to university level," Nasir Uddin said. "Don't you think that is a grand idea? I want the two of you to come and help me in my project." His eyes shone brightly, and his cheeks became rosy with pleasure.

"What has that got to do with anything?" Beena exploded. "You know we can't go to Bangladesh. Let's speak practically. You have to come here to live with us so we can take care of you. It's obvious you're in bad health!"

"I've thought of something." Nasir Uddin laughed sheepishly, his eyes becoming smaller. "Perhaps I can start a project in the flat. If I turn the flat into a project office space, then my students can live there and take care of me."

"What? Why would they do that? You think your students are dearer to you than your own daughter? Why won't you come live with me?"

Nasir Uddin, who had seemed to be speaking without rationale up to now, paused and pressed his lips together. "I could not burden you and Roberto," he said.

"What? It's not a burden to us. Roberto, is it a burden to us?"

"No." Roberto shook his head.

"If I return to my village and start a project there, I shall be the happiest man on Earth. I could build a proper building for the primary school. When a rickshaw-puller eats a plate of rice and goes to sleep, he feels that he is in heaven. Everyone on this Earth will have to die someday, but the greatest wish of a person before his death is to do the things his heart desires. I believe that for me also, following my dreams will give me the greatest happiness."

"What does that even mean?" Beena cried, bursting into tears.
"Don't cry."

"If you go back to Bangladesh, you will die. Who will take care of you?"

"Ammu, you can't be rigid about anything. You're bound to change your beliefs," Nasir Uddin said. "When I fled to Iraq from Bangladesh for money, my friend Shah said to me, it's the same problems and the same happiness everywhere. There isn't absolute security anywhere."

46. OCCLUDED VISION

Houston, July 2003

DESPITE HIS LOFTY SPEECHES, it was obvious to Beena that her father's health was failing. When he put bread in the toaster, he burnt it. Roberto's kitchen filled with smoke. Twice, Roberto steadied him when he was walking in the living room and was about to topple over. When he insisted on going for a walk for his exercise, in the heat of Houston, obviously intending to light up a furtive cigarette, Beena hurried to accompany him so that he would not fall or get lost. She worried about his gait. His body listed forward when he stepped. To Beena, he looked like he might tumble onto the busy road and into oncoming traffic at any moment.

One day, as they were walking together, Nasir Uddin at a fast pace and Beena following behind, he fell to the sidewalk. She couldn't tell how it had happened. Had his steps locked? Had he tripped? It looked more like he had dropped to the ground from weakness. He lay on his side, moaning, unable to heed her shrieked commands to rise as she pulled at his arms. His face was drained of blood and his eyes looked white and vacant, as if he was losing consciousness. Beena's heart thudded. A passing, youthful-looking

Asian man in medical scrubs helped Nasir Uddin halfway to a sitting position on the sidewalk.

"Why did he fall?" Beena asked the man in desperation.

"It could be many things, low blood sugar, imbalance," he answered in a reassuring tone. He had a smooth, young face. He introduced himself as a doctor in his second year of residency.

"What about cigarettes? Could it be smoking?"

"I would recommend getting him checked out by a doctor." The resident doctor held onto Nasir Uddin, bending over him and raising him by the shoulders, with his arms behind his back, till Nasir Uddin's eyes flew open. "Are you all right, sir? Let's pull you to your feet. Whenever you are ready."

Beena stared ferociously at her father and the man, her heart fluttering in panic. Her father did not have health insurance. She had not thought of these things before she had asked him to come.

Later that night, as they lay side by side on their backs in the darkness of their bedroom, Beena said to Roberto, "I'm really sorry. Are we a burden to you?"

"What? No."

"Was this a mistake? Our getting married? This is too much for you. You couldn't have known marrying me would mean all this."

"What? Was it a mistake for you?"

"No. That's not what I'm saying." Beena started to cry. She didn't know what she was saying. Perhaps it would have been better to leave America, to go home and be with her father.

"Beena, you keep arguing with your father to stay in America, and I think sometimes you are hurtful. Let him decide what he wants to do," Roberto said in the dark.

"Okay," she said in a small voice, turning away.

She thought perhaps Roberto meant that he didn't want her father to stay. It was impossible to know his true feelings. His face was covered by the darkness.

47. THE MECHANICAL ENGINEER

Houston, July 2003

THE TROUBLE STARTED ONE day with Roberto's car. It was ten years old, a used Toyota Corona he had bought in his first year in Houston, and it had not given him much trouble up to now. Still, as he revved the engine that day, it turned over, but it would not start. Roberto tried to start the car several times and then went back upstairs.

"I have to call AAA. The car's not working," he said.

At this, Nasir Uddin, who had been reading the newspaper on Roberto's old laptop sitting upright at the dining table (most of his day was spent reading the paper, watching the news, working on his book, and exercising for his diabetes), looked up sharply and said, "What's the matter? I can help." His eyes were intense behind the thick glass lenses of his spectacles.

"Ah. You're a mechanical engineer," Roberto said. "Sure."

Nasir Uddin rose shakily from the sofa to go to the bathroom. He always needed to use the bathroom before he went anywhere because of his diabetes. In a few minutes, he came back to the living room looking very upset. The bathroom door was locked! He had locked it himself the last time he had gone.

"Do you have a key?" he asked Beena.

"No, we don't have a key," Beena said. "My God, Abba, what have you done? Why do you always create a mess?" She looked at Roberto with apologetic eyes.

Nasir Uddin kept asking for some wire. When Beena wouldn't help him and Roberto looked around helplessly, he fished out a wire hanger from the closet in his room and started fiddling with the lock. He had rolled up his shirt sleeve, revealing a pink line running from the elbow down the right upper arm, the one that had fractured, where a tube had been inserted to drain the fluids after his surgery.

"You'll break the door," Beena screamed. She stood behind Nasir Uddin, watching him.

Nasir Uddin continued to turn the wire in the lock, taking it out sometimes to bend it into a new shape.

"No need to scream," Roberto said. "It's okay. I'll just call the mechanic."

"I got it. I got it," Nasir Uddin said, grinning as he pushed the door open.

Roberto told Nasir Uddin that he really had to leave for campus, so he would call AAA to take the car to a garage. Nasir Uddin looked at Roberto with sad eyes, small and watery behind his dusty glasses, but there was nothing to be done.

When Roberto returned home that day, Nasir Uddin kept asking about his car. Roberto told him that he had phoned the garage and the people at the garage had said that they had fixed it—it had been the fuel pump. Nasir Uddin kept asking Roberto for more details, until Beena realized that Nasir Uddin was very upset with himself. It struck Beena that her father knew about cars inside out, and yet he could be of absolutely no use to Roberto. This saddened her.

Later, Roberto came and challenged her in the privacy of their bedroom.

"I just realized why you were so upset with your father earlier.

It's on my account, isn't it? Because you feel that you're in my home, and you feel uncomfortable. You don't consider this your home, do you?"

"What? No. What's wrong?"

"I just accepted a job offer in Alabama, Beena. We should be celebrating. We should be packing and getting ready to move in the fall! Why is everything so gloomy?"

"I'm sorry," Beena said. "But your words make me think now there is a problem. That it's too much for you."

"No, that's not what I said. Just don't act so awkward."

Beena drew a deep breath. "All right. Salma is coming to visit on Saturday. Is that okay?"

"Why ask me? This is your home."

"I don't know," Beena said sulkily. "They're arriving in the afternoon."

He was irritable again. "It's not *my* home. It's *our* home. You don't need to ask my permission to do anything. You live here like a temporary guest." He turned away and sat down heavily at his desk, staring at his dark computer screen for a long time.

She looked at him in surprise. She had never known him to be so wound up or thin-skinned before about anything. "All right," she said in a cold voice.

He turned away and sat down heavily at his desk, staring at his dark computer screen for a long time.

At dinner, Beena argued with Nasir Uddin in Bengali while Roberto swallowed his food quietly. A doctor had told Nasir Uddin not to eat beef, because of his high cholesterol, so he was refusing to eat the beef curry Beena had cooked. He had not touched the food on his plate.

"Don't force him. I'm sure he'll eat if he's hungry...," Roberto began.

"Fine!" she said.

After dinner, Nasir Uddin sat down on the wingback leather armchair in the living room, with the tufted cushions and nail-head trim, watching the news. Roberto helped Beena pile the dishes in the sink, rinse them, and load them in the dishwasher, but there was no closeness between them as there had been at the serene cabin in Louisiana.

After drying his hands, Roberto moved to the TV room to watch the news with Nasir Uddin, who sat with squinted eyes and a frown on his forehead.

Beena entered the room with a bowl of dark cherries, saying, "If you live in Bangladesh, you'll live fewer years. Your longevity will decrease."

"Is that so?" Nasir Uddin laughed. "You reach a certain point in life when it doesn't matter to you how many more years you'll live. I have my home and my friends in Bangladesh, all the things that I could desire. I spent my whole life believing that's where I would die."

"Oh, and I'm nobody to you," Beena said.

48. CREAM OF THE CREAM

Houston, July 2003

SALMA AND RONNY ARRIVED in the afternoon, bearing fruits and
nuts for Nasir Uddin and bags of fried snacks from a Bangladeshi
grocery store. Nasir Uddin was very happy to receive his guests.
Since he had reached Houston, he had been calling his old friends
and students on the phone, finding one person's number from
another. In this way, he had been catching up with many old
contacts. Several students in Austin, Dallas, and San Antonio had
said that they wanted to come visit him.

"Uncle, how are you doing?" Salma asked, sitting down beside
Nasir Uddin on the sofa. "I am well, very well. It's good to see
you, Salma."

"It's not just us! I've brought the whole gang! They are all
coming." Salma giggled. She turned to Roberto and Beena.
"Don't worry. I brought snacks, lots of food."

"Abba, Salma was the one who recommended the doctor,"
Beena said. "It helped a lot, Salma. We took Abba to the doctor,
and the doctor said he was taking too much insulin. He doesn't
need the insulin. Now he just takes diabetes medication. Thank
you!"

"Sir, we respect and admire you so much." Ronny's round face shone with a genial expression. "You have taught us everything we know. All your students are doing very well here, working in top positions at all the big companies."

"Yes, that's true, Uncle," Salma said. "Everybody is filled with respect and affection for their dear sir."

Nasir Uddin gave her a toothy smile.

"These bags have samosas, egg rolls, kebab, piping hot jilapi, golap jum, and dry cake." Salma pointed at the brown bags lying limply on their sides on the coffee table.

"I'll put some tea on," Beena said.

Soon, there were more knocks on the door. Beena served black English tea and the snacks Salma had bought, still hot from the shop. Salma forced Nasir Uddin to eat an assortment of snacks on a quarter plate. Roberto kept going to the door to greet more guests. They walked past him awkwardly.

"Sir, this is Mehjabeen. She was your student." Salma introduced a young, lanky woman to Nasir Uddin.

"Oh! Which batch?" Nasir Uddin asked, his eyes gleaming.

Shona and her husband arrived, followed by Jahan Apa and her husband. Beena tried to catch Roberto in the kitchen. He was bringing down a stack of plates from the top shelf. She wanted to apologize for all the guests, strangers to him, filling up his home, but her apology only irritated Roberto. She left, upset by his frown.

When the doorbell rang again, Roberto did not stir. Beena rose to answer it.

"How are you?" Khaled greeted Beena in Bengali. He had come bearing a gift bag and a large, white cardboard box, which he said contained a cheesecake. He held out the box to Beena with both hands, smiling broadly and gazing into her eyes.

"Sir, this is Khaled, your most brilliant student." Ronny introduced his friend to Nasir Uddin. "He obtained the highest marks in the BUET entrance exam. And he was first boy of his batch."

"Yes, I remember. You were teacher for a while," Nasir Uddin said, gazing at Khaled affectionately.

"Yes, Sir!" Khaled said, springing onto a chair beside Nasir Uddin. "I brought you a gift." He handed over the small gift bag. "You wrote my recommendation letters when I applied to universities for my master's degree."

There were about fifteen people in the living room now. Roberto had pulled out every chair in his home, including the dining chairs. When he went to fetch the swivel office chair from his bedroom, Beena followed him there, and again said sorry, this was all too much of an imposition. This time, Roberto made eye contact and said it was fine, that this was important for Nasir Uddin, who had come all the way from Bangladesh.

When she returned to the living room, Nasir Uddin was opening Khaled's gift.

"This is a very nice fountain pen," Nasir Uddin said to Khaled, grinning with pleasure.

"Sir, I brought you a set of Feynman's lectures. I know how much you admired Feynman. You used to tell us stories about him," Jahan Apa's husband said.

Nasir Uddin looked very happy to receive the books, which he piled beside him on the sofa.

"Sir, I loved your machine design class," Shona's husband Bulbul said.

"Yes, you explained the concepts so beautifully," Mehjabeen said.

"So, what are you all doing now?" Nasir Uddin wanted to know about all his students' work.

As people bragged about their jobs and their positions at their companies, Beena's eyes widened. She'd had no idea where any of them worked. Now she found out that Ronny worked for a weapons manufacturer. Mehjabeen was a civil engineer. Shona's husband Bulbul worked in oil and gas. Salma worked downstream in oil and gas.

"Did you get a PhD?" Nasir Uddin asked Khaled.

"Yes, Sir. I was hired by a top company in Ohio after getting my PhD. And then I got this job in Houston, at H–."

"I think I was hearing on the news that your company has contracts in Iraq."

"Yes!" Khaled answered proudly.

"It is very sad, how Iraq is being destroyed." Nasir Uddin tilted his head downward. "It used to be a great country. It was very safe. Good economic development. Free university for everyone." His eyes behind his thick, dusty glasses appeared sad and distracted.

Khaled's face darkened. "No, sir. That's bogus," he said confidently. "We saved the Iraqi people. Now we will improve their economy through privatization. Western companies can go in there and create a new, modern country, Sir."

"Really?" said Nasir Uddin. His eyes were half hidden by his glasses and his mouth was open in a conceding smile, showing darkened teeth.

Beena retreated to the kitchen to make more tea. She felt cooler here, hot as it was from the stove where she was boiling water and the oven she had turned on to keep the snacks warm. After a few minutes, she returned to the living room carrying a tray bearing fresh cups of tea, with teabags in them. Nobody had touched the first round of cups, probably because the tea was too weak.

"Why work for a toy company?" Nasir Uddin was asking a man named Jahangir with a bald head and a clean-shaven face. "Do you find it satisfying? You must do something that you like, that challenges you and makes you happy."

"My job is satisfying, Sir." Jahangir bristled, but his tone remained respectful.

"What I want to say to all of you is that you would get much more satisfaction doing the kind of work that helps people. You all have brilliant minds. Have you considered returning to Bangladesh and helping in its development?"

There was no answer. The room filled with irritated movements. In the middle of this conversation in Bengali, Roberto excused himself, saying he had to go to the university. He had some work to do, he said. Beena tried to remember if he had mentioned this before.

"Sir, it's not possible to return to Bangladesh," Ronny mumbled.

"Why not?" Nasir Uddin asked.

"What will I do there, Sir? I would have to start from the bottom," Ronny said, in a firmer voice now.

"Listen to my idea. No, really. Listen. I want to open a school in the village. This will be a completely different kind of school. Each student will teach the students in the lower grades. What do you think of that idea? You can all come back with me to Bangladesh. It will be a great dream to realize."

"That's a nice dream, Uncle," Salma said sweetly, stirring sugar in her tea.

"Yes, come with me, all of you. What have you got to lose, Khaled?" Nasir Uddin turned to his most brilliant student, smiling with the corners of his mouth and his cheeks raised.

"That's not possible!" Khaled turned his face away.

"Really. Consider it," Nasir Uddin went on in a nagging voice.

"Why would I leave?" Khaled jumped up from his chair and stood over Nasir Uddin. "I am a respected engineer in a major oil company! H— is the most prestigious company in the world!" he shouted.

For the first time since Khaled had entered the apartment, Beena turned to look at him. His handsome face was twisted, and his neck throbbed in the purplish hue of the room.

"Come on." Nasir Uddin pressed his students, his mouth open in a weak, supplicating smile. "What is so great even about the greatest job? Why don't you all join me?"

No one replied.

"Abba, stop," Beena said, frowning at her father. She, too, felt uncomfortable because of his constant needling, his nagging voice, and his impractical words.

"Okay," Nasir Uddin said, laughing weakly.

"Sir, eat another samosa." Salma rose and carefully lifted a samosa onto Nasir Uddin's plate.

Khaled paced the room, tall and looming, his narrowed eyes scrutinizing his teacher with distaste.

Ronny glanced at his friend with a concerned expression, creasing his forehead, then he addressed Nasir Uddin. "Sir, we struggled for years to get to where we are. Now we all have comfortable positions in the US," he began politely. "Everyone here is very successful. We earn a lot of money. Each one of us earns close to half a million dollars. I bought my house for over a million dollars, Sir."

Khaled had been walking around the room. Now he turned sharply to face Nasir Uddin.

"Sir, how dare you judge me when I have accomplished far more than anything you have done? Yes, first you were my teacher, but later we were colleagues. Many of us in this room have patents in our names. We have engineers working under us. We are the cream of the cream. Bangladesh is a basket case country. There are no opportunities for me there. The labs at the engineering university cannot even run the quality of tests we run here."

"Is that so?" said Nasir Uddin, and he tried to laugh.

Salma had been sitting next to Nasir Uddin, checking her phone busily, not participating in the conversation. The corners of her mouth drooped sharply. Beena suspected that the visit was not going as Salma had planned. Now she rose abruptly. "Sir, I want to invite you to my house one day. We bought a big house. I want you to see it."

"Sure, I will," Nasir Uddin said.

Salma smiled. "Beena, are you free on July 4th weekend? Then come, bring Sir and Roberto."

Beena nodded mutely. Her mind was racing. That painful scene with Khaled when she had first met him had not been a mistake. Jahan Apa glanced at her watch. It was almost time for prayers, she said; she had to leave.

"I'll go as well." Khaled addressed his friends, averting his face from Nasir Uddin.

"Stay a little longer," Nasir Uddin begged them all. "Salma? Ronny? Khaled? Mehjabeen?"

"I've put water on for tea," Beena offered, for her father's sake.

"Stay? What for?" Khaled scoffed. "After you have insulted us, Sir? Do you want to insult us more?"

"Why, you've all driven all the way here to see me. Please stay a little." Nasir Uddin cried like a child. "Let's spend the evening together chatting."

Without answering him, the visitors walked to the door in a procession, following behind Khaled.

Nasir Uddin called to his guests again. "Wait! Let me come to the car with you. Let me put my shoes on."

"Sir, we are still here." Mehjabeen and Jahan Apa waited politely for Nasir Uddin to exit before them.

Nasir Uddin bent down by the front door to slip on his loafers. It took him a long time to bend, to find the right shoe for the right foot, and to pull on each shoe while squatting on the ground. His fingers were feeble and blocky. Beena waited impatiently behind her father. She wanted to run outside after the insolent Khaled before he drove away and make him pay for his words.

"Abba!" she cried. "What are you doing? Move!"

"Sorry." Nasir Uddin stood up. His feet were not entirely in his shoes yet.

When they finally emerged outside the building downstairs, the others had left. Mehjabeen and Jahan Apa and their husbands took their leave from Nasir Uddin, promising to invite him to their houses soon.

Beena followed her father silently back up the stairs, waiting patiently behind him as he mounted each step with difficulty. Back in Roberto's apartment, Nasir Uddin sat down heavily on the sofa, taking heavy breaths. It was obvious to Beena he was feeling poorly.

had the brains to peruse these, let alone remember what one plus one equaled. They stayed and talked late into the night. Other friends from farther away called him and begged him to visit them in Atlanta, California, and Alabama. They wanted to send him airplane tickets. One day, Salma threw a big party for him, inviting all his former students, including Khaled, and they were all very kind to him, sitting almost at his feet and listening to him talk, and later, at the end, bowing their heads and embracing him to say their good-byes.

At the airport, after he had checked in his luggage and collected his boarding pass, Nasir Uddin sat with Beena and Roberto at a coffee shop.

Drinking tea noisily from a paper cup, Nasir Uddin said, "It is best for me to leave. But for you, Beena, it is all right to stay."

Beena nodded, stirring sugar in her coffee.

"Don't take this decision so seriously, where you live. Every place is the same. It only matters where you can be happy. Don't give a damn about anything else in the world. Just do what you want and don't give a damn what others say. Be whatever you wish."

He took a last sip of tea and stood up to gather his carry-on luggage. Beena and Roberto followed him to the security check-in area, where he hugged them both goodbye heartily, smiling at them through shiny eyes, until he broke down and cried.

50. DARI BINNI

Dari Binni, 2003

FROM DHAKA, NASIR UDDIN traveled back to his village home. He flew by plane to Jessore. His nephew Mukul received him at Jessore Airport and drove him all the way to Dari Binni. It was the perfect season to visit the village. The earth was dry, and the temperature was cool. A few men walked with date juice pitchers on their shoulders in the early morning fog.

Arriving in Dari Binni, Nasir Uddin undid the locks and bolts of his childhood home. He wanted to arrange a grand feast for the people of his village. Sending messengers to their houses, he invited all the people of Dari Binni and the surrounding villages, and his relatives, cousins, nephews, nieces, and their families who had moved away to nearby towns. Two large cows and two goats were bought. Sweet curd was brought from Jessore. Several makeshift ovens were built in the courtyard. A long line of cooks worked outside under the open sky, peeling and skinning onions and potatoes, and lighting fires around large copper pots. According to the tradition of Jessore, the spices were cooked for a long time in fatty ghee. The ground red chili pepper mixed with the hot spices, cinnamon, cumin, cardamom, and cloves, till the beef was coated with fat and heat. A wonderful smell rose from the pots.

After everyone else had eaten, Nasir Uddin and his cousins and distant relatives sat on the veranda of his childhood home eating the prepared meal together.

"The way you are living, that is the ideal life," Nasir Uddin said to his cousins. "You eat off the land and wander under the trees that our fathers planted." He struck his forefinger in the air, gesticulating. The grease from an oily curry dripped down one corner of his mouth as he spoke.

Betel nut trees beside the house swayed gently in the breeze. Birds cried in the air.

Nasir Uddin's relatives piled more hard-grained rice and boiling beef curry onto his plate. "Don't talk so much, *Miah Bhai*. Eat," they cried.

But Nasir Uddin would not stop talking. Swiveling his head, he took in the green canopy of fruit trees, the shaded mud path, and the coexistence of the villagers with the animals and the land, and cried, "I thought educated people like me could improve on the village ways. But by living here, you are continuing the life that we lived. You kept this," he indicated his homestead and beyond, "and now I have a place to return to!"

"*Miah Bhai,* have some more!" A cousin dropped a delicious chorchori of tiny mola fish fried in onions and turmeric with green chilis and an abundance of oil on top of the rice on his plate.

There was electricity in the village now, but the house did not have running water or a modern bathroom with a flushing toilet so Mukul thought it would be inconvenient for Nasir Uddin to stay overnight. Rather, he suggested, Nasir Uddin could visit his sister Rajani in her home in Jessore.

They headed back late in the afternoon, with the sun low in the sky. A herd of cows returned home, kicking up golden dust.

As Mukul's newly imported Pajero sped on the tar road, Nasir Uddin watched a small village boy standing on a mud path beside the road. The boy, too, watched the car go past. Then he stirred and returned to running after a rubber tire, which he manipulated with a stick. The boy was shirtless. His thin body, with exposed ribcage and matchstick limbs, was covered with dust. He seemed untouched by anything in the world, unmoved by time itself. None of the events of the world concerned him as he concentrated on his rubber tire and the pleasure of his running feet.

ACKNOWLEDGEMENTS

This novel was long in the making, and there are many people to thank. First, there would be no book without my editor Kurt Baumeister and my publisher Leland Cheuk, to whom I owe everything. Chitra Banerjee Divakaruni, in whose workshop I wrote the first chapter, and to whom I submitted the manuscript in its first finished form. Robert Boswell, who led the first master workshop at the University of Houston, allowing writers to bring in whole manuscripts, whose praise and encouragement gave me the strength to stay with this manuscript for so many years. Numerous friends, including Keya Mitra, Jill Meyers, Nina McConigley, Mónica Parle, Jennifer Hannah, Nicole Zaza, Miah Arnold, Robert Liddell, and others whom I may be forgetting, who read this manuscript in its various forms. Antonya Nelson for shaping me as a writer and also for shaping the current structure of the novel. Other readers, including John Weir, Greg Oaks, Lawrence Hogue, Hosam Aboul-Ela, Claudia Rankine, and Peter Turchi, for all their encouragement, insights, and kindness. *Raven's Perch* and *1111* for publishing excerpts that are now excised from the novel, and all the other journals that have published me through the years and kept my spirit alive. Journalist Mohammad Habib (Sohel Bhai) for finding a lost poem and English Professor Asif Iqbal for verifying all my claims about a degree in English Literature. Ismat Haque for being the inspiration for my heroine and for answering every question about Dhaka University and a degree in English Literature. Carina Chowdhury, who designed my website and remained by my side updating the site and offering me every technological advice I needed. Chaitali Sen, who read and fixed the first chapter. My two children Maha and Luka who grew up while I was busy writing this book. My two brothers, early readers of the novel—Zahed Wahhaj, who vetted every scientific line, and Zaki Wahhaj, of excellent taste, who approved every aesthetic aspect. My parents Ziaun Nahar and Wahhaj Uddin, who saved every story I ever wrote and got it into my head that I am a writer. And, lastly, my husband Arif, who cooked and cleaned and took care of the kids while I wrote and revised and edited, who knew the answer to every question I asked, the name of every tree and river, and how the sun looks in the afternoon—thank you for reading multiple versions of multiple drafts at all hours of the day.

ABOUT THE AUTHOR

Gemini Wahhaj is the author of the forthcoming short story collection *Katy Family* (Jackleg Press, Spring 2025). Her fiction is in or forthcoming in *Granta, Third Coast, Chicago Quarterly Review, Pleiades, Prime Number Magazine (Press 53), Allium, Zone 3, Northwest Review, Cimarron Review, the Carolina Quarterly, Crab Orchard Review, Chattahoochee Review, Apogee, Silk Road, Night Train, Cleaver, Concho River Review, Scoundrel Time, Arkansas Review,* and other magazines. She has a PhD in creative writing from the University of Houston, where she received the James A. Michener Award for fiction (judged by Claudia Rankine) and the Cambor/ Inprint Fellowship. She is Associate Professor of English at Lone Star College in Houston.